THE ALLOTMENT AFFAIR

THE ALLOTMENT AFFAIR

C A Shepherd

1

"Quick, get your kit off," barked Juliet Parlour to her husband, "or we'll lose our conception window!"

"Said Juliet to Romeo," grunted Detective Inspector Mark Parlour, flopping backwards onto their king-size bed after a busy day at the station.

"Oy, this isn't a joke," his wife admonished him, prodding Parlour in the concave stomach before sliding her linen skirt down her hips.

And don't I know it, Parlour thought ruefully, wearily pulling himself upright and slipping his PC Plod boxers off. It really was time Juliet sorted out the laundry, or he'd be in Christmas undies forever.

They had been trying for some ten months now to conceive their first child, in the snippets of spare time afforded them by their respective professions of police inspector and secondary school teacher. Like many professional couples of their age and status, they had put their careers to the forefront and children on the backburner, almost taking it for granted that at the right moment, with the mortgage sufficiently whittled down and careers established at a suitably senior level, that offspring would occur. It had certainly come as a lesson in humility to the high-flying Parlours to discover that the Author of Life hadn't exactly blessed them in the fertility department and that babies were not going to appear on the doorstep along with the online shopping. Not that time was quite running out yet; Juliet Parlour was not yet thirty-nine. However, as she was only too aware, the chances of producing a healthy child decreased sharply the later conception took place, and new reports were even saying she had left it four years too late already. So time was of the essence.

Had it not been for the deafening tick-tocking of his wife's bio time-bomb, Parlour would have refused her sexual demands months ago. He infinitely preferred the natural bi-weekly, post football highlights rhythm of their love-making that had hitherto characterised their eighteen-year marriage to this stop-start mechanical exercise between the *Jonelle* sheets.

Parlour thought, not for the first time, how nice it would be to have some kind of private hidey-hole to escape from it all; a workshop at the bottom of the garden, say, or perhaps a plot at the local allotments, where he could brood in peace over a mug of black coffee. Not that his wife's sexual advances had ever been a problem in the past; it was just this awful, clinical, sex-on-demand that had dominated his after-work routine this past year or so that was so off-putting. He was not the type to wash down the stresses of the day in the pub, infinitely preferring a cuppa and some banter with his wife, to communing in the bar after hours with his colleagues from Billock CID. And in any case, as Juliet was constantly reminding him, alcohol could seriously affect the motility of his sperm. But it would be nice, at least, to have somewhere else to go just once in a while, some place just to sit and ponder the complexities of life.

I'll be taking up fishing next! Parlour grinned to himself, as he climbed in Juliet's open window of conceptual opportunity. Was this a midlife crisis, the desire to seek refuge from his wife? He had never felt like this before. No, it was just the stress of trying for a baby, wasn't it? Parlour dismissed the image of Deverton Allotments and distressed courgettes from his mind and tried to concentrate on his wife's sunbed-ripened melons as an *aide d'orgasme*.

***

Davidson Munroe, retired headmaster and vice-chairman of the British Alliance of Senior Citizens (Deverton Division), had no problems salivating over the fruits of his labour. Or rather, the vegetables.

And what a majestic crop of superior quality Upton leeks he had produced this year, just in time for the Best of British stall that would form part of the World Cuisine Festival to be held at Deverton Parish Church that coming Saturday. Upright, thick and non-bulbous at the base, they were a testimony to careful handling and fertile soil. Smiling smugly to himself, Munroe bent down to check on his recently planted crop of King Edwards, his knee joints cracking as he did so. He grimaced, standing up straight and arching his back, feeling a twinge of sciatica as he did so. A vain man, Munroe felt embarrassed by the little tell-tale signs of physical decline that were beginning to make their presence felt.

Still, nothing wrong with the little man downstairs, he grinned, subconsciously cupping the package in his chinos south of his middle-aged paunch.

"What are you smirking about?" Alicia Munroe, his wife of thirty-one years enquired, the hems of her flared trousers swishing on the wooden floor as she entered their shed at Deverton Allotments. A kind of *boho* Annette Crosbie in appearance, the infinitely more sophisticated Alicia found gardening about as exciting as a trip to the dry cleaner's. However, she had learnt to regard her husband's intense horticultural endeavours as a harmless alternative to other, less wholesome pastimes that befell middle-aged men.

"This, dear," Davidson Munroe replied, thrusting his leek in her bemused face. "That should wipe the smile off Mahatma Gandhi and his amazing Bombay potatoes!"

"It's *Salik Gani* and Bombay potato is a dish, not a variety – as you very well know," Alicia chided him, in defence of her good pal who also happened to own the plot next to Munroe's. The Deverton Allotment Association was a private initiative created for the dozens of Deverton residents who desired to experiment with vegetable growing whilst maintaining a perfectly manicured recreational lawn at home. Or at least that was the official marketing line; lording one's personally grown organic produce over the neighbours' inferior shop-bought specimens also had something to do with the popularity of the *DAA*, for eco-snobbery was as rife in the multi-car population of Deverton as elsewhere in middle-moneyed England.

"So what brings you here, anyway?" Munroe enquired of his wife. "Got a sudden desire to pull up some leeks?"

"I leave the pulling to you, dear," Alicia retorted. "Actually, I come with not so glad tidings regarding the World Food Fight."

Munroe frowned. "Is Pedlar refusing to grace us with his presence – consorting with the big nobs in London again, is he?"

He was referring to Roy Pedlar, the regional chairman of the BASC movement. Pedlar was a recent addition to the Deverton community, having moved into the late Terence Haynes's four bed detached in King Edward Mews, which had been let out several times prior to its eventual purchase by Pedlar.

"Oh no, Pedlar's coming all-right," Alicia replied, "it was he who bore me the tragic news…"

"For Cripe's sake, Leesh," Munroe barked, his greying eyebrows knitting together, "just spit it out and stop winding me up!"

Alicia pursed her lips together humorously, enjoying the suspense before lighting the fuse of her verbal bomb. She should have brought those paint colour charts from the home improvements store to show Davidson after all; she could have had great fun matching his face to the shades of red and purple proposed for their new back bedroom.

"Pedlar received a visit from His Holiness this morning," she informed him, her lips twitching.

"From Beauville?" her husband frowned, alluding to the rather dashing vicar of Deverton Parish Church, the Reverend Martin Beauville.

"Uh-huh," Alicia nodded. "He's banned your mob from the Cuisine Festival."

"What?" Davidson Munroe spat out.

"Reckons you'll hijack the event, defeat the object of the whole exercise…"

"Which is?"

"Spreading peace, love and multifaith harmony… and helping offload some ethically exchanged tinned prunes on their expiry date, of course."

Whilst bearing the Reverend Beauville no malice, Alicia Munroe was not averse to the odd pot-shot at the local parish church and its endeavours to spread the faith with what appeared to her at least, agenda-driven events of varying subtlety. To be fair to Martin Beauville, the World Cuisine Festival was a pretty original idea, and looked good fun, too, with local restaurateurs providing a variety of stalls offering samples of their national cuisines. A small charge would be levied for these starter-sized dishes, with the proceeds being split evenly between Deverton Parish Church's *Worship Wall* project and *Ethical Bean,* a trendy new charity based in the regional centre of Billock dispensing morally sound financial advice free of charge.

"Whatever happened to One Path to Heaven?" Munroe muttered, brushing the loose soil off his broad, suntanned hands.

"The Reverend Beauville believes there is much to learn from other faiths and cultures," Alicia replied a mite pompously, "and I have to say, I entirely agree with him."

Davidson Munroe snorted. His Jesus was decidedly white and middle-class and undoubtedly would have voted Conservative and read the Southern Parishes Express, were He to have His time on earth again. Munroe's mind travelled elsewhere as his wife continued a much practised monologue on the values of an open mind in today's diverse society. Alicia was just as middle-class and selfish as himself, Davidson thought. He didn't see her re-mortgaging the house to support one of the charities she was forever banging on about. And what did a few ethically exchanged bananas here and there do to alleviate the crippling debt that hung over many developing countries? Try as hard as he could, Munroe just could not see how democracy was achieved in military dictatorships by supporting whiney do-gooding rock-stars, who were simply out to boost their public profiles and revive flagging CD sales. The trouble with Davidson Munroe was that he was quick to point the finger, slow to pull it out and do anything useful himself. Alicia, despite her disinclination to leave the comfort zone, and her rather tokenistic attempts at altruism, at least made an effort to do the right thing.

"Hello, not disturbing anything am I?" a slightly high-pitched voice chirruped, a bony brown hand tapping on the side of the wooden shed.

"Dave was just waggling his biggest, juiciest *Allium ampeloprasum porrum* in my face," Alicia smiled humorously at her good friend, Salik Gani.

"Alicia, will you please refrain from calling me *Dave* like I was some spotty oik in a white van come to service the boiler!"

Munroe hated his wife's constant niggling wind-ups. This was her latest attempt to undermine him: - shortening the forename which he held so dear and which had been in his family as far back as the tree could be traced using the latest online technology - or at least the free CD-Rom that came with the Sunday paper. Or so it appeared to him. In all his self-important pomp, Munroe failed to notice the fond twinkle in his wife's eye and the way the left-hand corner of her mouth turned up as she pulled him a little further down the saddle of his high horse.

Salik Gani was used to such waspish exchanges, occupying as he did the neighbouring allotment. He was one of the rare members who did not boast a garden of his own, residing as he did in a small downstairs flat opposite the newsagent run by his family. Gani had purchased the plot from a legacy bequeathed him by a distant relative. He also owned a small, green-washed potting shed, containing several shelves of gardening products. Gani boasted a selection as global as Reverend Beauville's array of Ethically Exchanged foodstuffs, though, Munroe suspected, not imported quite so ethically into the country in the distant past.

"So what can we do for you?" Munroe enquired in the condescending, rather sneering tone he reserved for Alicia's less desirable friends. He could not see the attraction this wiry little man who helped run the local convenience store held for Alicia. The friendship had lasted too long to be another of her do-gooding projects. Had Gani not been so, well, *undersized*, Davidson would have been more than a little threatened by his frequent *sorties* with Alicia. As it was, he was simply a minor irritant, just another friendly little fly buzzing around Munroe's tomato plants.

"I gather the Reverend Beauville has banned the Nazi Pensioners from the Cuisine Festival," Salik grinned. Alicia snorted in delight. *That* was what was attractive about Salik Gani. He didn't give a flying *fuchka* about the ruling classes in the fearfully snobbish hierarchy that existed within the town of Deverton.

"How do you know that?" Munroe frowned, the hackles of his eyebrows rising as he looked down at the smaller man.

"Heard Pedlar ranting in the street to Beauville's new sidekick – what's her name?"

"Penny Rocket," Alicia grinned, referring to the rather down at heel ordinand serving time at Deverton Parish Church for the next couple of months as she trained for full-time ministry.

"It's *Roquet*," Munroe frowned at his wife. "Was he mad?"

"Spitting blood, *rivers* of the stuff," Gani replied humorously. He revelled vicariously in the petty rivalries that dominated the suburban enclave and took great delight in observing and reporting back to his friend and confidante, Alicia Munroe.

"Good Lord," Munroe replied, "I better get hold of Roy and calm the man down. Convert all that energy into a positive plan of action – these leeks demand an audience!"

Alicia groaned and placed her head in her hands in mock desperation.

2

Derek and Margaret Hebble were a self-righteous, anally retentive, inflexible married unit and Parlour despised and despaired of them in equal measure.

Derek and Margaret Hebble were also Parlour's in-laws of eighteen years and to make no bones about it, they irritated the heck out of him with their petty rules and regulations within the domestic fiefdom of 17 Parsley Gardens.

The milk of human kindness was value UHT skimmed when it came to the Hebbles. Theirs was a narrow existence in every way. With every month, every year that passed, another facet of society and of human experience in general became repugnant to them. They were, in effect, refugees in a pseudo underworld largely of their own mental making, with some help from the spiteful editorial team of the Southern Parishes Express, to whose viewpoints Derek and Margaret remained securely hostage. Whether safely ensconced within the leylandii and wood panelled fortress of Parsley Gardens or sat locked inside their sheepish excuse for a car, their doomed expression remained the same. Their eyes were full of foreboding for the disaster which would surely engulf society, on account of its sin; a sin which they had no hand in, yet which would sweep them away, too, on the crest of its evil wave.

As a kind of defence against this Bushesque *axis of evil*, the Hebbles, or at least it seemed to Mark and Juliet, became more fastidious about order and routine and tidiness with every week that passed, as if colour coding the sock drawer would somehow keep the proverbial wolf from the door. Their pathetic little attempts to exercise some form of control over life via an ever increasing array of domestic rules and regulations, did not go unnoticed by the opinionated Parlours, who were forever treading the fine line between insight and insult when it came to Juliet's parents.

Parlour swore he could see their heads visibly narrow as they sucked in their breath at yet another reminder that there was a grubby, unpredictable world out there where people were overweight or abused or addicted to substances, or had non-pastel skin colour, or were dysfunctional in some other way that was absolutely their own fault.

Sadly, their breed was not uncommon in society, especially not in the South of England. They could usually be seen sitting miserably at little round tables in Pubs with Carveries (during *Happy Hour*, naturally), muttering and judging all who passed through the doors. On a wet Sunday afternoon, they could also be found browsing in garden centres, picking up overpriced knick-knacks to send to suspecting relatives for Christmas. By clement weather, the Hebble breed found their way to local beauty spots, where they stayed seated in their car, a spotless windscreen enabling them to enjoy the sunshine yet remain unpolluted by excessive noise levels and undesirable behaviour in the world outside. There they would exchange pages of the *Sunday Southern Parishes Express,* sipping coffee from slim line stainless steel thermos cups. The Hebbles were the type of couple who took as their mantra the editorials of the said newspapers, finding it altogether easier to swallow simplistic polar opposites as presented to them on a platter, than engage with the complexities of an increasingly diverse society.

Though the views they espoused were strong, the mental infrastructure that supported them was decidedly fragile. Like a low-quality item of home assembly furniture, the Hebble Unit, once assembled, could not be easily dismantled into its component parts without the whole construction collapsing. For Margaret or Derek to query or recant on one strand of their philosophy would challenge the validity and life of the remaining parts, so ridden and interlocked was each fibre with their darkly defensive worldview.

"Coffee?" Margaret enquired, as Mark and Juliet neatly arranged their shoes on the lino below the hall radiator, a deferential action reserved solely for visits to the Hebble home in Chave, a leafy suburb of Billock, the rather soulless industrial conurbation where Parlour was based.

"Tea please," Parlour replied, remembering in time to avoid the thin brown gritty insult to coffee that would otherwise arrive in a tidy, some would say poxy, little cafetière with matching cups on a floral tray.

"Thought you were a coffee drinker through and through, Mark," Margaret Hebble frowned, hanging the jacket up that Juliet had left draped over the arm of the sofa, uttering a singular tut as she did so.

"Felt like tea for a change," Parlour lied, trying to ignore Juliet mouthing *Jackanory* across the room at him. He beamed. "You always make such a good cup, Margaret."

Margaret smiled a polite, tight little smile that didn't travel north, and then disappeared off to the kitchen, her velveteen M&S slippers making a soft squishing noise on the linoleum carpet protector.

"What's this, then?" Juliet frowned, once her mother had vacated the room. She picked up a thick glossy catalogue from the immaculate glass-topped coffee table. "*HomeGadget – innovative domestic solutions for all the family.*"

She snorted. "I can think of one domestic solution I'd like – don't think it'll be for sale in *HomeGadget* though!"

"That wouldn't be a *final* solution, would it, Jules?" Parlour chuckled rather malevolently.

Juliet giggled, putting her hand over her mouth hastily as her mother returned with a twee plate of shortbread fingers.

Margaret Hebble frowned and snatched the catalogue from her daughter's hand as if Juliet had just stumbled upon a Top Shelf magazine on her parents' coffee-table.

Parlour raised his eyebrows at his wife as his mother-in-law hastily stuffed the magazine in a sideboard drawer, cheeks visibly flushed. Suddenly sensing she had behaved rather oddly, Margaret regrouped. She smiled nervously.

"It needs to be collected, I'll forget if I leave it out on the table. We don't order much from it."

Yeah right, Juliet scoffed inwardly. The whole house was like an Earls Court Expo for geriatric gadgetry, from the long-handled loo brush in the bathroom to the increasing number of outside lights and timers that had suddenly started appearing in and around their property. The paranoia of old age had already started to set in, though the Hebbles were only just in their sixties. They had conceived Juliet in their early twenties, back in the days when a woman's sexuality lay open to busy speculation should she delay childbirth and opt for an education and career instead – or at least that was the case in the narrow circles within which their respective families operated.

"Well, best not shove it in some drawer then," Parlour remarked, shooting his mother-in-law a dubious look. Margaret looked flustered again. She hastily retrieved the magazine and placed it outside the white PVC front door.

Mark and Juliet shook their heads at one another. What had all that been about? But it was soon forgotten as Derek Hebble rushed into the living room.

"Quick, Marge, turn the telly on! I just saw Gordon and Mary at the March!" He pushed past his still floundering wife and flung back the wooden doors on the television unit, which in typical twee Hebble fashion, kept the TV out of view and dust-free. Parlour just didn't get it. What was so distasteful about a television set, for goodness sake? Everyone had at least one; there was no shame in it. For similar reasons, the computer was kept well out of view in a small upstairs room at the back of the house. Electronic gadgets were every bit as indispensable, as far as the wannabe paper-free Mark Parlour was concerned, as the oven or the fireplace, and you wouldn't keep them hidden inside cabinets, would you?

Gordon and Mary Tibbs were the Hebbles' oldest friends. They had been next door neighbours for some twenty-three years, a bond that had only been slightly challenged by the

Tibbs' ascent to the county town of Foxburgh some eighteen months ago. It was a popular step up, once the offspring had jumped ship, at least in their neck of the woods. In truth, the chief threat to the inter-couple harmony that existed among the four of them was Marina Chudder, née Tibbs, Gordon and Mary's elder daughter, who had produced three impeccably blonde and blue-eyed children, a triplicate tool for baiting the as yet grand-childless Margaret Hebble. In true trophy grandchild fashion, Mary Tibbs had adorned her spacious ground floor retirement flat in Foxburgh with the latest group portraits of the three decidedly Aryan mini Chudders. Far be it that the little minxes should soil her cream décor with their actual physical presence; no, a two dimensional image of them which was portable and could be taken to show those without children would suffice (it was an act of kindness, after all, to share one's extended family with those not so fortunate). Furthermore, a photographic image didn't answer back in the vernacular or spill blackcurrant squash on the carpet.

If Margaret Hebble wasn't fed up of the all-singing, all-dancing Von Chudder offspring yet, Juliet Parlour certainly was. Marina bloody fertility goddess Chudder was the bane of her life. If she had to listen one more time to how Marina had, like some modern-day martyr, knelt at the feet of mother earth and sacrificed a promising legal career to conceive children, she would throw up. What Mary Tibbs always neglected to mention was that the legal firm that employed Marina had tried on several occasions to boot her out, claiming she was not up to the job. Marina had simply jumped before she got pushed, playing the motherhood card to save face.

"What on earth….?" Parlour groaned as thousands upon thousands of senior citizens could be seen processing down Whitehall. Some were arm in arm; others bore placards with statements like *Glad to be Grey!* and *Grey Rights!* and more ominously, *Vote Grey - Because Life Needn't be Black & White!*

"It's the Grey Pride March," Derek informed his son-in-law, with a palpable degree of pride in his own voice. "Lots of our friends have gone up to town to march today."

Juliet nodded. "I read about it in the *Guardian* yesterday."

"How come I missed that?" Parlour frowned, staring at the bizarre scenes on the television.

"You probably missed the article; it was squashed in the corner of that interview with the Metropolitan Police Commissioner that you kept reading out to me," Juliet informed him. "It was pretty nauseating stuff, anyway."

"Oh nonsense," Margaret Hebble chastised her daughter. "They're only saying what we're all thinking, well our generation in any case."

"I'm glad you qualified that statement," Juliet frowned.

"Heaven help us," Parlour shook his head, as Gordon and Mary Tibbs did indeed grace their screen, walking arm in arm at the front of the almost military train of pensioners, dressed traditionally in dreary wintry colours. There was no way he was going to dress like a dull November day when he hit sixty-five, Parlour thought to himself, flicking a shortbread crumb from his charcoal grey chinos.

"They went up last night," Derek informed the others proudly. "Camped out on the street. Wanted pole position, they did."

"Mission accomplished, I'd say," Juliet remarked dryly. "Hey Dad, you're not involved in all this, are you?"

"What me, dear?"

"No dear!" Parlour giggled, mimicking a character from his favourite BBC sketch show that happened by chance to share his father-in-law's forename.

"Your father and I support equal rights for senior citizens," Margaret informed her daughter pompously.

Juliet snorted. "Oh come on, Mum, get real!" She flapped her hand disdainfully in the direction of the television. "This bunch of fat, middle-class *Gaviscon* addicts are hardly *suffering*, are they? It's more about being nasty and racist than equal rights, I'd say!"

"Juliet!" her father exploded, "I will not have you talking to your mother like that! When you get to our age…"

"I won't be as petty and small-minded, that's for sure," Juliet interrupted.

"Jules!" Parlour hissed, his eyes boring into her in a warning to drop it.

"More shortbread, Mark?" Margaret asked in a honeyed tone, diffusing the tension at least temporarily.

***

Detective Sergeant Cameron Goodlove was a strapping young man of little experience but considerable blag. With close-cropped black hair that hardly required the copious quantities of gel lavished upon it on a daily basis, the recently promoted sergeant had not been unfavourably received by the female contingent of Billock Police during his initial visit to the station the previous week. And thanks to a sharp sense of humour and chirpy disposition, he had been accepted with equal conviviality by the male dominated criminal investigation team housed therein.

He was yet to meet his new boss, DI Mark Parlour, but he had heard much about him, mostly couched in respectful and positive tones, though the words "irritating" and "smartarse" admittedly also occurred with some regularity and usually in close companionship to one another. "Spotty" and "ginger" also featured rather prominently; however as a reluctant early-riser, Goodlove was more bothered by the alarming frequency of "pernickety" and "punctual" in descriptions of his new boss at Billock CID. In actual fact, Parlour himself was rarely at his desk before 9am but by the same token, he was rarely absent from it a minute after.

Twenty-nine and single, Cameron Goodlove liked to subject his well-toned torso to a good buffeting from the local nightlife. A night-owl who wasn't averse to taking the odd bit of prey home to feast on, Goodlove was not best suited to an early start, a lifestyle that would surely be challenged by working in close proximity with a man as fast out the blocks as Mark Parlour. And this fact was not lost on Detective Chief Inspector Brian Sewell, seeking to raise the standards of excellence among his most promising cops, of which Cameron Goodlove was definitely a rose amid an unpromising intake. Or at least, bring some semblance of discipline to the young man's life – that would do for starters. And Mark Parlour, foxy in appearance and foxy by nature, if not in nocturnal habits, was just the man to do this, DCI Sewell was sure. All they needed now was a nice, fat, juicy, high-octane, non-routine investigation for Parlour to sink his teeth into again – grabbing Goodlove by the scruff of his broad neck and dragging the young pretender up to scratch in the process.

3

"If Lindsay Briscoe rams her two point four bloody kids down my throat once more, I swear I'll take a Sabatier to her!" Juliet cursed, flinging her car keys down on the table as she came home from church that Sunday lunchtime.

"Said Jesus," Parlour remarked dryly, shutting the front door behind them and slipping his jacket off. "And anyway, she has three – you always forget baby Josh."

"Honestly, some people!" Juliet continued unabashed. "Just because they fire out children like bullets from a shotgun, they think they can look down on us less fertile mortals!"

"I thought you and Lins were good mates," Parlour commented, checking the answer phone for messages, but for once, the light wasn't flashing. Most people knew by now that they attended the morning service at Deverton Parish Church, where Parlour helped with communion and Juliet was on the prayer ministry team.

"Yeah, so did I," Juliet replied, brow furrowed, "but just lately she's been a bit distant. I don't know why, she just isn't as… interested in others, I guess. Got a bit full of herself."

"Doesn't sound like Lindsay," Parlour frowned, flopping down on the sofa and hoping Juliet would take responsibility for refreshments.

"She's always been very pleased with her lot in life, I guess," Juliet continued, not obliging him on this occasion, instead flinging herself down on the adjacent sofa. "And who wouldn't be? Good-looking, rich husband with secure job in the City. Five bed detached at posh nob's end of Deverton. Three gorgeous kids with no discernible flaws. Four by four with Sat Nav, integral DVD and probably even a high-speed broadband connection! But she's never felt the need before to… I don't know… rub my face in it."

"C'mon Jules," Parlour admonished her gently, "it's just the kids thing, isn't it? You're feeling hyper-sensitive about not getting pregnant so every mention of her children seems like another cellar of salt in the wound."

"Maybe," Juliet conceded, "But I'm sure she never used to go on about them this much. It's *Charles and the Children Factory* overdrive at the moment, like she's lording it over me the whole time."

"Maybe she's feeling insecure about something," Parlour shrugged. Then he looked at his wife and they both shook their heads. Lindsay Briscoe insecure? Not in a month of church-attending Sundays!

"I guess I'll just have to make do with Ana," Juliet said a little self-pityingly, a trait Parlour found oddly endearing in his wife. She scooped up the slender black moggy they had acquired from the local cat shelter six months ago. As her full name of Anastasia indicated, the six-year old tabby cat had all but risen from the dead, having been resurrected to full health by the amazingly dedicated staff at Billock Blue Cross. There was a certain degree of truth in the assertion that cats were a popular pre-child plaything for self-centred adults seeking a gentle path into the more selfless world of caring for others. However, Juliet would like to think that she would have rescued Ana all the same. There was a powerful bond between them, Juliet sensed, and therefore an inevitability that they should be drawn to one another somehow, some day. Stroking the cool silken forepaws of her feline companion, Juliet closed her eyes and held her breath, trying to feel cells multiplying inside her. But all she felt was a gurgling in her empty stomach. She opened one eye and noted to her satisfaction that her husband had given up waiting and was approaching with the biscuit tin and two hot drinks for them.

"Cheers m'dear." She accepted the Deverton Parish Church Fifth Anniversary mug of steaming tea from Parlour.

"Uh-oh, catastrophe!" Parlour grinned, opening the *Walker's Petticoat Tails* tin, a Christmas gift from Juliet's parents, naturally, which had long since ceased to contain shortbread triangles. He showed his wife the empty tin.

Juliet held her hands up in mock horror, spilling tea down herself in the process.

"I feel a shifty Sunday sortie to Utopia coming on!" she grinned, referring to the Deverton branch of the popular top-end-of-the-market grocery outlet, which had replaced Melrose at the helm of the Esplanade. It wasn't the done thing in church circles to be seen shopping on the Sabbath, at least not at Deverton Parish Church, whose members tended towards a more rigid reading of Scripture, unlike the altogether more relaxed congregations Mark and Juliet had been a part of in their previous church lives. Parlour tried not to be legalistic about such Christian "hot potatoes" as Sunday shopping, whereas Juliet was far more prone to setting absolutes, which she tried, usually in vain, to guiltily live up to. In his experience, being legalistic left you open to being bitten on the bottom by your own moral precepts, as it was impossible to follow through with the required degree of consistency. However, Parlour's more relaxed attitude to what he deemed secondary issues in Scripture was beginning to rub off on Juliet, who was gradually mellowing with age. This could only be a good thing, in Parlour's view; he had gleaned from colleagues at Billock CID, as well as from the likes of Charles Briscoe, that children brought with them the need to compromise and find a way of life that balanced the practical, spiritual and emotional needs of all the family. Within this carefully constructed strategy for harmonious living, there was little room for untenable ideals and moral absolutes. So long as he wasn't doing his weekly shop on a Sunday, thereby increasing the profit margins of Sunday traders, Parlour's conscience wasn't unduly pricked by such trips to the local Utopia. It wouldn't do any harm to get used to moral compromise now. At least, that was his excuse for dashing off in the car as if his life depended on it that Sunday lunchtime to replenish the biscuit tin.

It never ceased to amaze Parlour just how busy the shops were on a Sunday. Conveniently ignoring the fact that creature comforts had won the day over uncomfortable Biblical precepts in his mind, too, it was with a considerable degree of hypocrisy that Parlour engaged in a silent rant on the evils of Sunday trading (at the macrocosmic level), whilst browsing amid the biscuits and confectionary aisle, rather aptly it had to be said, for a packet of *Ginger Thins*.

Locating the desired object, Parlour meandered in the vague direction of the *Basket Only* tills, stopping to pause at the idiot-proof signs that hung suspended from the ceiling above each aisle, informing the customer in generous screaming fonts which products were located below. Nevertheless, the newly extended branch of Utopia and its online service, E-topia, still felt the need to employ a troop of Customer Service Providers. Dressed in tasteful claret blazers and smart black slacks, the Maroon Coats, as they were known, were responsible for dispensing information of varying sophistication, from simple issues such as product location, to which wine best complimented this week's choice cut on the meat counter.

Unlike Billock Mega Mart, where the majority of the local population shopped, Utopia's "Maroon Coats" were not unskilled, lumpy social misfits, Parlour thought disdainfully to himself, whose distinct lack of social skills made a mockery of the *Happy to Help* motifs they bore on their badges. Without a lollipop in sight, this classy team of well-heeled and well-flossed customer assistants were a boon to the likes of Parlour, frequently in a rush and unfamiliar with the logic behind a product placement policy that saw condiments located above the frozen poultry section and potato snacks next to kitchen roll. Who on earth put brown sauce on their roast anyway? Not the sort of people who shopped at Utopia, Parlour thought snobbily.

But on this occasion, Parlour was not in a hurry and for once, had time to digest the information being directed at him, the consumer.

He chuckled out loud as he found himself in the *Ready Meals* aisle. *Ethnic Meal Solutions* he read to himself. Oh for goodness sake! Why did everything in life require a solution these days? It reminded him of Juliet's parents and their silly catalogue full of ridiculous gadgets for people with no more pressing concerns in their own lives than how to open a can of baked beans without getting sauce on their fingers. Solution was a word you used for paint products, anyway, wasn't it? Mind you, Parlour thought, there probably wasn't much difference in the contents anyway, with all those nasty colorants and chemicals such convenience food carried. They were probably far more careful about what they put on the shelves at Utopia, but nevertheless, what was the world coming to? What on earth was so difficult about grilling a fresh chicken breast and popping some spuds and greens in the microwave? Or plopping some pasta in a pan? You could whip up a nice sauce with a can of plum tomatoes, some fresh herbs and a clove of garlic in minutes. Simple nutritious meals could be achieved in the same time it took to let one of those nasty trays of play food toxify in the microwave, Parlour thought to himself, conveniently forgetting that it was generally his wife who took care of *their* meal solutions every evening.

"Shopping on the Sabbath? Tut tut!"

Parlour was interrupted from his self-righteous interior monologue by the old-school BBC baritones of Charles Briscoe.

"Oh you know," Parlour replied airily, slipping his good friend from church a wink, "conducting a bit of market research on behalf of the diocese!"

"With payment in *Ginger Thins*?" Briscoe grinned, prodding at the item in Parlour's hand in good humour.

"So what are you doing here – run out of spuds for the roast?"

But Briscoe had neither a basket nor a trolley with him. He shook his head. "Placing a wine order – got a bit of a family do next Saturday. Mum and Pop's fortieth wedding anniversary."

Parlour smiled to himself. He was amused by the pet names posh people often had for their parents. It wasn't as if Charles's father, Farque Briscoe, was from over the pond or anything – far from it, he was about as Old Boy Network as it got, as a High Court Judge with a large property in the Surrey barrister belt, where he golfed and whisted his leisure time away with wife Evelyn.

"Well, send them my congratulations, won't you?"

"Will do," Briscoe nodded and sauntered confidently towards the exit whistling, hands in pockets, every inch the confident head of well-set-up household.

It was as Parlour was browsing at the Sunday newspapers on a stand in the foyer that the unmistakeable tones of Roy Pedlar, regional chairman of the British Alliance of Senior Citizens, rose about the low level hum of the supermarket. A resident of Deverton, Pedlar, like Parlour, snubbed the local convenience store that was located in close proximity to both of their homes in favour of the major retailer at the helm of Deverton precinct, or *Esplanade*, to give it the name rather pretentiously favoured by the town planners. Whilst Parlour cited product diversity and superior lighting, as well as the absence of row upon row of dodgy "men's" magazines, as his reasons for electing to shop at Utopia rather than the Mini Mart managed by the Ganis at Deverton Triangle, Pedlar did not mince his words so leanly. As Salik Gani had been informed on many an occasion, this was England, and every Englishman should be proud to eat British dishes made from home-grown produce, not this pseudo-ethnic microwave muck housed in the little freezers in Gani's Mini Mart:- and all this despite Salik

Gani's keenest protestations that he, also, did not enjoy such products from the lowest common denominator school of cuisine, and that it was the lazy commuter population rolling off the train at eight pm that determined the products stocked therein.

Utopia's Global Produce Manager, it appeared, was refusing to support Pedlar's Great British Food promotion at Deverton Parish Church next Saturday afternoon. To add insult to injury, Trevor Tolt had responded favourably to a request from the Reverend Beauville to replace Pedlar's GBF stand at the *Celebration of World Cuisine* with a stand staffed by Utopia and stuffed with Utopia organic British produce.

"I'm sorry, Sir," Tolt was informing a crimson-eared Roy Pedlar, whose blood pressure was visibly rising, "but whilst *Utopia* fully supports the promotion of British produce, we cannot be seen to *discriminate* against our brothers and sisters in foreign climes, so a collaboration between us is entirely out of the question. I'm afraid the rather negative press your organisation has attracted of late will not do our corporate image any good, if we are seen to support your cause in any shape or form."

"Negative press? What negative press?" Pedlar snorted. "In friggin' lefty do-gooder papers full of typos and no regard for the Queen's English?"

"I do not wish to take this matter any further, Mr Pedlar," Tolt informed him in a tone of weary exasperation. "Now if you'll excuse me, I have a mango farmer from the Congo waiting for me on the phone."

Tolt disappeared through a door behind the Customer Service desk to leave Pedlar muttering furiously on the shop floor.

Parlour raised his eyebrows at a few fellow shoppers who caught his eye, grinned uneasily, then paid for his biscuits at the cigarette kiosk.

***

Meanwhile at the far end of Deverton Estate, where the majority of Deverton's vast population of four-by-fours could be found, Salik Gani was delivering the Sunday editions of the do-gooding left-wing broadsheets. His skinny shoulders baulked under the weight of his fluorescent orange paper bag, containing not only the newspapers, but the copious quantities of Sunday supplements and freebies. His cause was not aided by the Sunday Courier's decision to provide each reader with a paperback copy of *Eat Pasta, Lose Weight Fasta!* Who needs pasta, Gani thought to himself, feeling the pounds drop off him as he laboured up Maris Piper Way with his heavy load.

"Take your hands off my car!" a rasping upper class voice bellowed at him, as Gani slid on an empty plastic packet of Utopia Finest Farfalle and lost his balance. Gani muttered his apologies, and removed his hands from the bonnet of a luxury saloon car, which he had leant on to break his fall. *What was wrong with some people,* he wondered to himself, far too timid to give vocal expression to his musings.

"Sorry, Sir, lost my footing," he said instead, looking briefly into the hard eyes of an aristocratic type who seemed vaguely familiar.

So many of the inhabitants of Deverton had their heads stuck up their own backsides, Gani thought to himself, proceeding up Maris Piper Way. He stuffed a mini-encyclopaedia's worth of Sunday paper through the door of yet another mock Tudor five-bed detached at the seriously moneyed end of the designer village.

4

The Reverend Martin Beauville, six feet one inch tall with silky crow-black hair and sexy crow's feet around the eyes, stood forearm to shoulder with his recently acquired, diminutive minister in training, Penny Roquet, outside Deverton Parish Church late that Saturday morning. It was a comical sight. At five feet tall exactly, the greasy brown top of Roquet's mullet hairstyle barely came up to Beauville's shoulder blade.

She really could work a little harder on her appearance, Beauville thought, his musings straddling a rather worldly plane for a brief moment. That hair looked like something from *Shoot!* annual, 1986 edition. And as for those dreadful threadbare ankle-length skirts in faded floral print and those scuffed leather boots! Beauville was not of the theological school of thought that advocated buying all one's clothes from charity shops just because The Heavenly Father had a predilection for the inner chambers. As a figure often at the forefront of public affairs, at least at local level, it was important to command respect, in Beauville's opinion. He had dropped some subtle hints already that Penny might like to smarten herself up a bit, to no avail. Perhaps he would have to be a little blunter. Sometimes you had to be cruel to be kind, Beauville thought to himself, though he couldn't quite think of a passage from Scripture to support his theory. But the fact remained; it was difficult to be taken seriously by an increasingly sneering, unchurched public when one looked like one should be sitting outside Billock Station with some coins in a hat and a drugged-up sleeping mongrel. Still, Beauville thought, casting a disdainful eye down her sexually challenged contours, at least there wouldn't be endless silly rumours circulating about himself and the new ordinand. Nobody in their right mind would imagine they were an item. Roquet was your quintessential church spinster, damned to a life of celibacy, perhaps not by choice, but by sheer inability to slot into the romantic rat-race at even the most innocuous level.

"This promises to be a tremendous success," Roquet smiled benignly, her pale face dominated by thick, round glasses behind which hid weak and watery little piggy eyes of a vaguely bluish hue, "you must be very pleased, M-Martin."

It did not come naturally addressing the much respected and rather dashing vicar of Deverton by his Christian name. But she could hardly call him Reverend Beauville like one of his parishioners. Yet neither did she feel at ease calling him "Mart" in the tone of jokey familiarity that existed between Beauville and some of his male acquaintances within the fellowship at Deverton, the likes of that police inspector, Parlour, and the stockbroker, Charles Briscoe.

"Yes, only the good folks from Foxburgh Fisheries haven't turned up yet, everyone else who pledged their support seems to be here."

"Perhaps they're waiting for the fish to bite," Roquet joked feebly, surveying the array of vans of various shapes, sizes and liveries busily unloading in the church car park. There were quite a few traders from the French Market that came to Deverton every bank holiday weekend to sell typically French produce, or at least, the produce British customers sought to keep their fantasies of French village life intact. Parlour entertained a rather cynical notion that the traders were ex-pats residing in Hampshire and neighbouring counties, who loaded up with Bonne Maman and croissants at the local Sainsbury's then turned up at parochial outposts such as Deverton armed with some sticky labels and an array of gingham lined presentation baskets.

A gentleman in a butcher's outfit offloading produce from a maroon Renault van bearing the *Utopia* logo in white letters was enjoying some banter with the "French" contingent. There was also a white van from *La Dolce Vita* with its familiar logo of a rather rotund Italian waiter bearing a steaming pizza in his hand.   Roquet counted eleven other vans from various gastronomic outlets and food retailers from the Deverton/Billock area.

"Are Roy Pedlar and co here yet?" Roquet enquired of her mentor.

Beauville grimaced.   "He's rallying his troops in the community centre car park as we speak. Needless to say, they'll be over here in time for the paparazzi."

Several journalists from the regional news programmes and the local press were due with TV crew and photographers at noon, when the Deverton World Cuisine Festival was officially opened by Beauville himself and the local MP for Billock West, Fletchley Linlock.

"Good morning, Martin. Penny." Mark Parlour tipped his head politely in a southerly direction in acknowledgement of the trainee vicar.

"Aah, morning, Mark. Off duty, I hope!" Beauville chuckled. Parlour flung his arms open wide in a gesture to indicate that the faded jeans and casual shirt would suggest this was indeed the case.

"Come along to see the crack," Parlour grinned.

Beauville laughed. "Gosh, I hope there's none of that for sale or I will be in Mark Knopflers with the Bish!"

Roquet frowned, the exchange entirely lost on her. Though classical music was Martin Beauville's first love, he wasn't averse to a bit of classic car music. Roquet, however, required all her faculties to concentrate on driving and saved her *Seasonal Moods: Celebrating God's Creation* soundtrack cassettes for her little tape player in the kitchenette.

"You can never be quite sure with that ethically exchanged stuff," Parlour chuckled. "Jules brought some particularly vicious substance home in a packet from the One Church meeting last month. Masquerading as Ethical Exchange muscovado sugar, I believe."

"It's the desiccated coconut from the West Indies you need to watch," Beauville smiled back but then stopped in his tracks, nodding in the direction of an approaching TV crew from *Southern Aspect*.

As Beauville was interviewed on his input into the World Cuisine Festival, Parlour wandered off in the direction of the Church Hall, where various employees of the retail outlets involved were erecting stands and tables on their designated pitches, and exchanging hearty comments concerning the relative merits of their produce.

Parlour inhaled a heady mix of foodstuffs, some already fanned out on white trays on the table-tops, others being brought in as he stood there. The aroma of fresh pizza won the day for him, closely followed by the smell of freshly ground coffee at the Ethical Exchange stall and the salty-sweet perfume of smoked salmon canapés from the local self-catering company, *Meals on Big Wheels*, which delivered in a huge four by four with bull bars that would defend the vehicle stoutly against the most frenzied onslaught of male cattle.

However, his attention was diverted from the hub of activity in the hall to a scene outside the window, to the rear of the church building. It seemed Roy Pedlar had already made his way from the community centre car park and was mounting an attack from the rear.

Parlour frowned, heading in the direction of the back doors. Unknown to Martin Beauville, who was innocently chatting away to a single journalist and cameraman from the regional news programme, Roy Pedlar had stolen the limelight. Around two dozen journalists with Dictaphones and cameras from both national and local television stations were vying for pole position as he launched a bitter attack on Beauville's initiative.

Parlour pushed past the small crowd of locals gathering in the churchyard and marched over to the mob, at the centre of which stood the distinctive white-haired figure of Roy Pedlar, in all his Aaron-sweatered glory.

"You say you were refused entry to the event, Mr Pedlar," a strong-jawed girl from *Sky News* enquired in that stroppy Home Counties tone so prevalent among female journalists and newsreaders.

Pedlar proceeded to outline, in an evidently much-rehearsed spiel, how Martin Beauville, Vicar of Deverton Parish Church, had refused the Deverton branch of the British Alliance of Senior Citizens entry to his World Cuisine Festival, on the grounds that their Best of British stall promoting home-grown produce also promoted racism and intolerance. In a monologue laden with sound bites guaranteed to galvanise the grey vote into action, Pedlar called on the populace to raise aloft the flag of St George once more and to ditch "multicultural mash-mash" for the "real potato". With this, he brandished a fine specimen of the said vegetable in the air on what appeared to be a giant shoe-horn!

Give me strength! Parlour muttered to himself, shaking his head. This had nothing to do with the superiority of the British vegetable populace and everything to do with jumping aboard a convenient vehicle to make an ill-advised and unpleasant stand. He wandered past the posse of journalists and over to where male members of the BASC organisation, like a slightly creaky army platoon, were setting up wooden trestle tables, marshalled by the vice-chairman of the Deverton Branch, Davidson Munroe. Once the tables were up, members of the female auxiliary force spread gingham clothes of every hue upon the table tops. A mixed regiment from the Deverton Allotment Association then marched through the back gate bearing baskets of fresh fruit and vegetables, and a specialist branch of predominantly female workers then proceeded to arrange the produce in attractive displays of contrasting shape and colour. The centrepiece of the five table display was Davidson Munroe's prize Upton leeks and Roy Pedlar's Braveheart sprouts. Parlour had to admit, it was a well-planned and immaculate operation.

By withholding his troops until the press had arrived, Pedlar had insured Beauville would be in no position to turf them out of the church grounds without drawing negative publicity to himself and his own cause. Whatsmore, by paying those media students from Billock Institute to pose as a film crew from *Southern Aspect*, he had kept Beauville well out the way at the front of the church building. Yes, Roy Pedlar was feeling very pleased with himself indeed. The mass of vans clogging up the church car park itself and parked up on the main road outside to the front of the building, also insured that the majority of visitors to the event were acting on the advice of the stewards to park to the rear of the church – thereby accessing the grounds via the back gate, where the Best of British stall would be the first sight to greet them. The stewards, naturally, were also the genius of Roy Pedlar, the master tactician. Wearing fluorescent yellow waistcoats bearing the BASC logo on a back panel, Pedlar's elderly troops ensured all visitors to the event gained a healthy dose of propaganda as well as parking advice, by way of a leaflet highlighting the views of the British Alliance of Senior Citizens. The party literature was supplemented by a 50p off coupon for any item costing £2 or over on the Best of British Stand. It was horribly cynical, Parlour thought, inspecting the activity outside - and devilishly clever.

Want to BASC in your retirement? Join The British Alliance of Senior Citizens for a Secure Future! Parlour read from one of their flyers. He scrunched the leaflet up and threw it in the direction of Pedlar.

"Can't we get them for breach of the peace?" Beauville cried out rather desperately to Parlour, yelling to make himself heard above the din of Roy Pedlar's megaphone and the frenzied press activity. He stood hand on hips, clerical collar hanging loose around his neck, the patch of dark hair below visibly moist. He had just been tipped off that Pedlar had set up shop behind the church.

Parlour shrugged. "You're perfectly at liberty to throw them out the grounds, but whether that will do your cause any good is debateable."

Beauville groaned. "I can't win either way, can I? Blast Pedlar and his bunch of old cronies! Linlock's due any second now to open the Festival!"

It wasn't often one saw the suave and serene vicar of Deverton Church so riled, Parlour thought. But this was his baby, after all, an event in which he had invested a great deal of thought, time and effort.

"Well you know how the saying goes, all publicity is good and all that…" he countered to his friend.

"Perhaps," Beauville frowned dubiously, as a smart black Saab with driver roared up outside. The MP for Billock West, Fletchley Linlock, alighted from the back, a troubled expression upon his face as he surveyed the chaos outside.

***

The delicately perfumed aroma of Earl Grey tea wafted gently to the ceiling of the back room of Gani's Mini Mart at twelve thirty that Saturday afternoon, where Alicia Munroe was enjoying a cuppa and some McVitie's *Hobnobs* with the second-in-line to the small convenience store.

The shop was deserted on account of the events up at Deverton Church, and anticipating a boring afternoon of stock-taking with one eye on the football scores, Salik Gani was only too glad to admit his good friend and allotment neighbour, Alicia Munroe, over the threshold of Gani's Mini Mart.

In truth, Alicia's visit had rather less to do with seeking Gani's company and rather more to do with avoiding her husband's pompous posturing at the now hi-jacked Cuisine Festival. But what better way to wile away the hours until his return than in the easy company of Gani, discussing the relative merits of Megamart's Bangers'n'Mash over Utopia's *Saucisses à la purée*. Gani could not be termed a strict Muslim by any stretch of the imagination, favouring a good old English fry up wolfed down furiously at the local greasy spoon to his sister-in-law's traditional Bangla fish curry any day. This predilection for porcine entrails did not go down well with head of the family, Abdul Gani, who attempted with pitiful degrees of success to maintain Bengali customs in the home, a task made doubly difficult by their isolated position in the Deverton community.

"I tell you what, Sal," Alicia fondly addressed her companion, "How about I whip you up Munrovian Bangers and Mash chez moi? I haven't had lunch yet. I just need to grab some veg from the allotment. We'll be quite safe; the *Fartus Antiquarius* will be inciting the locals for a good couple of hours yet!"

"Shut up shop, you mean?" Gani threw his hands up in the air in a gesture of abject horror.

"Oh come on, you haven't had a customer since little Penny Whistle popped in for some *Salon Select*!"

Gani waggled his finger at her. "You very wicked woman!"

Taking the Mickey out of Penny Roquet the ordinand and her rather downtrodden appearance had become something of a popular sport among the residents of Deverton.

"Time for a quickie first?" Gani extracted a bottle of whisky from behind a row of grubby ring binders containing shop admin.

Alicia tutted humorously, but gratefully accepted a generous glass of Scotland's finest from her companion. It was sure to be the first of many; it was that kind of afternoon.

5

Parlour meandered into the main hall, where a couple of dozen locals were sampling fresh produce from the local culinary outlets. He made a quick tour of the various stands. They hadn't taken much money yet, though it was admittedly early days:- the event still had two hours or so to run. Through the window, he could see that a large contingent of the local population plus the majority of the press present at the Festival were actually concentrated around the BASC stall, where someone had come up with the bright idea of serving strawberries and cream with a complimentary glass of sparkling wine produced by the local vineyard at Fockham.

Beauville did have a small, but loyal band of supporters, however; Parlour noted with relief that some familiar faces from the church had shunned the hullabaloo outside and were gregariously making their way around the various stands, sampling the vast array of produce on display. One witty member of the public had enquired whether the local pharmacy had a table of indigestion products for sale at the Festival, too!

Juliet Parlour had joined her husband and could be seen licking her fingers and making appreciative noises at the *Pride of Billock* stand, alongside the Sheltons from church. They were soon joined by the Mogridge-Winstanleys, with their tribe of disaffected off-colour teenagers in tow that were dragged along to the church in various combinations each Sunday to lend a *raison-d'être* to the newly set-up youth group.

Martin Beauville just stood at the window and frowned, as he noted that the activity of the rebel gathering outside showed no signs of abating; indeed, Roy Pedlar appeared to have stepped up his efforts. Several of his hench-people were now waving placards in the air advocating, in no uncertain terms, that the community of Deverton and beyond should *Buy*

British. One protestor even had the audacity to bear a sign emblazoned with the words *Boycott Beauville!*

In the manner of those naff *Santa Stop Here* signs, Pedlar ad created some plastic arrows bearing the Union Jack. These temporary additions to the church flower beds, bearing the slogan *British Food Lovers Stop Here!,* pointed visitors in the direction of the BASC stand.

Beauville grimaced and shook his head. It was tacky beyond belief, but horribly effective. Despite the visible press presence inside the main hall, it couldn't be denied that much of the news interest was in the protest outside. Hopefully, that self-righteous old tosspot, Roy Pedlar, would make a complete ass of himself, thereby attracting only negative press to his cause, Beauville thought wistfully, without much optimism.

Beauville took a deep breath. His brain and his male pride told him to flex some muscle and have the BASC forcibly removed from the church grounds full-stop, and not just from the main event. But his keen sense of spiritual awareness told him to rise above their juvenile and small-minded act of intended sabotage and set about positively promoting the event he had conceived of and taken great pride in. Besides, God's church was supposed to be all inclusive; it was simply a matter of turning the other cheek - at least for now.

Time for some positive action! Beauville strode over to a group of local journalists sampling some ice-cream and espresso coffee from *La Dolce Vita*'s stand and invited them to take the *Ethical Exchange Chocolate Challenge*.

***

"I really think we should stay inside and support Martin," Juliet Parlour frowned at Dan and Judy Shelton. Curiosity had finally got the better of them; the Sheltons wandered out the back door of the church hall at one thirty to see what the fuss was about outside. Seeing his wife follow in their wake,

Parlour rushed behind with the intention of apprehending her. He didn't want them to be seen to be supporting Pedlar in any shape or form.

"What do we want? British Produce! When do we want it? Now!"

"What do we want? British Produce! When do we want it? Now!"

"What do we want? British Produce! When do we want it? NOW!"

"Cape Cod!" Mark Parlour exclaimed. His wife just snorted in disgust and turned her back on the dozens of grey and white-haired members of the local community. Not satisfied with waving placards, some were now brandishing large vegetables in the air to accentuate their point.

"Oh my goodness, it's the outlaws!" Parlour quipped with a rare paucity of originality, groaning in disbelief. "Jules!"

But his wife had already returned inside. Inviting cries of indignation, Parlour pushed through the throng of protestors and grabbed his mother-in-law's arm.

"Margaret, for goodness sake, what are you doing with these idiots? You'll get arrested!"

"Arrested for what?" Derek Hebble chuckled, self-confidence and self-righteousness bolstered in the presence of like-minded peers. "Being armed with an aubergine?"

"Inciting racial hatred, perhaps," Parlour said dryly, leaving his mother-in-law to stew over the possible implications. While she felt strongly that a stand should be made against the de-Britification of society, as Pedlar termed it, she was not one herself to flout the law, believing firmly in Conservative-Anglican principles of obedience to Queen and Country.

It was time to have strong words with Pedlar, Parlour thought. He was off duty but it would be negligent not to at least warn Pedlar that he could be in hot water very soon. And with Beauville, for that matter. Whilst he respected the vicar's desire not to flatter the protestors by acknowledging their influence over affairs, Parlour felt events were getting out of hand and posed a genuine threat to public order. He really ought to inform Juliet, too, that her parents were in danger of being unceremoniously dumped in the back of a secure police van if they didn't curb their misguided enthusiasm.

He attempted to gain Roy Pedlar's attention but Pedlar was studiously ignoring all attempts to silence him and continued to yell at the top of his voice down a red megaphone. Who was next in line, Parlour wondered. That retired headmaster fellow, wasn't it? What was his name… something pretentious, Parlour remembered. Munroe, that was it, *Davidson* Munroe.

But Munroe was nowhere to be seen. A fellow BASC member informed Parlour that the former Headmaster of Foxburgh High School had dashed off to the allotments in his estate car to pick up more vegetables for the protest.

Give me strength! Parlour muttered, slapping his forehead. They were in for a long and trying afternoon.

***

"Won't you let me have a try?" Penny Roquet begged Martin Beauville in the rather feeble, high-pitched voice that didn't augur well for her public ministry.

Beauville shrugged in a rather defeatist manner. Despite his own misgivings concerning the merits of such a course of action, he had been convinced by several respected members of the parish, Parlour included, that it may now be necessary to disperse the growing mob of protestors outside the church hall. What had started out as a couple of dozen of Roy Pedlar's cronies waving a couple of leeks in the air and bearing a few clichéd slogans on cheap day-glo card, had now turned into a major demonstration against perceived acts of Anti-British subversion within the hallowed walls of Deverton Parish Church. Fearing for the safety of their employees, several of the exhibitors at the Cuisine Festival had now removed their stands from the hall and had escaped before the unrest escalated further.

"You'll need the PA," Beauville informed her wearily. "You'll never make yourself heard above Roy Pedlar, megaphone or not."

Roquet trotted off dutifully in search of the church worship leader, Daniel Kelty, who would be able to fix her up with a microphone outside. Perhaps Daniel could rig her up a little platform, as she didn't enjoy the height advantage of Martin Beauville – not that he had enjoyed much success in his attempt to silence the BASC protestors with a passage on brotherly love. Far too subtle, in her view. Something more topical was required; yes, she had just the passage in mind.

***

"Well, I suppose we better get these sprouts home," Alicia Munroe giggled tipsily, some thirty minutes after their arrival at the allotment. She grabbed hold of the window sill of Salik Gani's potting shed as she staggered to her feet. "Oh, it's been fun!"

"I'll say, Mrs Munroe," Salik giggled, hiding the evidence of their revelry inside a plastic storage locker. "Elderberry vodka, whatever next?"

"Elderberry vodka jelly?" Alicia Munroe queried then burst into a fit of hysterical, alcohol-infused laughter.

"We have to make use of our home-grown produce, that's what I say," her companion slurred. "Will Dave be back yet?"

He struggled to manipulate the lock of the shed door with his spindly, inebriated fingers.

Alicia snorted. *"Am I bothered?* He'll bog off anyway when he sees you, so don't worry!*"

Gani giggled. He loved it when Alicia got hammered with him. She was so funny; her middle-class propriety and regard for the Queen's English went out the potting shed window.

41

"Come on back to my place," Alicia hooted, referring to her husband's shed opposite. "We've some sacks for putting the veggies in."

Salik Gani took the arm proffered him and they stumbled the fifty yards or so to Davidson's wood-stained shed. Alicia wobbled as she bent down to retrieve the key from underneath the ever-present bag of compost outside the door.

"That's funny," she frowned, struggling to push the door inwards. "I can't get this door open."

"Perhaps something's fallen down inside."

"It would have to be quite heavy," Alicia said with furrowed brow. She peered through the window and took a sharp intake of breath.

Please no! She cried, seeing her husband's body slumped on the floor. "Help me, Sal!"

Together they pushed their combined weights, which did not amount to much, against the door. It budged about six inches, enabling Alicia to grasp her husband's wrist with her finger and thumb. There was no pulse.

6

"So my recommendation to you all today," Penny Roquet persevered feebly amid a cacophony of jeers and boos, "is to heed The Apostle Paul's own words on this issue…"

"What do we want? British Produce! When do we want it? Now!"

The chant rose up again in earnest as the oily-scalped priest-in-waiting struggled to deliver her message.

"The Apostle Paul said…" Roquet continued weakly through the melee, determined to get her words out as she saw Martin Beauville striding across the churchyard below her elevated position on the flat roof of the church hall, where Daniel Kelty had hastily rigged up a microphone and lectern for the diminutive cleric.

"British apples, firm and ripe! We don't want any foreign tripe!"

"The Apostle Paul said, in the Book of Romans…"

"Shove your keeee-babs and your curry! We'd rather eat pig slurry!"

"Penny!" Beauville called out in vain, trying to attract her attention from ground level.

"THE APOSTLE PAUL SAID," Roquet shouted this time, making only the tiniest indent on the jeering crowed, *"I am fully convinced that no food is unclean in itself…. let us therefore make every effort.."*

At this juncture a decidedly over-ripe tomato skimmed past Penny Roquet's ear, splatting on the gable wall of the adjoining church building.

Undaunted, Roquet continued, ignoring Martin Beauville's arms gesticulating madly below, advising her in no uncertain terms to quit while she was relatively ahead. *"Let us make EVERY effort to do what leads to peace and to mutual edification. Do not destroy the work of God for the sake of…….. Aggghhhhhh!"*

Like some kind of assassinated crow, Roquet, stunned by an array of airborne courgettes, tipped forwards off the roof of the church-hall, her shapeless black cardigan flapping around her in the gentle March breeze as she fell unceremoniously into the hastily opened arms of the Reverend Martin Beauville.

Several dozen flashlights went off in unison as Beauville staggered backwards onto the lawn, his female priest-in-waiting spread-eagled on top of him.

"Food," Roquet concluded, microphone still in hand.

***

Mark Parlour had, much to his later regret, missed this vintage moment of *Carry On* style comedy, having decided to give no further credence to the exploits of his in-laws and their companions. He had left soon after dispatching a warning to his father-in-law, and had advised Beauville to call Deverton Police if matters escalated further. There was nothing more he could do and, more to the point, it was his day off.

As it was a chilly but sunny mid-March afternoon, Parlour decided to take the circuitous route home, as he needed to drop a book on digital photography into the home of his good friend, Charles Briscoe. He had forgotten the Briscoes were having a family do that Saturday and had taken the slim volume to church with him, in the hope of bumping into one of the Briscoe family at the Cuisine Festival.

As Parlour turned into Maris Piper Way, he heard the baritone arfing of posh people's laughter emanating from the large five bedroom detached on the bend of the road. Over the fence he could see the red and white stripes of a large marquee, housing no doubt a vast array of fine foods and quality wines as well as several generations of the Briscoe family.

Unsurprisingly, there was no response to his pressing of the doorbell, so Parlour opened the side gate and meandered into the well-heeled back garden.

"Mark!" a rather drunken Charles Briscoe bellowed, slapping his friend and fellow churchman on the back. Parlour winced; he was not a well upholstered man, weighing in at just under eleven stone, with these one hundred and fifty-two pounds of lean human flesh spread meagrely over a five foot nine frame.

Parlour exchanged pleasantries with the lantern-jawed blonde stock-broker, scouring the garden for Charles' father as he did so. The Honourable Mr Judge Briscoe was always good for a gas and was probably a little more articulate than his *bon-vivant* son at this moment in time. It had not escaped Mark and Juliet's notice that the usually sculptured features of Charles Briscoe were beginning to fill out a little, with these changes in the facial relief of Lindsay's handsome husband doubtlessly brought on by a little over-indulgence in the high life.

"Here, get some of this down your gullet!" Briscoe leered, grabbing a flute of champagne from a tray doing the rounds and handing it to Parlour. Parlour took a sip and winced. It was nice stuff, that was for sure, but too strong for him early in the afternoon.

"Looking for the old man?" Briscoe enquired. "You're out of luck, he's nipped off to get more wine."

"You've sent your Dad out for supplies on his own ruby wedding anniversary?" Parlour grinned. "Shame on you!"

Briscoe shrugged. "He's in his flash new motor, isn't he? Doesn't want Mum driving it home tonight, so he's not drinking."

"Very sensible!" Parlour laughed. Evelyn Briscoe was not renowned for her cautious negotiation of the highways.

"I hear your Dad's presiding over the trial of *Legs Eleven* at Foxburgh," Parlour continued, referring to the trial of Geoffrey Hardwick, the evil misogynist who had hacked eleven women to death in the vicinity of Billock Mecca, gratuitously removing their legs in some kind of grotesque symbolic act of personal retribution.

"Hope the bastard gets eleven life sentences," Charles bellowed, incurring a filthy look from his wife. It was neither the time nor the occasion for profanity, let alone talk of the Bingo Butcher, as Hardwick was also known.

"Anyway, brought that book around on digital photography," Parlour said hastily.

Charles Briscoe retorted with some hearty banter about Parlour using it as a feeble excuse for gate crashing their wine-fest, before seeing him to the gate.

***

The Reverend Martin Beauville was just brushing himself down when a reporter from Sky News flourished a fat microphone in his face.

"Donya Mickelson, *Sky News*, always first on the scene. Is it fair to say, Reverend Beauville, that today's Cuisine Festival has turned into more of a World Food Fight?"

Large chuckles all around. Martin Beauville groaned and decided honesty was probably the best policy. It had been a humbling experience in how *not* to manage parish diplomatic relations.

"You could say that, yes."

He attempted his most winning smile for the cameras, aware that his face would adorn the Sunday papers, doubtlessly along with an action shot of Penny's impromptu emergency landing.

But for the first time, good fortune swung his way that day – or so it seemed at that juncture – as a taxi screeched up outside Deverton Parish Church and a dishevelled Alicia Munroe all but fell out of the rear passenger seat.

She's either drunk or in a severe state of shock, Beauville thought to himself, unaware of how close to the mark he was on both counts, as Alicia burst through the church gates and bludgeoned her way through the huddle of press people.

"Alicia! Whatever's the matter?" the Vicar of Deverton Parish Church exclaimed.

She was trembling, quite unable to speak. Beauville placed his hands firmly on her shoulders in an attempt to calm her down.

"It's Davidson…. It's my Davey… he's…."

It was as if someone had pressed pause on the DVD:- time seemed to stand still for a second and the collective silence of bated breath hung palpably in the air.

"Come on, let's get you inside," Beauville said hastily, attempting to chivvy Alicia into the church building before three dozen Dictaphones were shoved up her nose and she was visually impaired for life by a flashgun *blitzkrieg*.

But it was too late; her body was frozen with shock and she stood rooted to the spot.

"He's dead!"

A gasp rose up followed by a frenzied clicking of digital SLRs as all semblance of integrity flew out the churchyard.

"Quick, get Mark Parlour," Beauville barked at Penny Roquet, unaware that Parlour had already left the event. He forcibly dragged Alicia Munroe out of harm's way and into the church, jogging her along to his office where he locked the door behind them.

***

Deliberately not in possession of his mobile phone that sunny Saturday afternoon, it was not until Parlour stepped through his front door in Spatchcock Drive just after two thirty pm that he received the emergency message from Martin Beauville. A flustered Juliet had informed him that Alicia Munroe had discovered the body of her husband slumped across the potting shed floor up at Deverton Allotments. Beauville had already driven up there with a catatonic Alicia Munroe, having had the good sense to immediately call for a police presence at the scene of a possible suspicious death, lest the lecherous reporters beat them to it. Hopefully their editors and legal departments would have the wisdom to shelve all shots of Alicia Munroe's dramatic arrival at the church following the shocking discovery of her husband's body, or face almost certain prosecution for prejudicing a police investigation.

"*Cape Cod!*" Parlour had exclaimed, unwilling, as ever, to take the Lord's name in vain. "Did she say what had happened? Blow to the head or…"

"She couldn't see clearly through the dirty window but she was able to open the door a crack and take his pulse – she couldn't get one," Juliet added soberly.

"She's absolutely sure?" Parlour frowned.

"Alicia's a St John's Volunteer, isn't she? I think she'd know."

Parlour nodded.

"Might just be a heart attack or something, he was a bit on the portly side…" Juliet suggested rather feebly.

"Let's hope it's nothing untoward," Parlour frowned, mirroring her thoughts. He grabbed his overcoat, phone and car-keys. "D'you want to come? Alicia might need someone there with her. Not sure if PC Cuddles'll be there."

PC Cuddles was the affectionate name given by her colleagues to WPC Cadley, the Billock Police Family Liaison Officer, generally called out to play teas maid and TLC dispenser when bad news needed to be broken or emotionally fused visits undertaken.

Juliet nodded and followed him out to his silver Merc, where she found her husband attempting to disperse a band of reporters on the driveway. Having heard Martin Beauville's command that Mark Parlour be contacted, they had immediately sought out his home address, with the aim of following him by car to the scene of the potentially newsworthy incident.

Deciding that on this occasion at least, keeping to the speed limit was not in the best interests of public safety, Parlour put his foot down and gave his wife the most thrilling five minutes she'd enjoyed in a long time as he screeched to the allotments at the far end of Deverton.

An ambulance and two squad cars were already present at the makeshift gravel car park at the top of the field.

He nodded to the local constable, Gary White, whom he saw on a daily basis. "Chalky. What's the news?"

"Singh and Tucks are down there with the paras. They're trying to get the back of the shed down, get a look at him without damaging him or any evidence."

"Good," Parlour nodded and taking his wife's hand, walked briskly down the straggly path in the grass to a shed on the left hand-side where a striped cordon had already been placed around the scene of the incident.

"There's Alicia over there with Martin," Parlour informed his wife soberly. "Stay with her, I might need to ask her a few questions in a minute."

Juliet nodded and approached the vicar and his charge.

"DI Parlour, Billock CID," Parlour informed the paramedics, who were waiting for Paul Tucker and Vee Singh to remove the back panel of the shed. Immediately, dozens of gardening products and plant pots tumbled from the shelves, a couple of which clonked the lifeless body of Davidson Munroe on their descent.

"Careful!" Parlour frowned, his knees cracking as he bent down to consider the figure slumped on the wooden floor. He donned some sterile gloves from the inside pocket of his jacket.

"Dead as a doornail," Parlour muttered, placing a finger on the sunburnt neck of the well upholstered middle-aged corpse. It was hard to imagine a figure less like a doornail in appearance.

"Mind if we roll him onto his side?" one of the paramedics enquired.

Parlour weighed up the options. He didn't want the scene touched, yet at the same time, if Munroe had simply suffered a massive fatal heart attack, he would look very foolish indeed calling in a pathologist and forensic team.

"Go ahead."

He winced as a pool of vomit trickled across the floor from the side of Munroe's mouth as the body was rolled onto its left side. Parlour watched as the female paramedic attempted to get Munroe's heart going but to no avail.

"Heart attack?" he enquired.

The male paramedic frowned. "Difficult to say. The vomit indicates he could have had a seizure of some sort, but I couldn't say for sure it's heart failure."

Parlour grimaced. That was not the answer he was hoping for. He stood up and looked around him. A mug of black coffee stood on a ledge by the small cobwebbed window. Parlour picked up the mug and tentatively sniffed its contents, mindful of the last suspicious death he had come across in the vicinity. In that instance, the churchwarden, Terence Haynes, had died of anaphylaxis, having had his cup of coffee spiked with peanuts.

Parlour turned his face away immediately; the liquid emitted a strong chemical odour, rather like that vile stuff Derek Hebble sprayed on his precious herringbone driveway to beat down weeds with attitude. He dipped his gloved finger in it. It was cold.

Parlour stepped over the body and considered the other contents of the shed. Just the usual implements and products associated with gardening, plus a number of well-thumbed items of popular fiction - clearly a haven to escape to, by the looks of it. Parlour grimaced, his knees giving another audible crack as he bent down to consider some objects at floor level. He retrieved a small piece of blue paper from the corner of the shed. It was the torn corner of a note, by the looks of it, for all he could make out were the letters "et"zzz written in small, precise, capitals, followed by an "x". Was that meant to signify a kiss? Parlour considered the possibilities. It could, of course, be a note from Munroe's wife; he would need to ask Alicia about that some time later when she had got over the initial trauma of finding her husband dead on the potting shed floor. Could this note have come from another source, however? Parlour turned the idea over in his mind, as he considered the scene before him. Davidson Munroe did have a bit of a reputation as a slimy chat-up merchant, but would he cheat on Alicia? Despite their little pot-shots at one another, the Munroes had always appeared to be a fairly well-oiled marital unit, coming together for social events, yet respecting each other's individual needs and giving each other space where necessary. Parlour decided the blue piece of paper was probably inconsequential. Who on earth, spouse or otherwise, wrote affectionate notes in block capitals in any case? The X probably signified something else.

Parlour replaced the small piece of blue paper on the floor for Forensics to bag and take off to the lab, should this prove to be a suspicious death.

He pondered a moment, weighing up the evidence before him, then put a call through for a pathologist and some forensic officers.

"Best leave him where he is for the moment," Parlour instructed the paramedics. "Let's face it, he's not going anywhere."

He frowned to himself. If Munroe had been murdered, how on earth had his killer managed to get out the shed, with his victim's body slumped so close to the door? Perhaps unusually, the door opened inwards. Maybe he had made a hasty exit just as Munroe was keeling over, before Munroe's body had hit the deck; he could have checked through the little window that Munroe had indeed breathed his last. Yes, that was probably how it had happened – if, indeed, foul play was involved.

Parlour wandered back over to his wife, the vicar, and the wife of the deceased. He put a comforting hand on Alicia's shoulder.

"I'm sorry, Alicia, I'm going to have to call a pathologist in. It looks like he had some kind of fit, but we're not sure why or how."

"Is it…" Martin Beauville fumbled for the words, trying to be tactful in dire circumstances. "… suspicious?"

Parlour looked at them wanly. "It could be."

Alicia Munroe let out a strange guttural sob then buried her head in her lap, perched as she was, rather bizarrely, on a small folding canvas stool. Juliet Parlour rubbed her back gently, completely at a loss at what to say.

Parlour frowned, suddenly spotting a small figure in dark clothing crouched in the corner of the shed outside which the others were sat.

"Mr Gani, isn't it?" he enquired, recognising the rather worse for wear figure to be the younger son of Abdul Gani, the elderly Bangladeshi man who managed the local convenience store.

"That's right, Sir," Salik Gani replied, a frog in his throat. He cleared his airways and stood up. He walked very carefully out of the shed and blinked as the sharp late afternoon sunlight pierced his eyes.

Parlour couldn't smell alcohol on his breath, but Gani looked, to all intents and purposes, thoroughly inebriated. So did Alicia Munroe, for that matter, but that could just be the shock of finding her husband out cold on the shed floor.

"Mr Gani, what are you doing here?"

"He was at the allotments with Alicia, they both discovered the body," Juliet informed her husband. Parlour put a hand up to halt her progress.

"Let Mr Gani answer for himself, please, darling."

But Salik Gani just stood there shaking, opening and closing his mouth like a cartoon fish, quite unable to utter a sound.

Beauville hastily grabbed his arm as Gani slid to the floor unconscious. A tiny silver hip flask slid out the side pocket of his threadbare grey slacks as he hit the ground.

Parlour ran a weary hand through his auburn hair and waved the paramedics over from the shed opposite. Bang went a relaxing Saturday night in with Jules.

"I'm sorry, Alicia," he informed the newly widowed wife of Davidson Munroe. "I'm going to have to take a statement from you… and meladdo here, once he's back in the land of the living."

Parlour grimaced and looked away. It was an unfortunate turn of phrase in the circumstances.

7

"Leave Gani in Interview Room Two to sober up – make up a coffee butler for him," Parlour commanded PC Nick Rossi, "and bring in one for Mrs Munroe and myself while you're at it."

Parlour disappeared into Interview Room One, where Alicia Munroe was already sat opposite DC Sean Denton.

"My constable's bringing through coffee for us soon," Parlour smiled blandly at Alicia Munroe, very much aware that he had to maintain a distance between himself and his fellow resident of Deverton, a lady known to him for some five years now. In his gut, he did not believe that the normally genteel wife of the retired headmaster had had anything to do with his murder – for murder it appeared to be - despite her unfortunate presence at the scene of the crime. However, he had a duty to take a full statement from her and count her as a suspect until he found evidence to the contrary.

"So recap on your day, Mrs Munroe," Parlour requested, nodding to Denton to make some notes.

Alicia shrugged. "Well I got up about 7.30 am, put some washing in the machine, made myself a cup of tea. Davidson got up soon after, had a shower and got dressed. He then made his usual weekend fry-up. I don't partake in this – the passive fumes alone add inches to my waistline, I'm sure." Alicia let out a brief, bitter chortle.

Parlour's eyes flickered with interest. "You didn't eat the same as him, then?"

Alicia shook her head. "No, Davidson had his bacon, tomatoes, fried bread, mushrooms and sausages; I had two slices of Bonne Maman on toast and some tinned prunes. It's too early in the day for me for all that rich food."

"And he cooked all this?"

"Of course," Alicia confirmed, wrinkling her petite nose in disgust. "I always said to him, if you want to send yourself to an early grave with all that cholest… oh dear."

Alicia let out a sob which she immediately muffled in a dainty white cotton handkerchief.

"And what did he do with the rest of the morning?" Parlour enquired, giving Alicia a moment to compose herself.

"He went to the allotments to pick some leeks and parsnips for his silly food demo, I called on a friend who's just broken her leg then did a spot of shopping at Utopia."

Parlour made a note.

"What did you buy?" Denton chipped in.

"Some paracetomol and a tube of denture cream – I only went to the pharmacy kiosk."

"Nothing else?" Denton enquired rather unsubtly.

"No cyanide in capsule form, if that's what you're implying," Alicia replied acidly.

She's very on the ball, considering her old man's just popped his clogs, Parlour thought to himself, making a note on his own pad of paper.

"That would have been about eleven o'clock," Alicia continued. "Davidson would have already been with Pedlar and co, setting up for their hatchet job at the church."

"So you didn't clap eyes on him the rest of the day?" Parlour confirmed.

Alicia shook her head. "Not until I found his body," she said quietly. "He went out about nine thirty, I left soon after to visit Anne."

"Didn't you want to support your husband over at the church?" Denton frowned. It all seemed a little odd to him.

Alicia laughed hollowly. "Support his jingoistic rubbish? I have more self-respect than that!"

"Did you have much in common, Mr Munroe and yourself?" Denton asked, with the subtlety of a breeze-block. Parlour tutted under his breath.

"We had separate interests and separate views on many things," Alicia replied coldly. "But we shared a bed, if that's what you're driving at. I loved my husband, always have done, always will. You don't need to read from the same editorial to be good together, you know."

"It's been said that your husband was rather popular with the ladies," Parlour began, treading very carefully. "Were you aware that Mr Munroe had a few... erm... romantic entanglements in the past?"

Alicia let out that same sad, hollow laugh. "Sarah Foxton, Laura Haddon, Melissa Eldridge... I can list them all with dates, if you like. There's one area where I *can* assist with police enquiries. But you won't find anything serious on him. Just a little bit of slap and tickle, none of them were underage at the time. Davidson and I have always had a more relaxed attitude than most to a spot of harmless flirtation."

Parlour looked a little taken aback, much to Denton's amusement.

"I knew what he was when I married him," Alicia continued impatiently. "There's more to marriage than..."

"Fidelity?" Parlour enquired archly.

"Sex," Alicia replied. "He never went all the way with his floozies, he knew the boundary. But it *was* about sex - sexual attraction - of course it was."

"How do you know it didn't go any further?" Denton frowned, who just could not believe that the express train could be brought to a last minute halt without overshooting the platform.

"I believed him," Alicia stated firmly. She seemed very sure of her ground, Parlour thought. There was an awkward pause. Parlour cleared his throat.

"And your relationship with Salik Gani was...?"

"Entirely platonic, Mr Parlour," Alicia smiled; the thought of her being romantically involved with the diminutive newsagent was entirely laughable in her book. "Salik has an allotment opposite Davidson's. We got chatting a few times, while I was helping Davey out. He's good fun, but there is nothing more to it, I can assure you."

"You have no children?" Denton persevered.

"What is this?" Alicia cried. "My husband's just been found dead in the shed, and all you can do is cast aspersions on our marriage!"

"DC Denton was just working out whether any relatives needed contacting," Parlour glared at Denton. They'd get nothing out of Alicia Munroe at this rate.

Alicia took a deep breath to calm herself. "It just never happened for us. My sister has children and now grandchildren – we didn't feel deprived. I do a lot in the community with young people, I'm training up youngsters for St John's ambulance at the moment."

Parlour nodded; he had been aware of that. Some of the teenagers from church had enrolled on the course led by Alicia Munroe. Parlour turned over a fresh leaf of paper.

"Moving onto this afternoon – you paid a visit to Mr Gani at the Mini Mart on Deverton Triangle, I believe."

"I was going to make myself a spot of lunch at home, but decided I'd see if Salik was around first. Deverton was deserted; everyone was up at the Church. I knew the Cuisine Festival wasn't his cup of tea, thought there was a good chance he'd be knocking around the shop. I know his brother takes Zoreena shopping in Billock with the kids on a Saturday, elderly Mr Gani has some friends he visits there, too. I think they go to the mosque, as well."

"So Salik *was* there and you chatted for a while before making your way to the allotments? What time did you get to Gani's?"

"About twelve fifteen. We had a cup of tea and some biscuits, then we decided to have a tipple."

"More than one, by the sounds of it," Denton commented.

Alicia shrugged. "Salik keeps a bottle of whisky in the back room. We had a few generous glasses then discussed going back to mine to do a spot of cooking – a shared hobby of ours."

Denton frowned. "Excuse me for sounding dull, but if you both like cooking, why wouldn't you want to be at a food festival?"

"Have you met Roy Pedlar?" Alicia frowned. "He must be the most pompous bore ever to walk this earth, Salik couldn't stand him. In any case, it was really just a glorified way of getting people in the church, and Salik avoids religious gatherings like the proverbial plague. He just about squeaks into the mosque once a month to keep Gani Senior happy. There's no way he'd voluntarily step inside Deverton Parish Church with all those smiley church people milling about, surreptitiously trying to invite you to their meetings by lining your stomach… sorry Mr Parlour."

Parlour grinned. "It's alright, Mrs Munroe, undercover *police* work's my domain! So why did you…."

"Go up to the allotments?" Alicia interjected. "I wish to goodness we hadn't, now." She sighed. "I decided we would go and pick some fresh veggies for our cook-up."

She shrugged, looking down at the table, blushing slightly.

"You know how it is when you have a few drinks… or maybe you don't," Alicia looked reproachfully at the clean-scrubbed Detective Inspector. "You get up to madcap things. They seem quite logical at the time."

There was a timely knock at the door and Nick Rossi entered with some coffee for the three occupants of Interview Room One.

Parlour played teas maid as Denton scribbled more notes.

"I'm sure," Parlour smiled blandly, not giving anything away on that score. "And when did you arrive at the allotments?"

Alicia frowned, trying to work it out. "It would have been about half one."

Denton frowned. "So you were in close proximity at the time of your husband's death, you even picked vegetables from his allotment, yet you neither saw nor heard a thing?"

He looked incredulous once more. Parlour hastily scribbled the words *we don't know it IS murder* on a piece of paper and shoved it to his junior colleague.

Alicia shrugged. "We picked some leeks and some sprouts and carried them into Salik's shed. We had a few drinks and a chinwag for a while, I couldn't tell you exactly how long we were there, but at least half an hour. Then we decided we needed a bag to carry the veg home, so I said, let's get one from Davidson's shed, he has a stash of spud sacks. That was when I couldn't open the door and…"

Alicia buried her head in her hands and let out a strangled sob.

"So you saw or heard nothing?" Parlour confirmed quietly, a moment later. Alicia shook her head. "Nothing at all. I guess he just went back there for more leeks while we were in Salik's shed drinking, and suffered a massive heart attack. We wouldn't have heard him, we were so far gone."

"Did Mr Munroe have a heart problem?" Parlour enquired.

"He had highish blood pressure, all those blinking fry ups, but nothing unusual. He was generally in very good health for a man of his age," Alicia stated.

"And did you see anything suspicious on the way up there?" Parlour asked.

Alicia shook her head.

"Were there any cars parked up at the allotment?"

"The allotments were deserted, there wasn't a soul in sight," Alicia replied slowly. Did Parlour imagine it, or did she frown ever so slightly?

He sensed Denton was straining at the leash to go for the jugular with Alicia Munroe and her unlikely tale, and placed a restraining hand on his forearm.

"That'll be all for now, Mrs Munroe. You can go home. Obviously until the cause of Mr Munroe's death is ascertained, we need you to stay in the area, in case you can help us further with our enquiries."

"That old euphemism," Alicia said coldly.

"And Mrs Munroe – Alicia…" Parlour began, standing up. "My condolences, Davidson was a great... erm… contributor to the community."

Alicia Munroe just glared at him and left the room, accompanied by Sean Denton.

Wonder if Gani's sobered up yet? Parlour wondered, wandering into the adjoining Interview Room.

But Gani was still draped across the table, one hand clutched to his stomach, a plastic ice cream pot next to him in the event of oral spillage. Gani would have to wait until the morning. Meanwhile, he could spend the night in police custody, unless he sharpened up soonish. He could be offered the perfect room with no interior décor to soil and a toilet at the ready.

8

"Darling, you came across very well," Juliet Parlour commented to her husband at ten-thirty that evening as the regional news, which she had recorded, came to a close.

Parlour grabbed the remote control for the DVD recorder and selected playback to watch the Southern Aspect report on the suspicious death at the allotment, this time a bonafide attempt to record newsworthy local events.

He grimaced as he saw himself in his heavy overcoat, a ginger wisp escaping the fine auburn hair usually Brylcreemed to perfection. Should have put a shirt and tie on, it didn't look good. And that was a particularly prominent zit on the left of his forehead, too. This televisual treat bore the caption *Mark Parlour, Senior Investigating Officer, Billock CID*. Oops, that was perhaps taking liberties; maybe he shouldn't have assumed to the press pack that had managed to trace him to the allotments that the case was his. Unlike the murder of Terence Haynes that had taken place four years previous, however, Parlour's wife had not been present at the scene of the crime, so he could not see why there should be any viable conflict of interests. DCI Sewell had been out of town when the death of Davidson Munroe had come to light; Parlour expected a phone call any minute following the broadcast of this news report.

The furore at the Cuisine Festival had also made the regional news, though not the anticipated *And Finally* slots on either ITN or Sky News, despite Pedlar's admirable ability to entice outside broadcast units from the national news stations to the parochial event. Much to Parlour's relief, the television stations concerned had honoured their agreement not to broadcast footage of Alicia Munroe's arrival at the church.

Poor old Martin, Parlour thought. Every innovative project he attempted at Deverton Parish Church seemed doomed to some scandalous failure. Still, the video footage of Penny Roquet flying through the air and landing on top of the vicar did have undisputed comic value. It certainly beat most of the decades old staged fuzzy clips of assorted North American dads falling into swimming pools that made up the bulk of those *Candid Camera* type shows.

Parlour and Juliet snickered as they watched the clip of Penny Roquet again.

"Poor Penny!" Juliet giggled. "She'll never live this down!"

"Neither will Martin!" Parlour grinned, but then sobered up. The events at Deverton Parish Church, even the rather disturbing presence of his in-laws at the fracas, paled into insignificance compared to the premature and puzzling death of retired headmaster, Davidson Munroe.

"Have you questioned Alicia and Mr Gani?" Juliet enquired.

"Gani's still out of it, it'll have to wait until morning. We've talked at length to Alicia, though."

"And?" Juliet prodded him.

Parlour shrugged. "She was up there in the allotment opposite, drinking with Salik Gani. Reckons they neither saw nor heard a thing."

Juliet frowned. "Do you think it's a case of the three wise monkeys? *See no evil, hear no evil, speak no evil?*"

Parlour shrugged again. "I find it hard to believe they didn't hear a thing, if Munroe *was* murdered, that is. But then again, if you were larking around with a mate, drunk as a skunk, would you necessarily hear anything? There's only one dusty little high up window in the shed, if they didn't happen to be looking out at the time, they wouldn't have seen anything. In any case, it could well be the case that the killer, assuming there was one, had locked himself in the shed and was lying in wait for Davidson Munroe to arrive. They didn't open the shed after all, until after his death. Gani and Alicia just picked some veg from outside."

"Hmmm…" Juliet sighed. It was all rather peculiar, she had to admit.

The telephone rang.

"That'll be Sewell after my dangly bits," Parlour groaned, grabbing the cordless phone from the coffee table. But it was Rossi from Billock Station. Apparently Gani had kept down a mug of coffee and was ready to give an interview.

"Got to go, Jules," Parlour said apologetically, dropping a kiss on his wife's head. "Gani's made a spectacular recovery and is willing to talk. I need to head back to the station. Hopefully I won't be long."

Juliet kissed him goodbye then replayed the news clip once more, this time putting it on a slow reverse picture mode, so that she could witness the even more comical sight of Penny Roquet flying backwards up into the air and landing on the church roof, like some kind of Church of England marionette doll.

****

But Salik Gani could offer nothing in the way of new information. He confirmed Alicia Munroe's statement that they had left for the allotments around half past one. They had picked some vegetables then returned to his shed for a few generous shots of home-bru vodka. Some time later, he couldn't say exactly when, they had decided to get some sacks from Munroe's shed to carry the leeks and sprouts home in. But they had been unable to open the shed door, and that was when they realised Munroe's body was slumped across the floor. He hadn't seen nor heard a thing and no, he had no reason for wishing Mr Munroe dead, had his death not been an accident.

Parlour had a hard time believing this wiry little man who helped run the local convenience store had had anything to do with the death of Davidson Munroe. Yet given that Gani had been in the immediate vicinity of the site where a suspicious death had taken place, at the exact time of its occurrence, and that he had, to the obvious detriment of the family name and business, shut up shop during opening hours to go there, had to make him Parlour's chief suspect. To make matters worse for Gani, he had been blind drunk at the time and could have conceivably acted out of character. Was this a racially motivated crime? Munroe had been second in charge, after all, of a party that sought to whitewash Britain. And Gani was not white, and had not been present at the Cuisine Festival. But then again, the visitor to the shed could have been one of Davidson's numerous women, or perhaps more likely, a jealous husband, come to eek revenge on the retired headmaster.

Parlour frowned as he escorted Gani to a taxi outside Billock Police Station. Hopefully the lab would get in touch soon and he could determine whether this was a murder enquiry or an unfortunate natural occurrence.

Juliet was still pottering around downstairs when Parlour returned in the early hours of the morning, quite unable to sleep with the unlikely events of the day still spinning around in her head.

"Well then?"

"Gani reckons he didn't see nor hear a thing. His account tallied with Alicia Munroe's.

"But he's such a harmless chap, I can't imagine for one minute he would murder…"

"Whoa!" Parlour halted her. "We don't know it *is* murder. Forensic haven't got back to us yet. But if it was, then Gani has to be our main suspect. After all, he wasn't at the Cuisine Festival. And he *was* at the allotments at the time of death, *and* he found the body with Alicia." Parlour paused for breath. "*And* he was smashed out of his skull on whisky and home-brew vodka. He was enjoying his own little Drinks Festival with Munroe's wife!"

"Oh boy!" Juliet whistled. "It doesn't look good for him, put like that, does it?"

The phone rang. Parlour cursed; it had been a while since he'd had a suspicious death to contend with, he'd almost forgotten the disruption it caused to his cosy evenings in with Juliet.

"Parlour," he responded curtly. "You what? In the mug? From where… oh I see."

He tossed the phone onto the sofa. It went without saying that Juliet would not breathe a word to an outside party; Parlour knew he could trust his wife implicitly on the discretion issue.

"He was poisoned, Jules."

"Not bloomin' peanuts again?" Juliet frowned, alluding again to the murder of the church warden, Terence Haynes, which had so shocked the designer town of Deverton a few years back.

"Someone put liquid paraquat in his tea mug. He took one swig of it and died instantly."

"Para-wot?" Juliet looked puzzled.

"Para-*quat*," Parlour replied. "Very strong, potentially lethal, herbicide. You know, for killing weeds and stuff."
"Yes, I know what a herbicide is, thank you," Juliet replied acerbically.

"You do surprise me," Parlour retorted lightly, for the upkeep of the garden was strictly his domain.

"So the killer just popped it in his mug and Munroe drank it while they were chatting?" Juliet frowned. It all seemed rather unlikely.

"I guess so," Parlour shrugged.

"Hold on though, wasn't Davidson Munroe at the Cuisine Festival?" Juliet queried. "I seem to remember him performing a kind of testosterone-laden Morris Dance with leeks while we were there!"

"He disappeared halfway through," Parlour recalled, "to fetch more artillery! He drove to his allotment to pick up more leeks and things. I remember now, because I was trying to have a word with him as Roy Pedlar wouldn't comply – Munroe was next in charge of the BASC Pensioners."

"But how would the killer know he was there, if Munroe had only popped over quickly?" Juliet wondered.

"Obviously Munroe was using the leeks as an excuse to keep an arranged appointment with someone," Parlour replied.

"So whoever it was made a cup of tea for Munroe which he'd spiked with this para.."

"Paraquat. Presumably, yes."

"And Alicia Munroe and Salik Gani were there at the same time?" Juliet confirmed, shaking her head. It beggared belief.

"They both maintain they neither saw nor heard a thing."

"Do you believe them?" his wife enquired. Parlour was an excellent judge of character, as a rule; a gift that had served him well over the years and which had accelerated his progress to rank of Detective Inspector. Parlour's refusal to rigidly pursue more obvious lines of inquiry when his instinct led him in another direction had seldom let him down, though it was often a risky strategy.

"I don't know either of them very well," Parlour conceded, "however they both seem pretty decent upstanding… albeit in this case, temporarily paralytic… members of the local community. Alicia Munroe helps out and gives financial support to a number of community based projects. Salik Gani is just an all-round nice guy, likes a bit of tittle-tattle and the odd flutter on the gee-gees, but nothing more sinister."

"Is he married?"

Parlour shook his head. "No, he's not. The proverbial bachelor, by all accounts."

"They're Muslim, aren't they?" Juliet frowned.

Parlour nodded. "I don't think the Ganis are particularly strict Muslims, though - well not the sons, at least. I gather Salik Gani likes a bit of a drink and Chalky White spotted him down *The Tall Ships* on *BOGOF Banger* night last week."

The phone rang again. This time it was PC Paul Tucker from the local station in Deverton. Juliet gauged from Parlour's short responses and worried facial expression that more trouble was afoot.

"That was Tucks," Parlour informed his wife. "Some racist thugs have gathered outside Gani's flat. I knew it was risky, letting him go home."

He grabbed his coat and keys again. "Go to bed, Jules. I'll see you when I see you – tonight's a write-off as far as sleep's concerned."

***

Salik Gani's one-bedroom maisonette was disadvantageously situated opposite the smattering of local amenities that serviced the immediate needs of the residents of Deverton Estate, and which was known to all and sundry as Deverton Triangle, though in reality it was more pentagonal in shape. From his front room, he could see into the dimly lit façade of the *Aromatic Duck*, the local Chinese takeaway; the metal shuttered, *Billock Courier* sponsored, eyesore that was Perry's Newsagent; the local launderette, its pale yellow walls under permanent threat from the local graffiti artists, and finally, Deverton Mini Mart, run by his own family, the flat above which was occupied by his father Abdul, brother Nazrul, sister-in-law Zoreena and his four nieces and nephews. On a normal weekday night, he could count on at least one group of disaffected teenagers loitering outside his lounge window, swigging cheap cider from bottles doubtlessly acquired by some older member of their gang. It wasn't the Ganis' fault; who could stop a young person of legal age from purchasing alcohol in their shop then selling it on to juveniles? The local plod, frequently busy over Billock way, where there was always more than enough to keep them occupied of an evening, had nothing to gain by meandering down to Deverton Triangle simply to caution a few under-age drinkers, or to move on some rowdy crowd who would simply sneak back ten minutes later.

Aware of the threat to his own personal safety from confronting lumpy white youths often twice his own bodyweight, Salik Gani had come to adopt a rather defeatist attitude towards unwelcome visitors to his front garden. Tonight, however, he was not so much anxious as downright terrified.

For in his front garden, and indeed amassing on the pavement and road outside, were at least thirty journalists with camera crew, some focused intently on his front window, others concentrating on the two dozen or so angry youths and residents, some of the elderly variety, shouting and catcalling for his intestines.

Gani had had a horrible feeling as soon as those paramedics had arrived and confirmed that Alicia's old man was beyond help, that he would somehow be linked with his death. Gani tried not to be cynical, but a combination of poor self-esteem and bitter past experiences at the hands of ignorant idiots, had filled him with little hope of being discounted from police enquiries. That was why he had cowered in the allotment, trying to suck every little last drop of Lowland courage from his monogrammed hip flask.

Though it saddened him greatly, as a second generation immigrant who had done nothing to harm anyone in his life, Gani had not been surprised to see such a swell of press people and local head cases outside his flat; goodness knows how many more there would be, had it not been the early hours of the morning. What he had not anticipated was the sheer intensity of media presence and speculation, and the mass boarding of such a crassly unoriginal bandwagon. Those bloody Nazi Pensioners were to blame, surely, stirring up all that Pro-British feeling at the posh nob vicar's Cuisine Festival thingy.

It was thus that Gani felt he had no choice but to call the police, whilst he still had glass in his window frames. Perhaps that Parlour chap that had questioned him at Billock Nick would turn up again. He'd heard from Alicia that he was a pretty decent bloke - though allegedly his in-laws had been brandishing spring lettuces in the air along with the other pompous prats from the group he and Alicia had hitherto humorously referred to as the BASC Separatists.

He crouched down under the window and attempted to peer out the gap at the bottom of the nets without attracting attention to himself, lest a few more bricks, or more edible hardware, were hurled his way.

He groaned. The crowd, if anything, had got larger. He put his hands over his ears and rocked on the floor as a flurry of highly unoriginal and deeply racist taunts punctuated the spring air in the early hours of Sunday morning.

9

"Thought you'd be having a lie-in," Juliet yawned, staggering downstairs to breakfast at 9 am that Sunday morning. Parlour was already sat at the table, slurping noisily from a bowl of Utopia *Flakes of Corn*, *The Observer* spread out in front of him.

"Couldn't sleep," Parlour grunted, scanning the inside pages for mention of the Cuisine Festival. But there was nothing. It was, as he imagined, no more than humorous Little England fodder for the tabloid press.

"So what news?" Juliet enquired.

"Ay?" Parlour grunted again, engrossed in the newspaper.

"Salik Gani! What happened last night over at the Triangle?"

"Oh, that," Parlour replied absently. "Tucks and I got him across the road to his brother's place then stuck some constables outside for the night."

"Bet you're popular, Saturday night and all that," Juliet commented, tightening her dressing gown and adjusting the collar, a nervous habit of which she had many. She poured herself some fruit juice and put two slices of *Kingsmill* in the toaster.

Parlour shrugged. "Sunday morning, technically. Still better than policing Billock on a weekend."

"'Spose," Juliet agreed. "Have you remembered that we need to pop around Mum and Dad's after church?"

"Oh yes," Parlour frowned. Juliet had left a library book there on their last visit which was now overdue. It made sense to pick it up while they had time, rather than take a detour there during rush-hour on a weekday.

"So you've been assigned the Munroe case, then?" Juliet enquired, determined she was going to make conversation with her husband over breakfast and interrupt his love-in with the *Observer* editorial.

"Mm."

"Mark!"

Parlour looked up at his wife's exasperated face. "Sorry, darling."

He folded the paper in four and tossed it behind him on the worktop, knocking over the box of Utopia pseudo Corn Flakes at the same time.

Juliet sighed.

"Yes, I got the anticipated tongue-lashing from Sewell about knowing my place etcetera but he's letting me have first crack at it. He knows you can't beat local knowledge and I certainly have that."

Juliet nodded. "Didn't you say you had some new guy starting soon?"

"Mm," Parlour smirked, "a chap by the name of Cameron Goodlove."

"Oh my!" Juliet giggled. "Is he for real?"

"Apparently he's built like a brick privy, despite the foppish name," Parlour replied. "He's already met most of the gang; I was out the office at the time. Seemed to go down well."

"Can't wait to meet him – what is he, DS?"

"Yep, newly promoted. Bit cocky, according to the Sewer, needs the experience to go with the confidence. Should meet him tomorrow."

"Oh well, I'll expect a full report at teatime, then," Juliet grinned. "Oh poo, I've just remembered, I offered to help Lindsay run the crèche at church this morning!"

"Brace yourself, then!" Parlour smirked. Juliet looked puzzled. "You know, for the latest instalment of *My Perfect Family*, sponsored by Colgate!"

Juliet groaned. "Don't you just wish they'd have a stomping good marital every so often like every healthy married couple?"

"Preferably in full view of the rest of the congregation, to give us all hope," Parlour agreed.

Juliet stood up as her toast popped. "Better get my skates on - need to get there a bit earlier to set up."

*****

"The crazy thing is," a pale and lined Alicia Munroe told WPC Nicole "Cuddles" Cadley, "is that I avoided the Cuisine Festival yesterday because I was sick of Davidson ranting on… now I'd do anything to hear his pompous nonsense across the kitchen table. The house is just so horribly quiet without him."

WPC Cadley nodded in sympathy, the proverbial accoutrement to the dismal grey-brown beverage dished up by a clearly distracted Alicia Munroe that Sunday morning. In her view, it was just good that Alicia was able to talk, not even twenty-four hours after her terrible ordeal at the allotments. Known informally at Billock CID as the "Grief Liaison Officer", Police Liaison Officer Nicole Cadley was pretty well-grooved in the art of visiting the recently bereaved and traumatised. From her experience, the sufferers, at least at this early stage, generally adopted a position on a volume-related spectrum of a kind, from the numbly silent at one end to the loud and angry at the other. In the middle were those who hadn't quite got to grips with whatever terrible twist of fate had befallen them, and who wanted to talk, wanted to make some sense of events. Alicia Munroe occupied this point on the scale. Perhaps in a few days, when the realization that her husband, dearly beloved or otherwise, wasn't coming back, not ever, the words would dry up and the terrible numbness would set in. Or perhaps it would transpire that foul play had snuffed the life out of Davidson Munroe once and for all, and then the bewildered ramblings would turn to pure rage. You couldn't tell at this early stage, without the full facts on the table, which way it would go. There were rumblings at the station that Munroe had been poisoned; soon the pathologist would hand over his report to Mark Parlour, and they would know for sure.

"Did you manage to make any of those phone calls to the family?" Cadley probed gently.

Alicia shook her head dismally. For all her rather infantile bantering with Salik Gani, she remained a proud and stoic woman and it was with some degree of self-loathing that she had put the handset down while it was still ringing her sister's number in Bognor Regis.

"Who do you need to call?" Cadley enquired, taking out her pocketbook. Parlour would appreciate the family info. She was already aware that the Munroes had no children.

"My sister, Margot, in Sussex. A couple of distant relatives of Davidson's in the Midlands. And..." her voice faltered once more. She buried her head in her hands on the farmhouse table.

Cadley waited.

"Lisbeth, my mother-in-law... oh, this will kill her. She's pretty flaky... I don't know if I should tell her, it'll finish her off, it will, I know it will..."

She'll find out pretty soon anyway, if the boys at the station are right, Cadley thought to herself grimly, her compassionate face bearing no trace of the malaise within.

"Did she see Mr Munroe often?" Cadley enquired instead.

Alicia nodded, blowing her nose loudly on a piece of floral kitchen roll. Her supply of dainty cotton hankies had long since dried up.

"My husband has been called many things in his lifetime, but one thing you could always say in his favour:- he was a devoted son. Davidson was forever popping over with something from the allotment. Not that she ate it, I shouldn't have thought, appetite of a sparrow... but I expect the care home did well out of him. Bless him..." Alicia stifled a large sob. "I'm sorry..."

"It's OK, it's fine to cry," Cadley reassured the older woman, squeezing her hand once more. "You won't embarrass me."

"What *am* I going to tell her?" Alicia Munroe spread her palms out before her.

"Well," Cadley replied slowly and thoughtfully. "If he visited often, I guess you are going to have to tell her the truth and pretty soon. Is she in full possession of her faculties, as they say?"

Alicia looked up. "She isn't in the least bit confused, or however they put it these days – just physically weak. Sanest person in the rest home, and that's including the staff." She afforded herself a tearful chuckle.

She looked up beseechingly at the young police constable half her age sat across the table from her.

"Can't I just tell her he died peacefully… in his sleep, say? That he had a massive heart attack and wouldn't have known anything about it?"

Cadley considered this statement. It not only revealed Alicia's desire to spare her mother-in-law some shocking news; it also told Cadley that Alicia did not believe for one minute that her husband had indeed died an innocent death. She would have to tread carefully here. By all accounts, choice winter vegetables were not the only seeds Davidson Munroe had been sowing up at the allotment. Despite there being a general consensus of opinion in the incident room at Billock CID that the suspicious death of the retired headmaster was somehow linked to the Cuisine Festival, it could not be ruled out that this was a crime of passion. Was Alicia Munroe aware of her husband's philandering? It was certainly common knowledge among the more senior officers at Billock CID, who had shared a clubhouse with Munroe at Chave Country Club. That would be a question for Mark Parlour and co, once pathology had made their findings available to the senior investigating officers. She was not here to ask leading questions but to support the bereaved in that awful emotional transit time between death and known cause of death, whilst simultaneously aiding Parlour in his enquiries by passing on any relevant information.

"Do I have to tell her anything at all?" Alicia continued, a little hope flickering her raspy tones. "Need she know? Can't I just say Davidson's not well and visit her instead?"

Cadley raised her eyebrows at the older woman to indicate the unfeasibility of this course of action.

"The family must be informed immediately, Alicia. We should know later today, if…" Cadley paused, unsure whether to rock the boat. Too late.

"If somebody did him in, you mean," Alicia interrupted, her voice cracking. *That was more like it*, Cadley thought to herself. A little bit of hysteria in the circumstances was quite healthy.

"Then, I suppose, it'll make the papers and she'll find out anyway."

"They'll name the victim, yes, if foul play is involved." Cadley nodded in concurrence.

***

It was just after eleven thirty a.m. when the Parlours pulled up outside Juliet's parents' house in Chave.

"Looks like they're out," Parlour commented, alighting from his silver sports car and locking it with the remote handset as his wife proceeded up the pristinely maintained herringbone driveway. She rang the doorbell, but as expected, there was no reply.

"Got the spare key?" Parlour enquired.
Juliet shook her head. "No, they said they'd be in."

"Probably out tossing leeks at innocent bystanders," Parlour grinned.

"Don't, it's embarrassing," Juliet frowned, who was deeply ashamed of her parents' right-wing leanings.

Parlour lifted a few flowerpots but found no spare key. He clicked his fingers. "They get the *HomeGadget* magazine, don't they? I bet you they've got the key hidden in one of those pretend pebbles!"

"Sadly you may well be right," Juliet groaned and rummaged around the rockery and shingle in the vicinity of the white PVC front door. "Bingo!" she grinned, selecting a rather too perfect grey pebble, like pumice stone in appearance. She shook it and it rattled. Parlour took a penknife from his pocket and prized open a little plastic flap on its bottom, revealing a secret compartment bearing the front door key.

"Hold on, what's this?" Parlour muttered, extracting a small piece of blue folded paper stuffed inside with the key.

"Mark!" Juliet exclaimed. "Don't be so nosey!"

She looked at her husband's furrowed brow. "What does it say, then?"

Parlour showed it to her.

"US 273 0900," she read out loud, "Signed *Inspector Gadget*."

She looked up at her husband. "My goodness, do you think it's some kind of American secret society? Perhaps they're working for the FBI!" She giggled as Parlour opened the front door.

"What are you doing?" Juliet enquired as Parlour began to rummage through the drawers of his mother-in-law's sideboard. "I've got my library book, they left it by the front door in case we called."

"Looking for the *HomeGadget* catalogue," her husband muttered.

"It was getting picked up last week, wasn't it? Remember Mum saying she needed to leave it by the front door? You know, when she went a bit doo-lally for a few seconds and we thought she was behaving rather oddly..."

Parlour clicked his fingers. "You're right. Oh well, it was worth a try."

"What are you on about, anyway?" Juliet frowned, stuffing the library book inside the grey canvas shoulder bag that Parlour so detested. In his view, it made his wife look like a mature student, under-dressed and slightly off the fashion pace.

"US 273 0900… sounds like a product number to me. I'm intrigued, that's all."

Juliet made a face. "I don't know what the big deal is. So the old fogy who distributes the magazine and goes by the ingenious pseudonym of *Inspector Gadget* has recommended some ridiculous tacky item to my dear parents just to make their lives that little bit more twee? I wonder what it could be? Crampons to facilitate their life on the edge?"

Parlour grinned. As a rule, sarcasm was not an attractive trait in his wife, but when it came to his in-laws, he could tolerate it in abundance.

"Come on, let's go," he instructed Juliet, shutting the door behind them, before replacing the key in the pseudo-pebble. "I'll stop by Gani's Mini Mart on the way home, haven't paid the papers in ages. Won't do for the local Copper to run up a huge tab at the local shop!"

The newspapers were the only product Parlour purchased at the one-stop, with Gani's Mini Mart being the sole deliverer of newspapers in the immediate area.

Juliet smiled to herself; running up a bill at the Mini Mart had not troubled her husband before. She suspected he would not be so concerned, had the store not been managed by the family at the centre of the murder investigation.

They pulled up some fifteen minutes later and Parlour alighted from his car.

Just for once, he thought grimly to himself, sidestepping a line of placard bearing pensioners and assorted hangers-on outside Deverton Mini Mart that Sunday afternoon, *it wouldn't do the Ganis any harm to shut up shop on the Sabbath*. Apart from an early finish on Friday, the Mini Mart was open seven am to ten pm every day. Nevertheless, it seemed like a rather foolhardy act of defiance in the circumstances. They would have had every justification, given the trying situation in which they found themselves, to take advantage of the flexible working laws for a Sunday and remain shut.

A small, but doughty, picket line had formed outside the Mini Mart, consisting of several of the less law-abiding senior citizens Parlour had encountered at the Cuisine Festival the previous day, plus, rather worryingly, a dozen or so hard-faced 18-30s of both gender, with sufficient anger and misguided prejudice inside of them to eagerly board the bandwagon stopping in the town of Deverton.

As Parlour attempted to enter the door of the Mini Mart to pay his newspaper bill, four shaven-headed youths in hideous "stadium" anoraks closed in to barricade his entry.

"What do you think you're doing?" Parlour enquired.

"Support Davey Munroe, boycott Paki produce!" They chorused.

"Excuse me?" There was an angry glint in Parlour's eye.

They repeated their mantra.

"And since when was Davidson Munroe a good friend of yours?" Parlour couldn't resist asking.

"'E stood up for our cultural 'eritage, didn't 'e," grunted one of the thugs. Parlour grimaced. If there was one thing that made him cringe, it was ill-educated people coming out with hackneyed political sound bites as if they were uttering pearls of profound wisdom. Making a martyr of old Day-Glo Munroe, whatever next?

A few mutterings by the more senior members of the picket line as to the status of Mark Parlour saw the barricade swiftly part ways.

"Thank you," Parlour said testily and entered the store.

"Good afternoon, Detective Inspector," Abdul Gani greeted Parlour with a tone of respectful gratitude for braving the morons outside his shop.

"Off duty, just come to settle my debts," Parlour smiled, reaching in his wallet for a twenty pound note. He hadn't paid the bill in a while. "Is your son still here?"

"He's upstairs with the rest of the family," Gani Senior replied sombrely, flicking through a notepad until he found Parlour's account. "Scared as a rabbit, poor boy. It's terrible, the things they've been saying, terrible. That'll be eighteen pounds forty, Mr Parlour."

"I quite agree," Parlour nodded, handing over a twenty.

"And how is Mrs Munroe?" Abdul Gani enquired.

God bless you, Parlour thought to himself. He would bet the other twenty quid in his pocket that the mob outside hadn't given one thought to the welfare of Davidson Munroe's widow that Sunday afternoon.

"Bearing up, by all accounts," Parlour replied. "I haven't been to see her yet; we have a uniformed officer who specialises in home visits for the bereaved."

He was careful not to say *victims of crime.* It was not definite yet that foul play had been involved, though given the fraught atmosphere that had gripped Deverton yesterday, it was hard to believe Munroe's death was an unfortunate coincidence, occurring as it did in the midst of an angry demonstration at the church hall, in which Munroe himself had played a pivotal role.

"Would you send her my condolences and very best regards when you see her?" Gani requested of Parlour. "Salik would like that. He cares very deeply for Mrs Munroe; she has been such a good friend to him. It's not easy living in a village like Deverton, we miss the Bangla community in Billock a great deal. We saw a business opportunity and we took it, but it hasn't been an easy ride for any of us."

Parlour nodded in sympathy. One could count the non-Caucasian members of the populace of Deverton on the fingers of two hands. He could well imagine the Ganis having problems integrating into the social void that was Deverton.

What we need here, Parlour thought, not for the first time, as he barged his way through the ugly mob outside and crossed the street, *is a pub or a community centre*. Or perhaps they could double up as one multifunctional social outlet for the natives of the new designer town. The church hall did not really count as a community centre, as however new and modern its rooms were, it still had the stigma of belonging to a religious organisation, and as such, it was not always easy to entice non worshipping members of the parish through its front doors.

Mind you, Beauville had done a pretty good job yesterday of getting the people of Deverton into the church building on Saturday, though perhaps in reality, those crazy BASC wrinklies had attracted the majority through the gates. Parlour frowned, recalling his in-laws' involvement in the tasteless melee that had ensued. He would have to have a word with them; it wouldn't do the credibility of either Juliet or himself much good in their very public professions of teacher and police inspector respectively, to have their family involved in such a politically volatile movement.

Parlour crossed the main road and headed for his four bed detached in Spatchcock Drive. Hopefully pathology had come back with the post-mortem results for Davidson Munroe, and he could crack on with finding out who really did have it in for the retired headmaster and vice-chairman of the British Alliance of Senior Citizens, Deverton Branch. He would eat his Brylcreem if that wiry waif, Salik Gani, had actually had anything to do with it.

10

"DS Goodlove, Sir," Detective Sergeant Karen Preece informed Parlour at nine o'clock that Monday morning.

"Send him in, Karen," Parlour smiled at his favourite officer and rose to his feet, awaiting his first view of the much talked-about newly promoted sergeant. Parlour's eyes rose skywards as the strapping young detective entered his office.

"You must be Cameron," Parlour smiled, shaking his hand. He'd heard some rather less than flattering comments about Goodlove's timekeeping skills, but he'd got here for 9am and that was good enough for Parlour. Just so long as he didn't start taking liberties and let the big hand slip too far beyond the vertical.

"Pleased to meet you, Sir," Cameron Goodlove smiled a little nervously, giving Parlour's slender hand rather too hefty a pump in his anxiety to impress.

"Don't have time to chat, sorry," Parlour apologised, slipping his suit jacket on and grabbing a wad of papers. "Just got the pathologist's report on Davidson Munroe – you've been briefed about the case, I take it?"

Goodlove indicated that he had indeed. "DS Preece called me at home yesterday."

"Good," Parlour nodded. He could always rely on Karen to play Jeeves and seamlessly attend to the small matters that kept the show on the road; in this case, enabling Cameron Goodlove to hit the ground running, thus avoiding wasting valuable police time bringing a new officer up to speed on the case.

"Right, follow me."

Cameron Goodlove had to abandon his normal lumbering walk to keep up with Parlour as the fleet of foot Detective Inspector deftly dodged through the dozy Monday morning staff meanderings and through several double doors to the Incident Room of Billock CID.

Parlour marched into the hub of activity and its occupants immediately fell silent. Goodlove was impressed.

"Davidson Munroe, found dead in his potting shed at approximately two fifteen pm Saturday afternoon – we have the pathologist's report."

Goodlove took the seat offered him by DS Preece and rejected the offer of a cigarette from DC Sean Denton. Perhaps later. Mark Parlour didn't have the appearance of a smoker about him, far too anal and clean-cut, best not rub him up the wrong way on their first morning.

"The post-mortem has revealed that Munroe died from… wait for it…"

"Syphilis!" yelled DC Darren Keough crudely from the back row. Cameron Goodlove guffawed rather too loudly for Parlour's liking and he gave him a stern look. Goodlove looked at his feet and wished he had polished his black Brogues that morning.

"… liquid paraquat… common or garden name, pardon the pun, weed killer." Parlour paused then parked his bony bottom on the desk and referred to his notes.

"Hunter's report indicates that Munroe died from ingestion of a bipyridyl based liquid herbicide at around two pm on Saturday afternoon, death would have been almost instantaneous. The herbicide, or weed killer, was placed in Munroe's tea mug from which the deceased evidently took a hefty swig."

"It wasn't suicide, Sir?" Karen Preece enquired immediately.

Parlour acknowledged her contribution with a definitive shake of the head. "The presence of non-digested paraquat down Munroe's chin and shirt front suggests he was force-fed the contents of the mug by a third party. That is to say, some of it missed his mouth, which would clearly be unlikely had Munroe administered the liquid himself. In addition, bruising to the face and neck area tells us that some kind of struggle took place - again indicative of force-feeding."

"Couldn't he have spat it out immediately, Sir, if it tasted funny, like? Perhaps someone snuck it into his mug. Perhaps he got the bruises earlier, digging up his leeks or something," DC Jenkins ventured.

"What, the leeks fought back?" DS Sean Denton guffawed loudly. But Parlour smiled at shy Welsh junior CID officer Ian Jenkins. It had taken some courage for him to ask a question in front of the others and Parlour noted the flush rising up the young man's neck.

He shook his head. "The liquid would still have contained traces of saliva, Ian."

"Could still have been suicide," Darren Keough countered. "He could have been in a bit of a state, Sir, his hands might have been shaky."

"Indeed, Darren. However, Davidson Munroe was a confident man and very much in his element that afternoon. We have no evidence to suggest he was in any shape or form depressed or disenchanted with life."

Parlour paused and surveyed the room once more. He had the full attention of all of his officers, and, he was pleased to note, Cameron Goodlove was now looking him square in the eye.

"We're not sure if this is entirely relevant at this juncture, however Hunter also found traces of a recently ingested slice of fruit cake among the contents of Munroe's stomach. Now obviously there was a lot of food doing the rounds at the World Cuisine Festival, and I do recall seeing some fruitcake on the tables personned by Pedlar's lot. Again, I couldn't say if this is relevant as Munroe may have just been a messy eater, but he also had fruitcake crumbs on his jumper, again possibly pointing to his being force-fed by a second individual."

A murmur went around the room.

DS Goodlove raised a hand in the air.

"It's alright, Cameron, you're not at school now," Parlour grinned, thinking you could spot a mile off who had worked for that T-Rex, Brian Sewell, at County HQ.

Goodlove turned a mild shade of pink and cleared his throat. "Sir, did you say the weed killer was put *in* his tea mug?"

Parlour shook his head. "When I visited the scene of the crime, I actually picked up the mug, assuming it was black coffee. I had to turn my head away immediately, the smell was so overpowering. It puzzled me that it smelt so strongly of chemicals, above and beyond the general smell of garden products in the shed. So I had it checked out, and it transpires that the mug contained pure unadulterated liquid paraquat, which in its purest form, closely resembles black coffee or coke. Now, this is where it gets interesting…"

Parlour paused to study his notes. "Because of the potentially fatal consequences of inhaling or ingesting paraquat, the world's main producer of the stuff, ICI, made some changes to its formulation in the 1970s. In the mid-seventies, they put what's known as a *stenching agent* in it…."

"Otherwise known as DCI Sewell," Keough bellowed. Brian "The Sewer" Sewell was notorious for filling enclosed spaces with particularly noxious bodily gases, to the extent that one year a Danger Highly Flammable Gases sticker had been attached to the rear bumper of his grey Lexus during a moment of drunken revelry by his juniors at Foxburgh CID.

This time Parlour did not glare at Goodlove for guffawing loudly.

"Ahem…" he continued. "In the late 70s, an emetic was added, so that anyone who took a tipple of liquid paraquat would throw up immediately. And just in case that didn't do the trick, they stuck some blue dye in it as well, so it couldn't be mistaken for coke or coffee."

"So… what are you saying, Sir?" Karen Preece enquired. "That the liquid in Davidson Munroe's tea mug pre-dated this stuff?"

Parlour nodded. "That is exactly my point, Karen. You can't buy paraquat in this formulation in this country and indeed, you haven't been able to for thirty odd years."

"So it was a very old bottle of the stuff?" Goodlove frowned.

"Or it was introduced from another country where rules governing herbicide formulations aren't so stringent," Parlour stated.

"Gani!" Keough exclaimed. He slapped his thigh. "I knew our friend the paperboy was mixed up in this somehow!"

"Darren, I consider that a racist assumption," Parlour warned him. "All I meant was, whatever killed Davidson Munroe was not bought in this country in recent times. Therefore it was either brought in from outside somehow – not easily done in this day and age – or has been knocking around in someone's shed for nigh on 30 years or more."

"Could it have been ordered on the internet?" Preece frowned.

"What – on E-bay?" Keough scoffed, as was his custom.

Parlour tipped his head to one side to consider Preece's question. "It would still be extremely difficult to get it into the country but it's worth checking out, sure."

There was a pause as Parlour's crew considered the new information that had come to light concerning the death of Davidson Munroe.

Parlour stood up. "It seems fairly obvious to me that Munroe's death was no accident, so this is officially a murder enquiry. I need Deverton Allotments shut down and a thorough search made of the contents of every shed, as well as all refuse on site. Failing that, we may need to do a house to house, or garage to garage. Let's see if we can find the stuff that killed Munroe; that would make a good starting point. Someone needs to check out Gani's hipflask, too, for traces of weed killer. Though I am loathe to jump to conclusions concerning Salik Gani and to invite accusations of racism, it cannot be denied that he was present at the scene of the crime, therefore I would like a thorough search made of his property. I myself will pay our friend Mr Pedlar a visit and see if anyone had a particular grudge against Munroe, either within the ranks or from outside, from either a political or personal standpoint."

Parlour snickered slightly. Munroe's reputation as the local middle-aged Lothario was common knowledge in Deverton.

"DS Goodlove, you're with me," Parlour commanded and gathered up his papers. Goodlove raised his eyebrows humorously at the rest of Parlour's staff, having fitted seamlessly in with the gang at Billock CID. His body language belied the nervous excitement building up inside at accompanying the much respected Mark Parlour on his first murder investigation as a Detective Sergeant.

Parlour noted a flicker of disappointment in Karen Preece's eyes. He would reassure her later that she was, by a country mile, his best copper, and therefore didn't require chaperoning. It was of considerably more benefit to the team - and to the investigation - if Preece was exercising her initiative independently of Parlour.

"Karen…" Parlour turned to her and smiled sweetly. "I need someone with a bit of sensitivity to visit Alicia Munroe and find out about Davidson *The Man*. Apparently he's had more bits on the side than The Sewer's four bed detached!"

DCI Sewell and his much built-on property in Billock was the butt of many a joke in CID.

"Alicia Munroe is allegedly aware of all his past shenanigans. However, I'd like you to do some additional delving, ex colleagues, fellow gardeners, etcetera – explore every facet of his personal and public life. See if he had anyone on the go recently, you know the sort of stuff."

Karen Preece nodded and returned the smile. It was certainly a more interesting prospect than visiting that nasty old tosspot, Roy Pedlar.

"But first of all, could you organise a thorough examination of Deverton Allotments – I want that weed killer found."

Parlour shuffled his papers and stood up.

***

"Gosh, what a beautiful little girl!" Juliet Parlour exclaimed, bending over a small infant of mixed race sat in its buggy in the queue at Deverton Post Office that Monday morning. Billock Community School had been closed down indefinitely whilst damage caused by a gas explosion in the school boiler room could be assessed and repaired. Juliet had only found out that morning, when she had arrived at the school at 8am as usual to find members of staff milling around in the car park, and the gates locked. Though it was majorly inconvenient in terms of missed schoolwork, Juliet could not deny just how welcome some unanticipated time on her hands was.

Talk was that the school would definitely be closed that week and perhaps even some of the following week. Juliet decided to get lots of niggling odd jobs out the way first, leaving the rest of the week free to get a little ahead with school work and – hopefully – enjoy a few lunches out with her husband. Juliet Parlour did not believe in the existence of luck, good, bad or otherwise; however it did seem mighty unfair that Davidson Munroe should go and pop his clogs in a suspicious manner the weekend before she had some free time to meet Mark for lunch. Now he would be burning the candle at both ends, and if he did manage to cadge an hour off here or there to meet her, his head would be full of suspects and motives, his mobile phone going off every ten seconds.

Juliet looked up at the baby girl's mother, a slightly stocky yet well-dressed and attractive lady of singular race, whom Juliet estimated to be in her early thirties.

"What's her name?"

"Jemima Ermintrude," the woman replied, her eyes twinkling. Juliet gave her a long hard look then giggled nervously.

"Sorry – couldn't resist it," the younger woman grinned. "Why does everyone give their children such silly names these days?"

"Cos we're all individuals, ain't we?" Juliet replied, feigning a cockney accent.

The other woman laughed then sobered up a little. "This is Sacha."

Juliet smiled. She liked this friendly lady.

"And how old is she – three?"

"Blimey, you don't have a clue, do you?" her new acquaintance chuckled. "No kids, I take it?"

Juliet blushed. "We're the original DINKYs. Is it that obvious?"

The other woman just smiled. "Sacha's thirteen months. She's just had her first birthday, the week we moved house, actually."

"Ooh, you've just moved into the area?" Juliet exclaimed, seizing the bait dangled her.

The woman explained that she had recently purchased a small flat on a development on the far side of Deverton, a good two miles from the Parlour's four bed detached in Spatchcock Drive.

Juliet extended a hand. "Juliet Parlour."

The woman removed a hand from the buggy for a moment. "Michaela Brevitt. But everyone calls me Micky."

"Is that m-i- double k – i?" Juliet grinned.

"Do I look like a bimbo?" Michaela frowned, but the corners of her eyes were upturned.

"No," Juliet replied honestly. She smiled more sincerely this time. "Must be pension day or something."

There was a long queue at the post office; it seemed that half of Deverton had decided, along with Juliet, to get their errands out of the way first thing that Monday morning.

"So what do you do?" Michaela asked her as they shuffled a little nearer to the temporary cordons that enticed customers to form a snake-like queue before waiting to be electronically summoned to the next available cashier.

"I'm a secondary school teacher, German and English," Juliet replied.

Michaela made the customary *rather you than me* speech that greeted all teachers sheepishly admitting their profession to others.

Michaela Brevitt explained that she was PA to the Director of a marketing company in the city, but that she was on an extended career break until Sacha started school. Juliet wondered where Sacha's father was, but decided to leave that delicate question for a later date. Deverton Post Office was neither the time nor the place for enquiring after the marital status of a complete stranger. Michaela Brevitt had no such qualms.

"And you're married, I take it?" she enquired, nodding at Juliet's expensive white gold wedding band.

"Mark's a police inspector with Billock CID," Juliet informed her. "You'll see him on telly from time to time, he's the skinny one with the ginger hair! He's done a couple of *Crimewatches* and been on the local news a fair few times. You might have seen him on *Southern Aspect* on Saturday, actually. He's investigating the death of…"

Juliet paused. She did not usually discuss police business with complete strangers, and especially not in the local post office. Her pride in Mark, coupled with the ease at which she found herself conversing with this young woman, had temporarily loosened her tongue.

But Michaela was oblivious to her sudden malaise. She clicked her fingers. "That retired headmaster guy that snuffed it! Yes, I did see him on the news – your husband, that is. He came across very well – I work in marketing, I notice these things!”

“Yes, he did,” Juliet beamed. Though his pernickety-ness drove her mad in the home environment, she was very proud of the professionalism Mark brought to his job.

“Oh well, see you later,” Michaela smiled, as the electronic announcement ordered her to proceed to Cashier Number Four. It was a peculiarly *southern* end greeting, that one, Juliet thought, as she, for her part, shuffled along to Cashier Number Eight at the far end of the counter. In other parts of the country, the recipient of such an *adieu* would be scratching their heads, wondering at just what point in the conversation they had arranged to meet up again that day!

Juliet smiled to herself, her load suddenly feeling lighter, and not just for handing over a parcel to the lumpy occupant of cash desk number eight. She realised her spirits had been lifted by the cheery conversation with her new acquaintance, and made a mental note to tell Mark all about it later. Perhaps it was an indicator of how difficult she was finding Lindsay’s company these days; it was refreshing to bump into a smart full-time Mum who appeared to have a conversation piece that *didn’t* revolve around children.   There was hope for her yet, should she be blessed with offspring in the near future; it was possible to have children and not be a completely humourless stressed out baby-bore!

***

“So what did you make of our grieving widow, then?” Parlour enquired of his new colleague as they returned to Parlour’s car later that morning. He had decided to pay a visit to Alicia after all, instead of kicking his heels waiting for Preece to organise a search of the allotments. Roy Pedlar was not available for interview until midday, which had scuppered Plan A.

Goodlove paused and chewed his gum intensely. Parlour clicked in annoyance; the oral exercise equipment was going to bug him. Perhaps it was that nicotine substitute gum to stop the younger man from smoking – in that case, it was to be encouraged. However, Parlour doubted it; within seconds of meeting him, his keen nose had registered the tell-tale smell on Cameron Goodlove's breath and clothing.

"I thought she was … well, about right, really," Goodlove replied thoughtfully. He flexed his fingers, his knuckles cracking. *Double-flipping-jointed as well*, Parlour grimaced. *I've got myself a knuckle-crunching, gum-chewing copper as my sidekick - great!*

"What do you mean by that?" Parlour enquired, starting the engine up and heading for Deverton Allotments. A warrant had been obtained to search the private property owned by the Allotment Association and Parlour was keen to see how the team personned by Karen Preece was progressing with their search for lethal herbicide.

"Well… they obviously had a happy marriage, but she didn't live in his pocket by any stretch of the imagination. So she's shocked and grief-stricken, naturally… but not falling apart. She's a strong woman. I don't get the feeling she's going to retreat from life in any way. Once she's got through the initial shock, she's going to want to know why, and once she knows the whys and wherefores, she'll move on."

"So you don't think she's involved in any way?" Parlour asked in the slightly softer, smooth tone that indicated he was testing out a colleague's reasoning and adopting the role of devil's advocate.

"You mean, did she bump him off? What's her motive?"

Good strategy, put the ball back in my court, Parlour noted. He smiled. It was good to be challenged.

"Money? Davidson would have a hefty pension. She could escape and live the boho high-life somewhere? Cuba's pretty good, I hear…" Parlour turned sideways to face Goodlove. "Passion?"

"What, with the pint-sized paperboy?" Goodlove scoffed.

Parlour shrugged. "They're pretty close, by all accounts. After all, Alicia was with Gani while her husband was busy waving his leek in the air! You'd think she'd turn up to support him, whatever her political views, but where was she? Having a cosy *tête-à-tête* with Gani in the back parlour!"

"You don't seriously think they were having it off, though, do you?" Goodlove pulled a face. Clearly the proposition was highly unattractive to him.

"You never know what goes on behind closed doors…" Parlour commented.

"Wheesh!" Goodlove exclaimed, "remind me not to frequent Deverton Mini Mart!"

"Or Deverton Allotments!" Parlour laughed as they headed for the said location.

"So who did the dirty deed, or was it a joint venture?" Goodlove grinned.

"Gani was the perpetrator, I'd say," Parlour replied, going along with the mock theory. "They'd joked about bumping off Davidson, but Gani decided on the quiet it wasn't such a bad idea after all, and in a fit of drunken stupor, performed the evil deed with something he found in one of the old codger's sheds that he'd stashed in that hipflask of his. That's why Alicia isn't totally falling apart. She's shocked at what's happened, yet at the same time it's released her to be with the man of her dreams…" Parlour snorted at the end of his spiel and shook his head. "I don't think this is a crime of passion, at all, actually. It's political, if you ask me. It's just too much of a coincidence that the vice-chairman of some right-wing pensioner party gets himself killed on the afternoon of a rowdy demo."

"That still doesn't preclude Gani, though, does it, Sir?"

"No, it doesn't," Parlour conceded, "but I don't think he'd be stupid enough to get caught out of his face at the scene of the crime if it was him!"

"But the report from Pathology did say Munroe had paraquat all over him. If Gani was as pissed as a newt, he may well have spilt some on him when administering the stuff."

Parlour snorted. "Have you forgotten something, Cameron?"

"It's just Cam, boss."

"*Cam.* Munroe was a big chap, well past his prime admittedly, but nevertheless a puny little waif like Salik Gani would be no match for him."

"Of course not," Goodlove admitted sheepishly, feeling a little foolish. There was a lull in the conversation. "So what next?"

"See if Karen's bunch has turned up anything suspicious at the allotments. Then see if I can get hold of that pompous butt-wipe, Roy Pedlar."

Parlour made a face as he rolled up to the grassy hillside that contained the privately leased gardening plots. That was one visit he was not looking forward to, having witnessed one of Pedlar's unpleasant tirades at first-hand in Utopia the other Sunday.

"I do hope you're wearing a bra!" Parlour yelled down the hill to Karen Preece, as he spotted his sergeant huffing and puffing with a spade on a plot of land near where Munroe's body had been discovered. Unlike Charlie Dimmock, though, Preece did not require any upstairs support mechanisms, being rather meagrely blessed in the bosom department.

Preece made a gesture that could be counted on the middle finger of one hand as Parlour approached.

"This is what I like to see, Cam," Parlour informed his new colleague humorously. "A DS who's not afraid to get their hands dirty! Any joy, Karen?"

"Nah," Preece grimaced, tossing a spadeful of sticky mud over her shoulder. "We're waiting for Pooch Patrol."

Parlour grinned at the reference to the local police dog handler, Jeff Wilkes, and his police dog unit consisting of three general purpose German Shepherd patrol dogs.

"You'll let me know immediately if you find anything, won't you, Karen?" he requested. "I'll need to get permission for a house to house otherwise. Could well be stashed away in someone's garage."

"Will do," Preece huffed, ramming down hard in the boggy clay.

***

Roy Pedlar shared a pristine, but non-ostentatious detached property in King Edward Mews with his wife, Lucinda. The residence had once belonged to the late Terence Haynes, the last Deverton man to be murdered prior to Davidson Munroe. Since Haynes's untimely death nearly five years ago, the house had been let to a series of moneyed professionals before Roy Pedlar had come in with an offer to match the over-inflated asking price. It seemed nobody wanted to occupy the former home of a murdered man – until now.

"Nothing special, is it?" Cameron commented as Parlour rang the doorbell.

"What were you expecting?" Parlour grinned. "A Union Jack at full mast? A Rule Britannia door chime?"

Before Goodlove had a chance to retort, an imposing figure with white hair combed back from his forehead answered the door.

"Detective Sergeant Cameron Goodlove and.."

"Detective Inspector Mark Parlour, Billock Police," Pedlar completed for him. "I've seen you on television. They say TV adds four pounds to your body weight, I'd say more in your case."

"I like to keep myself trim," Parlour replied coldly, following Pedlar's back up a cream papered hallway to the spacious living room that had formerly been occupied by Wing Commander Terence Haynes and his disabled wife, Davinia. How odd that No.8 King Edward Mews should come to be home, once more, to a right-wing authoritarian, Parlour thought to himself, lowering himself uneasily onto a stiff dark green Chesterfield sofa.

"Pompous prat!" Goodlove said sourly to his senior colleague as Pedlar left the room briefly to organise tea for the two detectives – or at least, to organise his wife.

"Let's try and keep an open mind," Parlour hissed at him before Pedlar re-entered the room.

"So, gentlemen, what can I do for you this morning?" Pedlar boomed, standing in front of the fireplace with his hands behind his back, making full use of his height advantage to intimidate Parlour, who was perched rather effeminately on the edge of the sofa.

Goodlove arose from his armchair and pulled out a pocketbook and pen. He was a good two inches taller than Pedlar. Parlour smirked at his ploy and decided to let Goodlove initiate verbal proceedings.

"So Mr Pedlar, as you will be only too aware, your deputy was found dead at Deverton Allotments at approximately two pm on Saturday afternoon."

"Yes, yes, terrible affair," Pedlar nodded, without any trace of emotion whatsoever.

"We can now confirm that this is officially a murder investigation," Goodlove stated.

"Well, that was bloody obvious!" Pedlar snorted.

"What do you mean by that?" Parlour enquired immediately.

"You lot wouldn't be crawling all over the place if Munroe had just snuffed it of natural causes, would you?" Pedlar remarked sarcastically, displaying a stunning lack of sensitivity. Parlour gave him a long, hard look; Pedlar simply stared him out, the corners of his mouth slightly upturned in a malevolent sneer.

"What was it? Rat poison? Slug pellets?"

"Paraquat, Mr Pedlar," Goodlove stated.

This time Pedlar did raise his eyebrows. "Really? Must have been a pretty lethal concoction."

"It was thirty odd years old," Goodlove replied. "Before they made it safer."

"How on earth did the murderer get hold of that?" Pedlar frowned. Parlour watched him intently.

"That's what we're hoping to find out, Mr Pedlar," Goodlove responded.

"Well, you won't find any here," Pedlar informed him firmly. There was an uncomfortable pause for a second before Pedlar swept his hand out in a grandiose gesture towards Parlour.

"Search the place, please, be my guest. But you'll be wasting your bloody time. I have no idea who did Munroe in, and I certainly do not own any illegal chemicals. You may not share my politics, Mr Parlour, but I can assure you, I would not murder a fellow citizen of this country and I most certainly do not subscribe to housing hazardous substances on my property, or anywhere else, for that matter."

You're the hazardous object in this house, matey, Parlour thought to himself. Time for a change of tack; this wasn't getting them anywhere.

"Why don't you sit down, Mr Pedlar?" Parlour asked smoothly. "We have some routine questions we need to ask you. It won't take long."

Pedlar frowned, before reluctantly taking a seat opposite Parlour in an ugly, winged, high-backed leather chair that mirrored his stubborn, unyielding nature.

"What was your relationship to Mr Munroe, Mr Pedlar?" Goodlove began.

"He was next in command of the Deverton BASC, as you very well know," Pedlar replied tartly.

"With BASC being the…" Goodlove consulted his notebook, feigning ignorance, a deliberate tactic to bring Pedlar down a few notches.

"British Alliance of Senior Citizens," Pedlar interjected impatiently. "Some people call us a political party; I prefer to think of us as more of a *movement*."

"And how long had you known Mr Munroe?" Goodlove continued, ignoring the invitation to show an interest in Pedlar's political aspirations.

Pedlar knitted his white eyebrows together. "About three years, I'd say. I saw him at a few BASC meetings down here while I was still based in Surrey, and of course much more when I set up regional HQ here. He started coming along to our meetings when he retired. He was Headmaster at Foxburgh High, I'm sure you're aware. Very well respected in the community. Munroe worked wonders at that school, turned it right around from one of those gawd-awful left wing experiments with mixed ability classes and no semblance of discipline, to a very tightly-run ship with grammar school values. Brought back shirts and ties, introduced…"

"National Service?" Goodlove enquired. Parlour smirked and looked down at his notes.

"I wish they would, Detective Sergeant, I wish they would," Pedlar replied, unphased. He uttered a few more impersonal eulogies to Davidson Munroe that had more to do with spouting right-wing propaganda than bemoaning the loss of a valued acquaintance.

"Are you aware of anyone who might have harboured a grudge against Munroe?" Goodlove continued, once he could squeeze a word in edgeways. "Either politically or personally?"

Pedlar frowned. "He was known as a bit of a womanizer, but he never actually cheated on Alicia as far as I know.

Perhaps some jealous ex? Some woman's husband? I really couldn't say."

"Did you ever have a disagreement of any magnitude with Munroe?" Parlour enquired.

Pedlar shook his head. "He enthusiastically embraced BASC values and I had no cause to feel anything other than brotherly comradeship towards him."

"And you're not aware of any problems or issues between Munroe and another individual?" Parlour persevered.

"If you're intimating some kind of in-house squabble, you're barking up the wrong tree entirely, Mr Parlour," Pedlar replied smoothly. "I suggest you widen the lens and consider who might want to sabotage the valuable work the BASC is doing in this fine nation of ours. It surely can't be a coincidence that a valuable member of our community and a proud British citizen is murdered at the exact same time a multicultural event is taking place at the local Church of England, of all places. Surely you should be focusing your efforts on those who don't espouse or practise British values, not pointing the finger at conscientious citizens of this country."

Was it a dig at Beauville or a slur on the Ganis, and Salik in particular? The latter, Parlour suspected. Either way, it was a cheap shot from a thoroughly nasty piece of work, Parlour decided. He stood up.

"That'll be all for now, Mr Pedlar. We'll see ourselves out."

"We never got our tea, boss," Goodlove hissed as they shut the front door behind them.

"I wouldn't let my cat drink from his garden pond, Cam," Parlour replied soberly. He shuddered. The likes of Roy Pedlar only existed in crass television dramas… didn't they?

11

One of the major advantages of Juliet being off school, Parlour thought to himself later that evening, was that she had the time and energy to cook up a real feast for them!

"This is pure sex on a platter!" he congratulated his wife, stuffing another forkful of hot'n'spicy cannelloni in his mouth at six twenty that evening. "Best sex I've had in ages, in fact."

Juliet winced, his barbed reference to their *perform on demand* intercourse not lost on her.

"Sadly ineffective in the conception of baby Parlours, though," she replied dryly, helping herself to a mound of salad with the plastic tongs.

"So how's your day been?" he enquired, deciding a change of subject was in his best interests.

Juliet shrugged. "So-so, though I did meet someone in the post office this morning – a lady with a baby girl. She's just moved to Deverton, Micky she calls herself. She's on a career break from some high-flying PA job in the City. We got chatting in the queue, she was good fun… a rare breed in Deverton."

Whilst the designer village was a pleasant enough place to live, bar the odd suspicious death, it could not be denied that it contained an inordinately high number of individuals who took themselves incredibly seriously, thereby lacking the ability to laugh at themselves and life in general. Michaela Brevitt, with her good-humoured banter, had been a breath of fresh air.

"Where's she moved to?" Parlour enquired. It would be good for Juliet to make friends with a mum her own age who wasn't lording her fertility over her. Might give her some pointers as to what life would be like with little ones without making her feel inadequate.

"Those new flats over the other side of Deverton, off Maris Piper Way."

"Those trendy yuppie pads with balconies?" Parlour enquired brightly, unable to suppress his tendency to be impressed by wealth. "How can she afford that, as a single Mum at home?"

"I don't know that she *is* single," Juliet replied, "She just didn't mention Sacha's…"

"Sacha?" Parlour smirked.

"She didn't mention the little girl's father," Juliet continued regardless, "it seemed rude to pry. Anyway, she's probably on a paid career break - if she's that good at her job, they wouldn't want to lose her. It's some megabucks position, by the sounds of it."

"Why move here?" Parlour enquired, frowning slightly.

"Look, Mark," Juliet replied impatiently, for she wanted to move on to the more pressing issue of who murdered Davidson Munroe, "it was just a quick chat in the post office queue; if I bump into her again, I'll invite her around, so that you can give her the third degree!"

Parlour held his hands aloft. "Alright, alright, keep your wig on!"

"So how's the murder investigation going?" Juliet asked, calming down again.

Parlour waved his head from side to side. "So-so."

He outlined to his wife the probable manner of Munroe's death and the interesting findings relating to liquid paraquat. Karen Preece and co had found no incriminating evidence up at Deverton Allotments and Parlour would need to request permission for house-to-house enquiries to take place, in order to make a search of sheds and garages on domestic properties for a bottle of old paraquat. This search would probably be targeted in the first instance towards certain individuals, unfortunately including the Ganis, and the police dog unit would undoubtedly be employed to speed up the process – though, as Jeff Wilkes had pointed out – the dogs' exposure to the canister of original unstenched, undyed liquid paraquat sent down from a lab in Huddersfield would need to be carefully managed.

"And how is Alicia today?" Juliet enquired.

"Bearing up. I took DS Goodlove with me to snoop around the house while I did some subtle probing."

"Oh, what's he like?" Juliet had forgotten that it was Cameron Goodlove's first day at Billock CID.

"Bit laddish for my liking, but seemed up to speed. He handled that idiot Roy Pedlar pretty well."

"Pedlar? What did he have to say for himself?"

"Much as you would expect," Parlour replied. "It was an atrocious assault on the life of an upstanding member of the local community, Munroe was a fine British citizen ad nauseam. Of course, he's pointing the finger at Gani, without saying as much."

"And are you?" Juliet frowned, who could no more picture the little man who served at the newsagents murdering someone as she could envisage Martin Beauville enjoying a romantic weekend in Paris with Penny Roquet.

"What's the motive?" Parlour shrugged. "If it was an attack based on pure racial hatred, why poison the organ-grinder's monkey…"

It was an ill-advised choice of words in the circumstances.

"… why not bump off Pedlar? He's the nasty bit of right-wing work shouting his mouth off, after all. Munroe was just a bumptious, self-important individual looking for a project to occupy his retirement."

Juliet nodded. "You're right. Unless there's something we don't know about, some issue between Gani and Munroe."

Parlour frowned. "You could say that about Munroe and anyone. We're just all, whether consciously or subconsciously, jumping to race-based assumptions because Salik Gani happened to be present at the scene of the murder. Perhaps this was something to do with Alicia – though I don't think for one minute she did it. She's too… unsorted, if you know what I mean. She would try and behave in some kind of consistent manner if this was her doing, whether that was extreme grief or measured composure. She wouldn't be veering all over the place like she is at present – in my experience of spouse killers."

"You mean, she hasn't staged a telly appeal yet?" Juliet smiled. It never ceased to amaze her just how many convicted murderers had made emotional pleas for the capture of their partner's killer on national television. It was now almost the case that whenever such appeals were made, viewers automatically looked to the person making the heartfelt speech and questioned their innocence and integrity.

"I did warn Pedlar about performing a similar stunt to the one he pulled on Saturday again," Parlour informed her. "But he's adamant he won't rest in his grave until he's achieved a mono-cultural Britain – his words, not mine."

Juliet shuddered. "Whatever next? Leek slogans on Asian shop windows?"

Parlour smirked then sobered up as his brain called up disturbing black and white footage from Nazi Germany. He had left Pedlar's house in King Edward Mews feeling distinctly ill at ease. There was a nasty racist undercurrent to Pedlar's monologues that left him feeling somehow dirty inside for having shared the same airspace with him for twenty minutes.

***

Alicia Munroe hauled herself up from her seat at the kitchen table and rubbed her numb posterior. She had been sat there, head resting on the backs of her lightly liver-spotted hands, for the best part of an hour.

I suppose I better get on with something, she told herself listlessly. How loudly the kitchen clock ticked and how noisy that dripping tap was. She would have to change that washer herself, now that Davey wasn't around to do her odd jobs. Alicia felt her head tighten as the emotions welled up inside, but the tears wouldn't come. It was the oddest physical sensation, like automatic doors were closing in on her head, squeezing her brain cells together with no physical release.

She walked gingerly over to the washing machine, for her legs had all but gone to sleep while she had sat immobile at the table. The widow of Davidson Munroe scooped the washing out of the Whirlpool 1400 and into a yellow plastic laundry basket waiting beneath the circular door. She picked up his 38 inch waist khaki chinos, and a half-sob, half grunt emanated from her mouth. These were his favourite casual trousers, the ones he had been wearing first thing on the morning he'd died, before an accident with some fried tomatoes at breakfast time had enforced a change of clothing upon him. She pressed them to her pale, lined cheek, clutching them tightly to her as if her very life depended on it, before her attention was drawn to a fragment of blue paper in the crevice of the rubber seal on the washing machine door.

Sitting on her haunches, Alicia picked the paper out the door and unfurled it. The biro writing was smudged on the damp paper but was just about legible. She shuffled over to the table and balanced her rectangular gold reading glasses on the end of her nose. A burning sensation rose up her oesophagus like liquid paraffin and Alicia emitted a loud sob-grunt, before running into her bedroom and flinging herself on the bed. She beat the mattress with her fists. He'd promised her no more. *The rat the rat the rat the rat the rat....*

✳✳✳

"How's your brother?" Michaela Brevitt enquired of Nazrul Gani as she nipped into Deverton Mini Mart for a packet of chocolate Digestives at seven thirty that Monday evening.

"How do you think? Like a fox on Hunt day," Nazrul Gani replied, scanning the biscuits into the shop till.

"You can just see how their nasty little racist brains are working around here, can't you?" Michaela commented, handing over one pound seventeen exactly in loose change. Flip, the prices these local convenience stores charged! Still, it was good to do her bit for the local economy. "Even the ones you'd credit with more political savvy, like our dear local MP…"

"Fletchley Linlock…" Nazrul said, wrapping his tongue slowly and salaciously around the name of the local MP, for it was a name that demanded such oral gymnastics.

"Salik just isn't the killing sort, anyway," Michaela continued. "No fire in his belly – and I would know, tried to get him to come to my meeting tonight, but he wasn't having it. He keeps his head down so far, he's practically head-butting the pavement!"

Nazrul Gani chuckled. "That's why you don't have Sacha with you?"

"That's right," Michaela grinned, "Got her organising party affairs at thirteen months. Totally brainwashed already. Actually, she's tucked up in bed; the guys have just turned up, with no readies. My cake lady's let me down at the last minute, so here I am raiding your biscuit shelf!"

"Here, have these on the house," Nazrul smiled, handing her a huge bag of mini poppadoms. They're not selling too well this week."

"Cheers, Naz," Michaela smiled back, knowing she enjoyed his spiritual support if not his physical presence at her gathering. She jogged back across the road and into her black hatchback. Michaela then drove the short distance to the Knightsbridge development and turned the key in the lock of number thirty. Hanging her brown suede jacket up in the hallway, Michaela Brevitt threw the packet of biscuits over to the other committee members of the Respect and Tolerance Party UK.

<h1 style="text-align:center">12</h1>

"What the… oh, it's you."   Alicia Munroe's voice fell listlessly as she pressed her back against the wall of her rather narrow entrance hall to admit Salik Gani that Tuesday morning. Disguised in a black hoodie and baggy black jeans that entirely wiped out what vague semblance of a bottom he possessed, Gani had made a spirited attempt to avoid recognition and had escaped the claustrophobic clutter of his brother's flat above the Mini Mart via the rear-facing bathroom window.

"Sal, I really don't feel up to much, I'm no company," Alicia began, meandering into her kitchen, the usual authority she held within her own domestic domain all but dissipated.

"Leesh, we've got to talk," Gani replied, removing the hoodie to reveal his more usual upper body attire of long-sleeved polo shirt in a non-descript colour, testimony to a non white-separatist machine-wash policy. He plonked himself down at the kitchen table. "They're going to pin Dave's death on me, and you and I both know there's some other explanation. You've got to help me!"

Alicia Munroe raised a weary hand in the air. "I've told the police until I'm blue in the face that you had nothing to do with it, what more can I do?"

Gani frowned. This was not the Alicia he knew and loved. "Leesh – someone's *murdered* your husband, *your husband*, and *I'm* – that's me, your best mate – am going to cop the blame for it. Don't you want to get to the bottom of this?"

Alicia sighed. "Salik, at the moment I just don't care."

She wandered out into the garden, absent-mindedly nursing a cold cup of tea in her hand.

"You *don't care*?" Gani exploded in a rare show of rancour.

Alicia turned around and looked him firmly in the eye. "Salik, read my lips – I don't give a toss who murdered *my husband*. They're welcome to him. The bastard was cheating on me!"

A stunned silence hung suspended in the air above the back door where Gani was standing, finally interrupted by the shrill sound of the doorbell.

"Ignore it," Alicia commanded. "It'll just be Billock Plod with more routine questions that they need to routinely ask every morning."

But Gani was in no fit state to answer the door.

"Mr Gani!" the Hampshire tones of DC Darren Keough sounded out from the front of the house. "We know you're in there, would you come on out please, this is the police."

You don't say! Alicia Munroe groaned inwardly. She opened the shed door and pushed her dumbstruck friend inside. Then she proceeded back up the hallway to answer her front door.

"Mr Gani left the house a few moments ago," Alicia Munroe informed DCs Keough and Jenkins. It wasn't a lie; he had vacated the kitchen for the back garden two minutes previously.

"Yeah, right," Keough scoffed, attempting to invite himself in.

"There's really no point..." Alicia began, holding firmly onto the door to barricade him out.

"We'll be the judge of that, Mrs Munroe, thank you," Keough retorted. Alicia wavered a moment before stepping aside to let them in.

"Shoes off, first!" Alicia reminded him in a retrograde moment of feisty pre-widow pomp as Keough shot upstairs. The infinitely more deferential Detective Constable Jenkins did so before disappearing in pursuit of his colleague.

Keough reappeared moments later. "Slipped out the back, did he?"

Munroe just shrugged, unable to quite bring herself to lie to the police. She was, at the end of the day, a law-abiding citizen.

"Well when you see him, can you tell him he's under arrest. Our friendly sniffer dogs just unearthed some elderly weed-killer in Gani's flat, of the variety that was used to poison your husband."

"You can tell me yourself," Gani said with a quiet fury in his voice, appearing from the back garden.

***

"Derek! What the fudge cake are you doing here?" Parlour exclaimed on entering Billock Police Station early that Tuesday afternoon. His father-in-law was sitting sheepishly in the waiting area at main reception.

"They want to question me about the contents of my garage," Derek Hebble replied meekly. "Margaret's got her Book Group meeting at the house, didn't want people talking, so I've volunteered to come up here instead."

Parlour stood non-plussed for a moment. "They want to question *you* about the contents of *your* garage? Derek! Have *you* got dodgy weed-killer stashed in there?"

"No, no, of course not!"

"Oh Derek, this has nothing to do with your Nazi Pensioners, has it? You know Jules and I don't condone your involvement in…"

"No, no, it's nothing like that," Derek interrupted hastily.

Karen Preece tapped Parlour on the shoulder and he turned away from his father-in-law.

"Sir, we've pulled Salik Gani in for questioning. He gave himself up at Alicia Munroe's house."

"Thanks, Karen." Parlour turned back to Derek Hebble. "Derek, I have to go. I'll call by later, if they haven't banged you up!"

Shaking his head, Parlour followed Karen Preece into the lift. What on earth had the silly old tit been up to? Jules would throw a wobbly.

***

It transpired that a dirty old plastic container of weed-killer dating back to 1972 had been found stuffed up through a hole in the fabric base of Salik Gani's bedstead. It was of a variety sold in several parts of Africa and South-East Asia over three decades ago, though not in the UK. It had been most likely smuggled into the country in an age where customs checks on chemical products or human bodies were not nearly as stringent as they were today.

Despite Gani's protestations that he had never seen the weed-killer in his life before, he would be held in custody for the next twenty-four hours as a mad rush to find substantiating evidence against him ensued.

Parlour shook his head, pulling Detective Sergeants Goodlove and Preece into his office and shutting the door behind him. He took a swig of coffee from one of the beige ribbed cups issued by the station vending machine then grimaced. Clearly the machine was nearly out of powder for it had the same wishy-washy consistency as one of Margaret Hebble's affronts to coffee.

"It doesn't make sense, Sir, does it?" Goodlove frowned, squeezing his giant frame into an itchy black office chair.

"What doesn't, Cam?" Parlour asked smoothly, reclining in his revolving chair.

"Well, why kill Munroe?" Cameron reiterated. "Why didn't Gani go for Pedlar – he's orchestrated this whole Monocultural Campaign in Deverton after all."

"So you think Gani did it, then?" Parlour enquired, slipping Preece a sidelong glance.

Goodlove shrugged. "The evidence is overwhelmingly against him, isn't it, boss? He was present at the scene of the crime, drunk as a skunk, ditto Alicia Munroe who is therefore an unreliable witness. We find weed-killer of an apparently similar type to that used to murder Davidson Munroe stashed away in a pretty good hiding place in his flat. He made sure not to leave it in his potting shed; that would be too easy to find."

"Why hide it at all?" Parlour asked smoothly in the smart-arse manner for which he was renowned. "You'd get rid of the evidence, surely?"

"You think it was planted there, Sir?" Karen Preece enquired.

"Smacks of it, wouldn't you say?" Parlour replied, folding his hands behind his head. "The killer knew the potting shed would be a bit too obvious – everyone would know it had been planted there, so he or she hid it in Gani's flat in a not immediately obvious place, to make it look like Salik had tried to conceal the evidence."

"So how did they get in Gani's flat?" Goodlove wondered. "He's been holed up at his brother's place across the road and we've had police surveillance on his own flat to stop the village idiots trashing it."

"It was probably planted there some time after the murder, once they learnt that Gani had been present at the scene of the crime," Parlour replied. "I haven't read the full report yet. Perhaps they broke into the flat from the back entrance... I should imagine it wouldn't be too difficult to escape police notice. No disrespect intended, but it's pretty boring keeping watch on an empty flat; I'm sure the officer concerned took their eye of the place a couple of times. I expect you could sneak in fairly easily."

"I can't see any motive for Gani, in any case," Preece frowned. "So many people have told us he's harmless, not an aggressive bone in his body. Likes to take the mick out of Pedlar and co but nothing more sinister than that. Anyway, he's a pretty weedy bloke, isn't he – pardon the pun. It'd take someone at least equal to Munroe to ram that weed-killer down him..."

"Unless they were threatening him with a weapon as well," Goodlove counteracted.

"I hadn't considered that, actually," Parlour conceded, nodding in approval at his new colleague. There was a pause.

"So what next, boss?" Karen Preece enquired, standing up and stretching her long limbs. Tall, dark and distinctly uncurvaceous, Preece was the direct opposite of Juliet Parlour in terms of physical relief. Nevertheless, there was something boyishly attractive about her; she exuded a subtle sensuality with her sharp intellect and cool logic that triggered a subconscious reaction in Parlour's own sinewy limbs.

"Well, I'm still waiting for the lab to get back on a match between the paraquat that killed Munroe and the stuff found at Gani's flat. Meanwhile, I need to have another little chat with Alicia Munroe," Parlour said regretfully. He felt she should be left in peace to grieve her husband's untimely death. Parlour did not sense in his gut that she was in any way responsible for his murder, yet there were a few awkward questions only she could answer. He had got the impression that Salik Gani had been hiding some vital fact from the police concerning Davidson Munroe; perhaps Alicia would shed some light on the matter.

He looked at his two junior colleagues. "I have the feeling Gani knows something, but he's not sharing the information - probably out of loyalty to Alicia. They're as thick as thieves, those two, by all accounts."

"Do you want me to go?" Preece offered, fed up of muddy allotments and dusty garages. A cup of fancy tea in a bone china mug and some home-made cheese scones in Alicia Munroe's front room sounded a far better option.

Parlour shook his head. "Thanks, Karen, but I think she needs some continuity. She's seen so many different officers this week; I think she's more likely to talk to me when she doesn't need to go over old ground again."

"Don't talk to me about going over old ground!" Preece groaned, considering the blisters on the top of her palms.

Parlour rose to his feet. "Right, guys, that's me for the day. Got to go and see my father-in-law about some stash in the garage!"

***

"Mark, you better come in," Margaret Hebble said tearfully, opening her white PVC door to her son-in-law at five fifteen that afternoon. "Derek's in the conservatory with Juliet, I have to tidy up after my ladies."

Parlour snorted inwardly. How much mess could half a dozen middle-aged ladies in a reading group make? Knowing Margaret as he did, he suspected one shortbread crumb on the carpet merited the full Dyson treatment. Or perhaps she was just consumed with embarrassment that Derek's little secret had been uncovered in such an undignified fashion and was seeking the solace of some vigorous vacuuming and polishing to work off the anger.

He meandered into the PVC conservatory, or the Sacred White Temple as Juliet acerbically referred to the scrupulously clean and entirely soulless Victorian style monstrosity adjoined to the back of the Hebbles' four bed detached. It was an ugly conservatory, in Parlour's view, who far preferred the less frilly look when it came to most things in life, with the possible exception of his wife's underwear.

"Hello, darling," Juliet stood up and kissed her husband. Knowing it would embarrass his father-in-law and in eager anticipation of the Harold Bishop-esque malaise that would follow, Parlour deliberately lingered two moments on his wife's lips before pulling away and attempting to relax in a floral basket chair. That was another *bête-noire* of Parlour's:- conservatory furniture. Lightweight and invariably ugly, what on earth was wrong with putting normal furniture in there instead? It wasn't as if the rain got in, and a simple twiddle of the blinds would stop the sun streaming in and fading the fabric.

Parlour opened his PDA and brought up a screen listing the items found in Derek Hebble's garage.

"Two Sony 40" HD Ready digital LCD televisions; a Phillips 42" HD Ready digital plasma television; three Sky+ boxes; a Hitachi Freeview box; two Panasonic DVD recorders; a Sony home cinema kit; two Apple i-Pod Nanos; one Samsung MP3 player; one JVC Mini System; one Technics Mini-System; one Nikon digital SLR; two Olympus compact digital cameras; one Canon DVD camcorder; one Motorola PEBL mobile; one Sony VAIO laptop; one Acer notebook and – wait for it – *thirteen* TomTom sat navs!"

Parlour drew breath; his wife buried her head in her hands. There was an uncomfortable pause before Parlour snapped shut his electronic notebook and slipped it back in his pocket.

"Why, Derek?"

"I thought I'd already been questioned at the station," Parlour's father-in-law mumbled sulkily.

"Where did it all come from?" Parlour persisted.

"Won 'em all," Derek muttered. "Competitions. You know, in Mother's magazines, local radio, TV phone-ins… you name it, I enter it."

Apart from Margaret, Parlour thought lewdly and not entirely without malice.

Derek looked up sorrowfully at his daughter. "I suppose you think I have that compulsive obsessive thingy, or whatever it's called."

"That's more Mother's domain," Juliet replied, with a certain degree of bitterness. Her mother's ferocious cleaning habits drove her up the wall. She shook her head. "I don't understand, Dad. It's not as if you're strapped for cash; you could afford to buy some decent bits of electronic kit if the desire took you."

"This isn't about a new-found desire for the latest gadgets, though, is it, Derek?" Parlour probed gently. Derek Hebble said nothing, just stared miserably at the floor.

"And Mother had no idea?" Juliet frowned, still shaking her head.

"She doesn't set foot in the garage, does she?" her father replied with a bit more vigour this time. "Afraid she'll get a milligram of motor oil on her best tweeds."

It was the first time Parlour had heard such venom in his usually benign father-in-law's tones.

And that was the whole point, Juliet thought to herself, suddenly understanding the psychology behind such a bizarre course of action. This was about maintaining some semblance of control and personal identity in Margaret's fun-free dictatorship.

"Oh come on, Jules," Parlour teased, in an attempt to lighten the atmosphere. "Don't be too cross with him. He has to put up with Margaret 24/7 – that's enough to drive any man to silly competitions in supermarket magazines!"

"Not a real man," Juliet muttered under her breath. She looked up. "Why can't you do something useful, like win us some free tickets to something? Mark's already seen to it that we have every electronic gadget known to man! How about that Bon Jovi concert at the Bowl? Or better still, apply for *Millionaire* and get some hard cash? Then I'd get my Four by Four!"

"Arthritis in the old hands is too bad!" Derek replied, attempting to wiggle his rather gnarled fingers. "I'd be no good at the fast fingering."

Parlour winced as some deeply unpleasant sexual imagery involving his in-laws flashed across his mind once more.

"Poor old DS Goodlove," he chuckled instead. "Had no idea you were my pa-in-law; thought he'd made a major stolen goods coup!"

"Can we just leave it for now?" Derek Hebble grumbled, seeing his wife approach through the sliding door.

Parlour stood up and pulled Juliet to her feet.

"I'm sorry," Juliet said wistfully, once they were stood outside once more.

"What for?"

"You know – Dad wasting police time and all that."

Parlour squeezed her waist. "Don't be silly; they thought it was hilarious down at the station that Cam dragged in the DI's father-in-law for questioning on his second day at work! Anyway, we might get a few new gadgets out of it!"

But Juliet didn't see the funny side. Clearly this was some kind of cry for help, this desire to acquire objects and stash them away. Wasn't that the reasoning child psychologists applied to youngsters who displayed this behaviour? However, her father was not a child… but Juliet was beginning to have her doubts, what with the findings in the garage and his sudden involvement in, what appeared to her, an infantile and ill-advised political stance.

Parlour, aware of his wife's tendency to attach too much significance to events and over-analyse them, wound down his window from the low-slung driver's seat of his sports car as she stepped into her Fiat Punto to follow him home to Deverton. "Don't be too hard on him, Jules. It must be mindlessly boring putting up with your mother and her germ-free environment day in day out; it's probably the only thrill he ever gets, winning all those electronic gizmos!"

"Perhaps he should request a transfer to Deverton," Juliet called across to her husband. "Plenty of action around our way!"

Don't I know it, Parlour thought wryly to himself. He must read through his notes tonight and attempt to spot some missing link to aid him with this murder enquiry. Salik Gani would have to be released tomorrow lunchtime, unless hard evidence could be produced linking the bottle of paraquat found in Gani's bed to Gani himself, in the form of fingerprints or traces of chemicals on his skin or clothing. The hipflask had already proven a non-starter.

Talking of hard evidence, Parlour thought to himself, smiling at his own joke, he must check out a certain men's health issue with Nick Hunter, the pathologist working on the Munroe case.

13

"Hello again! Micky, wasn't it?" Juliet Parlour enquired, feigning casualness as she bumped into Michaela Brevitt in the Household Cleaning Solutions aisle of Utopia at half past eleven that Wednesday morning. She smiled at baby Sacha, who was belted into a stylish black *Mamas and Papas* buggy, and brushed her dark head lightly with a rather nervous hand. She was new to the business of toddler ingratiation.

"Hi there, Juliet," Michaela smiled. "Run out of loo cleaner! Had some friends around the other night – male friends, say no more!" She brandished a black plastic container of *RimReaper* in the air.

Juliet chuckled, wondering precisely what sort of gathering this had been. She must find out if Michaela Brevitt lived alone with her daughter; it was going to bug her otherwise.

"I just needed some milk, but the Mini Mart is shut."

Brevitt frowned. "Shut? It never shuts!"

"Salik Gani was taken in for questioning yesterday morning – the place is rife with reporters and racist thugs. Mark was called out last night to get rid of some local yobbos making the family's life hell. Didn't you know?"

"No!" Michaela exclaimed. "I was in Reading all day, only got back late last night. I had to stop off en route to pick Sacha up from a friend's in Newbury then got stuck in traffic on the A34 - surely the most boring road in the world. So what happened?"

"Look – do you fancy a coffee?" Juliet enquired, waving her hand in the vague direction of Utopia's café, with its burgundy faux leather sofas and gargantuan tub chairs, guaranteed to house even the most generous of bottoms.

Brevitt wrinkled her nose. "You have to queue forever while they fart about frothing the milk. Tell you what, why don't you come a round to mine? I have a couple of chocolate biscuits left over from the other night."

"Deal!" laughed Juliet, who would go willingly to the homes of complete strangers for a chocolate biscuit, a trait she would be wise not to pass on to any future offspring.

"I have the car, I've just come back from the Dry Cleaners," Brevitt informed her.

They paid for their shopping then left the airy, some would say soulless, supermarket and into the car park.

Nice car, Juliet thought, as Brevitt remotely unlocked a smart black Alfa-Romeo 147 hatchback. Understated but classy – a bit like Brevitt herself, Juliet thought admiringly.

She helped put the shopping in the boot as Michaela strapped Sacha into her car-seat then pretended not to notice in the rear view mirror as she saw Michaela promptly remove it all again to put the buggy in first.

I don't have a clue about all this baby malarkey, Juliet thought to herself from the passenger seat. *Of course the shopping would get squished with the buggy on top. Doh!*

Juliet pondered a sticker on the back windscreen bearing a picture of a black rodent. Under the rodent was the slogan RATUK and a web address. She considered rather densely for a couple of moments whether the car had been purchased by some Czech-owned garage or something, before she realised it was in fact two words, RAT UK, to tie in with the rat logo. Whatever was RAT UK? Not wanting to appear too intrusive on only their second meeting, Juliet decided to wait and see if the issue arose naturally in conversation. Juliet Parlour was not as assertive and as self-confident as she liked to think she was and often neglected to step in where most people wouldn't hesitate to jump feet first.

Juliet watched out the corner of her eye as Michaela drove smoothly from the shops at Deverton Esplanade along the winding road to the far side of the town, a couple of miles from the Parlour's property in Spatchcock Drive. She couldn't help but admire the together young woman with her smart car and cute baby girl. A designer Mum for a designer town, Juliet thought to herself. She had yet to see Michaela Brevitt's flat.

The younger woman hung a left to the new apartments rather fancifully entitled "Knightsbridge Park" and slunk down a herringboned drive to an underground car-park, strictly for residents' use only. Michaela Brevitt rolled up to a parking space bearing a gold plaque on the wall in front of it, on which was engraved the number thirty. Then she alighted from the car. This time, Juliet waited for Michaela to take the bags out herself, before lifting a couple from the ground and following her up the staircase. Sacha tottered alongside Michaela; clearly she had been walking for a good few months, Juliet could recognise that much.

"Let me just get Sash a snack and I'll be sorted," Michaela informed Juliet and started rummaging in the cupboards.

"Shall I put the kettle on?" Juliet queried, not wishing to assume she would get a filter coffee from Michaela Brevitt, though the evidence so far suggested this was a distinct possibility.

"Nah – I've got a filter machine," Michaela duly replied. "The coffee's in that silver canister by the microwave, if you know what you're doing."

"Right-o," Juliet replied, who did know what to do with a coffee maker, if not with babies and buggies.

As the smart black Italian filter machine chuckled away to itself, Juliet meandered around the flat, arms folded, surveying her surroundings. Michaela certainly had a lot of nice stuff; every item of furniture from the leather sofa down to the remote control holder, looked like it had come from some exclusive designer store years ahead of its time. Suddenly their own beech furnishings seemed passé and distinctly *nineties* in comparison.

She frowned as her eyes fell on a pile of A4 brown boxes in the hallway bearing the self-same RAT UK slogan as seen on the Alfa Romeo rear wind-screen. She was itching to peek inside one of the boxes but it was a small, if luxurious, apartment, and she couldn't rely on Michaela not spotting her. Juliet was also dying to know if there was a Mr Brevitt or a Mr Anything Else on the scene. Male friends were certainly in abundance, if her earlier comments concerning bathroom hygiene were anything to go by.

"So what brings you to Deverton of all places?" Juliet enquired instead, as they settled down on the Italian cream leather sofa to drink their coffee. Sacha was now ensconced in front of *CBeebies* with some *Utopia* Low-Sodium Prebiotic Wholewheat Dinosaurs and a beaker of vitamin-enriched milk, watching some bizarre pre-school programme featuring a miniature man with bad ginger hair flying around on a giant wooden spoon. Juliet supposed she would have to become *au fait* with such lurid televisual imagery should she produce the desired offspring in the next year or two.

"Wanted to get out of the city," Michaela explained, not entirely convincingly. "Just fancied somewhere a bit cleaner to bring Sacha up. Deverton's ideal for me; it's just about commutable, and I do need to go into work from time to time, it's a condition of my career break. You know, keep on top of new developments etc."

"We like it here," Juliet nodded, "though it has been said it's rather bland in Deverton – well, compared to other bits of Hampshire."

Brevitt shrugged. "It's what you make it, isn't it? There *are* a few characters here, the guys that run the shop on the Triangle are a good laugh. Well, at least, they were before some homicidal maniac went on the loose."

She shook her head as Juliet outlined how the police had arrested Salik Gani at Alicia Munroe's house the previous day.

"It makes me sick," she exclaimed, with a vehemence that surprised Juliet. Michaela Brevitt seemed so poised, so controlled; it was a shock to hear her express such an angry sentiment. Still, righteous anger made one economical with niceties, Juliet thought; or at least that was the excuse she gave herself every time she "went off on one" about something or other, a not too infrequent occurrence at Spatchcock Drive.

"What has that guy done to hurt anyone?" Michaela continued. "It's out and out racism. He was in the wrong place at the wrong time with the wrong skin colour, that's it in a nutshell."

"He was blind drunk at the scene of the murder; circumstances *do* kind of point against him," Juliet cajoled, defending her husband's honour. "I don't know if that makes it a racist decision, taking him into custody, does it? I'm sure Mark would be duty-bound to ask anyone in for questioning who was found in possession of a lethal chemical substance implicated in a murder, especially when they were found inebriated at the scene of the crime."

"He was having a drink with a friend, that's all!" Brevitt defended Gani rigorously. Sacha looked up anxiously from the television as her mother raised her voice.

"Look!" Juliet held her hands aloft. "I don't think he did it, either, for what it's worth. Why are *you* so bothered, anyway?"

Confidence restored, Juliet just stared at Michaela. She was missing something here; Michaela Brevitt seemed passionately concerned for the welfare of Salik Gani, far beyond pure neighbourly interest or community spirit.

There was a brief hiatus before Michaela got up and took a business card from the book shelf.

"I haven't been entirely straight with you, Jules – hey, is it OK to call you Jules?"

Juliet nodded, though in actual fact, she only really liked her husband abbreviating her name in that way. Though she would hate to admit it, she was rather in awe of this *doyenne* of self-confidence.

"It's true I'm on a career break, and it's true I wanted to be in commuting distance of London. However, I'm also chairperson of a national pressure group."

"RAT UK," Juliet interjected.

"That's right," Michaela nodded, guessing Juliet had seen the car-sticker and the boxes in the hallway.

"I saw your car sticker… and the boxes in the hallway," Juliet confirmed.

"They're flyers," Michaela explained. "We're aiming to kybosh the BASC's demo in London in a few weeks, though not in the manner that Roy Pedlar and co sabotaged that church event down here."

"The World Cuisine Festival."

"Yes. I couldn't make it to that, unfortunately," Brevitt said with genuine sorrow in her voice; she would have almost killed for such media coverage.

"So RAT… an acronym, I presume?" Juliet enquired.

"Respect and Tolerance," Michaela explained. "We campaign against racial hatred and xenophobia. We set ourselves up four years ago to provide an opposing voice to the nasty right-wing nonsense Pedlar and co are touting around the country."

She fetched a yellow and black leaflet from a box next to the computer and handed it to Juliet.

RAT UK, Juliet read, *Promoting Respect and Tolerance in the Regions.*

Want to rid Britain of Darkies?
Then rescue GB from the Dark Ages!
Join RAT, for a smarter Britain.

She smiled at the now earnest young woman opposite her. "Good word-play on Darkies."

"We're appealing to people's intellectual vanity," Brevitt informed her. "You see, even uneducated people don't like to think of themselves as stupid; we're trying to get the message across that smart people look beyond skin colour and accept cultural diversity..."

"Only thickoes are racist and xenophobic," Juliet interrupted, smiling humorously.

"Well I wouldn't quite put it like that," Brevitt frowned.

"Isn't it all a bit *yoof culture*?" Juliet enquired rather disparagingly, *and a mite patronising*, she wanted to add but didn't.

"Not really," Brevitt frowned. The party had a little more depth to it than that; this was more than a Benetton style fashion statement. "The average age of our executive leadership team is 40."

With the dubious integrity of a politician in the making, Brevitt neglected to inform Juliet that the addition of the retired Robert and Antonia Killington to the party leadership bumped the average age up to forty something; the other four members of it were all in their twenties and thirties.

"And is there a membership fee?" Juliet enquired, trying to beat down the small bubbles of excitement rising up to the surface like carbon dioxide molecules in her favoured Irn-Bru tipple. She had been looking for some cause to sharpen her teeth on for some time now, and church offered her little in the way of political lobbying. A few little rants about selfish people who didn't buy Ethical Exchange chocolate was hardly satisfying her inner urge to live on the edge and make a difference.

Brevitt smiled. "There's no fee to be on our mailing list or to partake in demos, no. However, we do suggest a voluntary donation of at least £25 annually to help fund our work. We don't seem to have a problem persuading people to part with their cash; even our student members recognise the importance of our cause and are only too willing to stump up some beer money to aid cultural justice in this country."

Ooh, she's good, Juliet thought to herself, a little grudgingly. She must take a leaflet home to show Mark, he would be interested, she was sure. Though not as inclined as his wife to air his political views in public, Juliet knew he also despised the ghetto culture that was beginning to sweep across the UK and indeed much of Western Europe. It was a culture – in Parlour's view - fuelled by misguided social ideals and a refusal to communicate and compromise in an adult fashion by all parties concerned.

"So is it just about stamping out racism?" Juliet asked, considering the flyer in her hand.

Brevitt shook her head. "It's about recognising the rights of any minority groups in society, this isn't just about race. At a more proactive level, it's about exposing the lies behind the polemics of Roy Pedlar and co."

"Curious you should end up in the same town," Juliet commented slyly, flashing her eyes at the dark-haired woman opposite.

Michaela just grinned covertly. "Let's just say, a flat came up on the commuter belt that placed me in proximity of a major threat to our ideals!"

"So you're going to try and sabotage the *Grey Pride* march at Whitehall, then?" Juliet enquired.

Michaela cocked her head. "I'm not sure if sabotage is the right word. We'd like to think we were a little more *civilised* than the BASCies. But we'll make our presence felt and our voices heard, that's for sure. The arrest of Salik Gani on my own doorstep has made me more determined than ever to put Roy Bloody Pedlar in his place. That man is manipulative and a thoroughly nasty piece of work; most of those old dears have no idea what they're signing up for, they just want to be part of some kind of jingoistic *Dad's Army* style pensioners' club."

"I'm surprised you never got Gani himself on board," Juliet mused.

"He isn't interested," Michaela said with regret in her voice. "I've tried on a number of occasions to get Sal or Naz involved; but they just want to keep their heads down. They won't even take part in the *RAT RACE* fun-run we're organising in Hyde Park. They say it's bad for business to get politically involved in anything, especially in the current climate. I'm a bit disappointed, to be honest. We've had zero luck around here getting new members; people don't seem to realise that political apathy leads to nutters like Pedlar getting a foot in the door."

There was a lull in the conversation before Juliet finally plucked up the courage to assuage her curiosity regarding Brevitt's marital status.

"You live here alone, well just you and Sacha?"

Brevitt smiled to herself; she had wondered when Juliet would get to that.

"Yes, I do."

"And Sacha's dad – is he local?" Juliet enquired.

Brevitt shrugged, still smiling vaguely. "He's somewhere in London, I believe. I couldn't really say."

They split up and she doesn't want to talk about it, Juliet registered. She stood up. "I really must get back. I've been avoiding a mountain of school work. It's been great talking to you and thanks for the coffee."

"No problem," Michaela smiled, rising to her feet. She followed Juliet into the hallway.

"Ooh, I like your leather," Juliet commented, fingering a black leather biker jacket on the coat-hooks.

"Why don't you try it on?" Michaela smiled.

"Can I?" Juliet laughed and tried it on for size. It fitted perfectly. She looked herself up and down in the mirror. Gosh, she looked quite hip and sexy.

"You look great," Michaela nodded appreciatively. "You can have it if you want it."

"Yeah, right!" Juliet laughed.

"No, seriously, I've really filled out since I had Sacha, there's no way that'll ever fit me now. I was going to sell it on *EBay,* to be honest."

Juliet looked dubious.

"Look…" Michaela tried it on and Juliet noted indeed that Brevitt could barely squeeze her muscly child-rearing arms and generous bosom inside, let alone zip it up.

"If you're sure…" Juliet said hesitantly. What on earth would Mark say? It was a bit too *in-yer-face* for him, she was sure. But with the big four-o milestone coming up in the not too distant future, this could be just the ticket, Juliet thought to herself. She hummed and hawed for a few seconds, for respectability's sake.

"Cheers then," she accepted gratefully and put the jacket over her shoulder.

"Can I give you a lift home?" Brevitt enquired.

"No, it's alright," Juliet replied, considering the small toddler who had nodded off in a heap before the telly. "Don't disturb Sacha. Anyway, you're just around the corner from a friend of mine. I said I would call by sometime this week, I've been putting it off to be honest, but there's no excuse now I'm here."

Juliet smiled wanly, wondering if Lindsay would yet again succeed in winding her up that day.

But it had proved a bad time to call, being slap bang in the middle of the children's lunchtime and Juliet had once again cursed her own gaucheness when it came to families with children. Lindsay's chastisement of her for coming around at such an impractical time only heightened Juliet's insecurity regarding her childless status. How immature, how positively *virginal* she must appear to the likes of Lindsay Briscoe and Michaela Brevitt.

Still, at least she had a husband, and one whose career was on the ascendant, thought Juliet a mite bitchily. It had not escaped her notice how jowly the otherwise devilishly handsome Charles Briscoe had become of late; Parlour had commented that Briscoe was slipping slowly into the self-indulgent whisky-laced bunker of moneyed professionals who'd reached the zenith of their career and could only briefly stop still to admire the view from the top before falling from their perch.

It was a good half hour's walk back to their home on the other side of Deverton and Juliet regretted turning down the lift from Michaela. She was not to know that Lindsay Briscoe would make her feel so unwelcome. A year ago, she would have had no hesitation in enquiring immediately when *was* a convenient time to call, but Juliet's increasing frustration at not falling pregnant, in tandem with Lindsay's rampant smugness at her own fortuitous lot in life, had caused an unspoken friction between them, and so Juliet simply left it at that and muttered her apologies.

Juliet had a horrible feeling Lindsay was going to catch her off-guard one day soon, though, and then the poison would spill forth from the boil of unexpressed anger – and probably from Juliet's mouth, being the less self-controlled of the two women.

Such thoughts filled Juliet's head as she tramped up Upper Foxburgh Road, the busy road linking the two sides of Deverton in an east-west direction, the leather jacket over her shoulder creating a damp patch of perspiration across her back.

***

"Take Mr Gani back to Deverton, please, Cam," Mark Parlour instructed DS Goodlove early that Wednesday afternoon. In the absence of firmer evidence linking Salik Gani to the elderly bottle of paraquat found in his flat, Parlour had no choice but to release the rather downtrodden local shop worker from police custody. According to Gani, a bathroom window he always left a notch open on leaving the house had been released from the catch and was flapping against the frame. Furthermore, some imprints had been made in the earth below the window. There was no tread on the prints; their creator must have worn bags over their shoes. That was, if this person even existed. It would have been well possible for Gani to have entirely engineered this "evidence". But given there was no tangible proof either way that the bottle of weed killer had been planted in Gani's bedroom, Parlour could not justify keeping him in custody a moment longer.

Stubbled and thoroughly devoid of spirit, unlike at his previous encounter with Parlour that fateful Saturday afternoon, Salik wandered bleakly out of the police station in Goodlove's wake, a pathetic weedy figure of a man beside the strapping young Detective Sergeant.

He sat mutely in the passenger seat of Goodlove's non-descript executive lease-car, refusing the cigarette offered him by the jocular younger man.

Goodlove attempted light-hearted conversation about football transfers and show-biz tittle tattle but soon gave up as it became apparent Gani had neither the energy nor the spirit to offer up anything in the way of a response.

Twenty minutes later, Gani had been safely deposited at the Mini Mart where two uniformed officers would keep an eye on the shop until the initial furore over the murder of a white, middle-class local had died down. That Davidson Munroe had not been particularly popular among the general populace of Deverton was neither here nor there; that an Asian man had been found at the scene of the murder and had harboured the probable means of murder within his own property, despite any firm evidence linking him to the crime, was highly significant. PC Vee Singh frowned to himself in disgust as he took up his post outside Deverton Mini Mart. The hypocrisy of these wolves in sheep's clothing was nauseating.

14

Alicia Munroe proceeded soundlessly and soullessly up the hallway to the telephone table, where the cordless phone, reclining in its plastic deckchair, was bleeping coldly at her. She could not feel her legs as she walked; some physical force entirely out of her control instructed her feet to move in the direction of the leather-topped desk.

"Deverton treble seven four four two," she replied dully. Why did people bother repeating their phone number? Alicia Munroe frowned to herself. This was one of these foolish habits Davidson had got her into which made no sense whatsoever. It was a relic from a pompous bygone age… oh dear, was that how she viewed the years of their marriage already?

"Alicia?" queried a high-pitched, educated voice.

Who else? Alicia wanted to reply acerbically but hadn't the energy to.

"Yes?"

"Lins Briscoe. I was wondering if you could help me with an order for the Hampshire Homebodies? They have their annual social on Friday afternoon. I know you're probably not in the mood for baking, but I thought it…"

"Might take my mind off things?" Alicia interrupted, smiling wanly to herself. If only baking Victoria sponges were the solution to this torturous to-ing and fro-ing between grief and anger. "What do you need?"

"Oh just a dozen of your delicious cheese scones, a walnut loaf and a St Clement's – I need them late morning Friday."

"Where's the meeting – the Church Centre?"

"Gosh no; it's at somebody's home," Lindsay replied in a surprised tone of voice, as if this was entirely self-explanatory – which arguably it was.

"Come around at noon on Friday then," Alicia instructed her and put the phone down before any uncomfortable niceties were uttered. Lindsay Briscoe had built up quite a tidy little earner servicing the sugar cravings of Deverton's non-working female population. Her home-baking business, which bore the rather silly name, in Alicia's view, of *Tumtations*, had proven a profitable side-line for the mother of three, so much so that she had taken on an extra pair of oven-gloved hands in the shape of Alicia Munroe. Lindsay very much hoped that the sudden death of Davidson Munroe would not put a premature stop to the mutually beneficial, if somewhat functional, working relationship between the two women.

***

Two hours cooped up in the flat above the Mini Mart with Zoreena and her four irritable pre-school children was all it took to awaken Salik from his self-pitying torpor and galvanise him into action.

"I'm moving back across the road," he informed his shocked elder brother as he appeared downstairs with a shabby sports holdall.

Naz looked up, but fortunately there was only one elderly granny searching the ambient shelf for bargains, completely oblivious to events till-side.

"Ssh!" he hissed at Salik nevertheless. "Are you out of your mind? Those mad idiots won't give you a moment's peace! You'd be safer sleeping in the bloomin' allotment!"

"Not a bad idea, that one," Salik conceded, not entirely in jest.

"Please, Salik, I'm begging you…"

But it was too late, his younger brother had already vacated the shop and was making his way across the road. Naz looked frantically around him. The shuffling female pensioner at the back of the shop was hardly going to raid the till. He sprinted out the shop towards his brother's retreating back, but it was too late.

The colour drained from Salik Gani's cheeks as he came to face to face with foul-smelling brown faeces around his PVC letterbox and some barely concealed graffiti of a white supremist nature on the brick wall.

"We tried to clean it off this morning, before you were released – the graffiti, that is… it's a bugger to get off without the proper kit," Naz mumbled.

Salik rose his hand in the air and motioned for silence. "Go back to the shop, Naz. It's not your fault. I'll deal with it."

He turned and faced his brother. "I'm an innocent man, I'm not going to hide anymore."

"Brave words, brother," Naz frowned. "And very foolish as well in the circumstances, if I may say so."

He shook his head and returned to the Mini Mart.

***

Royston Pedlar surveyed the two dozen strong gathering of BASC members assembled in the function room of *The Grand Old Duke* public house in Lower Chave and frowned. He had expected at least another half dozen or so to show their face at this important strategy meeting. Aaah, there was Gerald Pimcock with the minibus now. Pedlar had sent out the local Ring-a-Ride volunteer to round up the non-drivers amid the local membership to boost numbers at the meeting.

He rubbed his hands in glee as he noted that Pimcock had returned with a full complement and marched outside to frogmarch the less sprightly BASC members of Billock and its environs through the outside doors of the function room, with the aim of speeding up proceedings. He had only rented the room out for two hours and that included clearing up time.

Ten minutes later, with coats removed and public conveniences safely negotiated, Pedlar called the meeting to order.

"Good afternoon, fellow Baskers. I'd like to begin this meeting with a minute's silence in memory of our dear friend and Vice-Chair, Davidson Munroe."

Heads were bowed and a sixty second silence immaculately observed.

"Thank you, Ladies and Gentlemen."

Pedlar pulled some half-frame reading glasses from a spectacle case placed alongside the overhead projector and flicked on the machine. A low-level hum filled the air as his elderly followers waited for him to outline his agenda for that afternoon.

"I'd like to begin by reminding you all of our motto:- *The British Alliance of Senior Citizens – Protecting British Culture for the Senior Citizens of Today and Tomorrow.*"

A noisy cheer rose up and Pedlar guffawed heartily, his collar and tied chest puffing out proudly as he towered above his minions. He did not notice the uneasy glance Margaret Hebble exchanged with Mary Tibbs, to the right of her.

***

"So they've let you back out to play," Alicia Munroe commented wearily, stepping aside to let Salik Gani through her front door.

"Not travelling incognito today then?" she further enquired as she waited for him to remove his trainers and overcoat.

"No more hiding, Alicia," Gani informed her. "I didn't bump off your old man and nobody's going to pin that one on me just cos an Asian guy finds himself in the wrong place at the wrong time."

"Bold words," Alicia commented, raising her eyebrows with rather more energy than she had mustered up so far since the death of her husband.

She motioned for him to join her at the kitchen table, dusty from flour and the remains of a home-baking session.

"Back in the swing of things?" Gani enquired, accepting a mug of tea from his friend.

Alicia shrugged. "Not really. Got a cake order, that's all. Thought I might as well get started, they'll freeze down fine. Can't guarantee I'll be in the mood Friday morning – Lindsay needs them Friday lunchtime."

"Very wise," Salik nodded, though with little real idea of how Alicia must be feeling inside. "Still help her out a lot then?"

"Now and then," Alicia replied, sounding bored of the subject already. It was a profitable enough venture for her, but could she be bothered anymore? It wasn't as if she needed the money; Davidson had ensured she would be well provided for in the event of his death, untimely or otherwise. Alicia wasn't sure that she would be able to find the energy anymore for helping others, everything just seemed so pointless at the minute, and therefore so easy to wriggle out of. Mind you, most things in life were futile and forgo-able if you thought about it, Alicia decided in the rather lacklustre manner that had descended upon her now that the initial shock of Davidson's murder had worn off. She had dipped into the Bible tracts that that sweet but drippy trainee vicar had left her with on Tuesday, but rather than reading up on God's mercy and comfort, Alicia had become sidetracked with the Old Testament story of Job. Now there was a candidate for Prozac, if ever there was one. That man definitely had depression, Alicia concluded. Who said the Bible didn't relate to modern issues?

"Alicia – there is something bothering me," Gani informed her.

"What's that, then?"

"Alicia!" Salik exclaimed, shocked at the stony expression that remained on Alicia Munroe's face, an expression that seemed entirely devoid of grief for a deceased spouse of thirty odd years. "Could you just sound a little bit concerned that your husband has just been murdered?!"

"Why should I be bothered?" Alicia enquired, rising only slightly to the bait. "I find out he was having it off with some floozy in the potting shed without having the common courtesy to inform me…

"Whoa! Who told you this?" Gani frowned.

"I found some silly note in the washing machine, it obviously fell out his trousers… it wasn't the only thing to escape from his chinos."

A tear rolled down Alicia's cheek, belying the show of casual indifference.

Gani squeezed her hand across the table, incurring a fine dusting of self-raising flour on his sleeve for his exertions.

"It was from some woman arranging to meet him there that afternoon," Alicia informed him miserably.

"What did it say?" Gani inquired, brow furrowed.

"It just said *meet me at the allotments at 2*, that's all."

"Oh Alicia! That could have been from anyone!" Gani exclaimed.

"It was a woman's handwriting," Alicia sniffed. "I could tell."

Gani snorted. "What are you on about?"

"It was tiny and rounded – and printed, too. Very neat. Men don't write like that."

"Some do," Salik frowned again. Naz didn't have the most manly hand in the world.

"Trust me, it was a woman's," Alicia cut in. She shook her head, staring down at her fingers. Gani noted that she had removed her rings.

"It's not the first time he's got involved with another woman, Sal," she informed him quietly. "But he hasn't cheated on me in a long while, or so he led me to believe. There have been a couple of flirtations with young girls over the years – you know, ex-pupils and student teachers. Never anyone under-age, nothing dodgy like that. And he'd never bedded any of them. Just a bit of slap and tickle, he said. Part and parcel of his personality, old Gung-Ho Munroe. Nothing to worry about. But now…"

A strangled sob escaped from Munroe's mouth. Gani squeezed both hands this time, but Munroe immediately pulled one away to furiously wipe the tears away. That man was *not* worth crying over.

"Now I just don't know what to think. He was murdered - *poisoned*, for goodness' sake. People don't go around murdering over a minor flirtation. He'd severely cheesed off someone, and a quick bosom grope in the allotments hardly warrants putting poisonous weed killer in his mug – wouldn't you agree?"

She looked at Gani through blurry eyes.

"What have you done with this note?" he frowned. He felt that Alicia was jumping the gun a little.

"I flushed it down the loo," Alicia replied.

"Don't you think you should have…"

"Shown the police?" Alicia interrupted him. She shook her head. "Whatever I think of him, I don't want the whole of Deverton knowing he was at it with some tart in the potting shed. I have some pride left, you know."

"So you'll let me take the rap instead?" Gani cried, rising to his feet, an expression of tortured hurt contorting his features.

Alicia pulled him back down. "C'mon, nobody seriously thinks you did it. Only a few small-minded idiots with nothing better to do than stir up trouble, because there's fudge all else to do around here."

"Those few small-minded idiots have covered my door in dog shit and lobbed a brick through every window of my house!" Gani exclaimed. "And in any case, they found this note telling Davey to meet someone there at 2pm – *I* was flippin' well there at 2pm, wasn't I?"

"*It wasn't you.* There's no hard evidence linking you to the crime; anyone could have written that note, just as anyone could have broken into your flat and planted weed killer in your bed. They've released you, haven't they?"

"They'll find some way of stitching me up," Gani muttered blackly. Alicia shook her head.

"Not with Mark Parlour heading the case. He's a decent man, he won't make facts fit the theory."

"I'm not so sure, Alicia," Gani said glumly, sinking back on this chair, his earlier enthusiasm waning as suddenly as its onset. "Even he can't ignore the weight of evidence against me."

There was a minute's silence before Gani raised his head. "Who's to say it couldn't be something to do with Pedlar and co? Some bit of in-house fighting? Maybe it was a set-up, a ruse to get Davey to the allotments for two o'clock."

Alicia shook her head gloomily. "He went there of his own volition, the police have already established that. He ran out of bloody leeks…"

She thought fondly for one moment of her husband's pride at his well-developed crop of leeks, but immediately banished the sentiment. It was so confusing, this juggling act, trying to house fondness and hatred in her heart at one and the same time. It would be far easier just to hate; just to write off thirty-one years of marriage as a sham. Or at least for now, where emotions had to be kept simple just to get through the day.

15

"It's your mum!" Parlour hissed, peering through the beech wood horizontal blinds in their bedroom at ten past five that afternoon. He hastily pulled his boxer shorts and trousers back on and grabbed a fresh polo shirt from the drawer. It would take too long to button his work shirt and he didn't want her to know that he had been at it with her precious daughter and only child.

"Decent of her to wait for you to come," Juliet grinned, staying put on the bed, ankles raised up on some pillows to aid the passage of sperm on their journey north.

"Aren't you going to get up, then?" Parlour frowned, taking a thin silver comb from his back pocket and carefully teasing each auburn strand back into place. It was a rather effeminate action that amused Juliet greatly.

"I'm sure Mother will understand, when I produce a healthy little Hebble-Parlour!"

"You can explain why you're late downstairs with a healthy glow, then," Parlour retorted, and hurried down the staircase to answer the front door.

"Margaret – how lovely to see you!" Parlour lied, ushering her straight into the living room. "Jules is just resting upstairs, she'll be down in a jiffy."

"Oh dear, has she had a bad day?" Margaret frowned, persistently worried for her daughter's welfare, though her daughter was more than capable of holding her own in the big wide world, and indeed, was infinitely better equipped to do so psychologically than her anxious and highly-strung mother.

"No, she's just had a few late nights recently," Parlour grinned, meandering into the kitchen to put the kettle on, Margaret trotting along obediently behind.

"Hello Mum, this is unexpected!" Juliet frowned, as she appeared downstairs ten minutes later. It wouldn't do to look too pleased to see her mother, lest it should increase the frequency of parental visits at this very busy time of day.

"Your father doesn't know I'm here," Margaret informed them anxiously. She brushed her skirt underneath her legs nervously as she perched uneasily on the edge of one of the Z chairs that the Parlours had been fond of ten years ago. It had to be said, they appeared a little dated now and Juliet was hankering after some leather tub chairs to replace them.

"Can I get you a cup of tea?" Parlour enquired, stopping short of inviting her to dinner, much to his wife's relief. However, Margaret Hebble was unlikely ever to accept such an invite, so set in the routine was she of cooking and dining with her husband at all times. Parlour hoped fervently that Juliet and he would never become so inflexible that they couldn't adjust to circumstances and seize opportunities and impromptu invitations as they pleased. Parlour wondered if it was just another generation thing. Derek Hebble would probably have a hernia, faced with the task of preparing and cooking a meal for himself after all these years of having it construed and constructed for him. He thought rather scornfully of such men, who were so narrow in their roles and abilities that they remained all trussed up in the ropes of routines dictated to them by their wives. Parlour was inclined to look down on others, whilst exaggerating in his own mind the frequency of which he himself played the Noughties All-Rounder in the home.

"No thank you, Mark, I must get back soon. Derek thinks I've just nipped off to Utopia for some bits and pieces we can't get in Chave," Margaret replied.

"So what's up?" Juliet asked impatiently, throwing herself back on the chair and sitting cross-legged. Parlour balanced on the arm of the chair and waited for Margaret to download.

"We had one of our…meetings… this afternoon."

The Parlours teasingly left it to Margaret Hebble to elaborate, though they were fairly sure what kind of meeting she was referring to.

"You know, the um…"

"Nasty Nazi pensioners?" Juliet enquired, sarcasm lacing her meringue-light tone.

"There's no need for that, Juliet," Margaret said curtly, pursing her lips. "It's called the…"

"British Alliance of nasty Nazi pensioners," Juliet grinned. Parlour frowned at her and placed a restraining hand on her forearm.

"Roy Pedlar held a meeting this afternoon at the Duke of York, 2pm, isn't that right?" Parlour enquired smoothly.

Margaret Hebble looked taken-aback. "You knew already?"

"We had a retired copper go and see our friend Mr Pedlar in action," Parlour informed her soberly.

"Oh," was the only reply his mother-in-law could muster.

"He's a thoroughly nasty piece of work, Margaret, you really should watch the company you keep," Parlour informed her, exaggerating the actual danger posed by Pedlar at this moment in time to put the frighteners on his mother-in-law. Derek may be beyond reach, but Margaret was far more likely to be scared off, if perceived to be flying in the face of the authorities.

"Oh come on," Margaret protested. "He's just a decent, if a little bombastic, senior citizen trying to stand up for his rights, trying to bring back British values… you'll find most of us older folk resent the way our country's being taken over by immigrants and European statutes."

"Margaret, there is nothing decent about a man who causes a riot in a church-yard and who issues long-armed shoe-horns to all who join his gang!"

"You know about the shoe-horns?" Margaret wondered, looking even more troubled.

Parlour frowned; he had said too much.

"So what did you come to tell us?" Juliet enquired. She would ask Mark about the geri-gadgets later.

"It's just that… well… I'm concerned about… OK, about Roy Pedlar," Margaret finally spat out, staring at the ceiling in discomfort.

"A-ha!" Parlour exclaimed triumphantly.

"Mark – let her speak," Juliet frowned.

"Sorry."

There was a longer pause which saw Margaret Hebble open and shut her mouth several times to speak before finally coughing and giving audible form to the words taking shape in her mouth.

"Roy Pedlar didn't appear to be as…worked up… about the murder of Davidson Munroe as I thought he would be. I was only saying to Mary yesterday that we would have expected quite a bit of… rancour… from him. Especially since they arrested that Indian chap from the Mini Mart."

"He's Bangladeshi," Parlour interrupted dryly, "but do continue."

"So what did he say?" Juliet enquired impatiently.

"Well not a lot… we had a minute's silence in memory of him… then Mr Pedlar simply stated that the … murder… was undoubtedly the work of someone trying to sabotage the work of the BASC. He just called for us to be extra vigilant and to step up our efforts to promote British values and British culture, as this was what Davidson would have wanted."

Parlour nodded. He could check out these details with retired Detective Chief Inspector Tanner of Foxburgh CID tomorrow.

"So no Joseph Goebellesque racist rantings then?" Juliet enquired sarcastically. She really was quite aghast that her parents should choose to spend their retirement engaging in such a thoroughly pointless and nasty pursuit as giving credence to Roy Pedlar and his alliance of narrow-minded trouble-makers.

"He didn't mention the Ganis or make any other erm… culturally related… comments on the subject," Margaret informed them.

"That is strange," Parlour agreed. There was a moment's silence as they considered the potential reasons for this unexpected response to Munroe's murder. The obvious conclusion to be drawn, of course, was that Pedlar himself was somehow involved in the successful attempt on Davidson Munroe's life, and as such, did not wish to draw undue attention to events and implicate himself in investigations. However, he was already implicated, albeit indirectly, by virtue of the timing of Munroe's death and the events running up to, and indeed, concurrently with the murder at the allotments.

"I really must get back," Margaret Hebble said nervously, standing up. "I don't want Derek to suspect I was here. He doesn't realize I'm starting to …"

"Have misgivings about Pedlar?" Parlour enquired tactfully before his wife could wade in with something unhelpful that would get Margaret's back up and discourage her from confiding further in them.

Margaret just nodded curtly.

"Well thanks for popping around, Margaret," Parlour smiled, seeing her to the door, leaving a bemused Juliet in the living room.

"I just felt you should know… how he was today," she stated hesitantly.

"You did the right thing," her son-in-law reassured her.

She paused for a moment, opened her mouth to talk, then closed it again. Parlour waited patiently; he was sure she had some other information she felt duty-bound to impart to him.

"Yes?" he enquired finally.

His mother-in-law took a deep breath. "You might like to pop into Utopia on Monday morning. They're doing a promotion on ethically exchanged products, I believe."

And with that, she left the property and walked briskly to her little silver Daihatsu, not turning her head once as she returned to her car to make the short journey back to Chave.

Parlour frowned. She'd evidently bottled it, but what had Margaret wanted to tell him? He scratched his scalp and returned slowly to the living room.

"Well then, well then, the worm has turned!" Juliet grinned, raising her thick fair eyebrows at her husband.

Parlour tutted. "That's no way to refer to your dear mother!"

He threw himself back on the sofa and folded his hands behind his head, a typical lounging pose for Mark Parlour.

"So what next, super sleuth?" Juliet enquired, shoving a Twix mini in her mouth. It was if Juliet was already pregnant, the way she had been shovelling comfort food in her mouth these past few weeks.

"Whatever happened to your Lent vows?" Parlour frowned, kicking a cushion that was annoying him off the sofa.

"I never said I was giving anything up, did I?" Juliet replied uncouthly with a mouth full of sticky caramel and milk chocolate. She swallowed the chocolate bar. "Just said I was going to try and eat more greens."

"You did this a few years back," Parlour snorted. "You had lettuce sandwiches in your lunchbox then came home and demolished the contents of the biscuit barrel night after night. What's the point?"

"Well at least I can rely on you to pop across to Utopia on a Sunday to replenish my stocks!" Juliet commented sarcastically and pulled herself to her feet.

"Where are you going?" Parlour frowned, his stomach rumbling as Juliet picked up her keys and wandered into the hallway to get her jacket.

"Just up to Venny Row," Juliet called back. "Martin Beauville informs me that some retired couple have moved into the house on the end. Thought I would call around and invite them along to the service on Sunday."

She leant over the sofa and dropped a kiss on her husband's lips. It was then that he noticed the leather jacket.

"Jules!" he exclaimed rather aghast. "Where on earth did you get that… biker jacket thing?"

"Cool, isn't it?" Juliet commented nonchalantly, though her heart was beating furiously underneath it. She had feared Mark would react in this way. He was so conservative when it came to clothes.

"Where did you get it?" Parlour persisted. "Oh Jules, you didn't…"

"Keep your carrot-top on!" Juliet grinned. "I didn't pay anything for it. Micky gave it to me. It doesn't fit her anymore, got arms like a truck-driver since she had Sacha."

"Micky?" Parlour frowned.

"You know, the lady I bumped into at the Post Office the other week."

"Oh, your sloany New Labour professional placard-bearer?" Parlour grinned.

"Her name's Michaela, Michaela Brevitt," Juliet informed him curtly. She slung her handbag over her shoulder and left him frowning at her leather-clad back as she departed for the exclusive Venison Row development.

"Gosh, our garden needs tidying up," Juliet thought to herself five minutes later, as she surveyed their property in Spatchcock Drive from the elevated position of the new arrivals' driveway. The house in Venison Row offered an illuminating aerial view of the Parlour's garden from the rear aspect.

Juliet's eye strayed to the red Audi saloon in the driveway as she waited for someone to answer the door. She blinked as she recognised the black rat logo on the rear windscreen, the self-same sticker Michaela Brevitt had borne on the back window of her Alfa-Romeo.

Her gaze flickered back to the chunky oak front door as it inched open. The middle-aged male occupant of the house gazed rather dubiously at Juliet. It didn't occur to Juliet that the biker jacket made her look a little less comfortable to the older generation.

"Hello there!" Juliet greeted the wary face at the door, cocking her head to try and gain a proper view of its owner through the acute angle.

The voice sounded friendly enough, Bob Killington thought to himself, and opened the door a little wider.

Juliet extended a hand. "Juliet Parlour, I live down in Spatchcock Drive – you can see our back garden from your house." She indicated in the direction of their property.

Killington noted with satisfaction that she was pointing to the large four bed property that belonged to the Detective Inspector chap. His wife had recognised Parlour, as he stepped into his car the other day, to be the ginger detective that had featured on the local news the other day when that BASC fellow had been bumped off.

"DI Parlour's wife?" he enquired quite innocently. Juliet forced herself not to growl an angry retort and assert her desire to be recognised as an individual in her own right.

"That's right," she smiled blandly instead. A more observant individual, such as Bob Killington's wife, would have picked up on the frown that furrowed Juliet's brow in concurrent motion with her upturned lips.

"You'd better come in. Not in trouble already, are we?" he grinned, stepping to one side to let her in.

"My husband doesn't send his wife to do his donkey work, thank you," Juliet informed him a little more frostily this time. What a ridiculous notion. She slipped her jacket off. The relief from Bob Killington was palpable on realising that Juliet Parlour was as respectable as themselves in her chain store work trousers and angora v-neck sweater.

She followed him into a kitchen diner and was immediately greeted by a tall, triangular lady in her mid-sixties with no breasts to speak of but ample hips.

"This is my wife, Tonky," Killington informed Juliet, indicating to his spouse with an outstretched palm. Juliet did her best to stifle a giggle.

"I can speak for myself, thank you, Bob," Tonky informed her husband curtly. She smiled broadly at Juliet. Juliet smiled back; she was a woman after her own heart, though perhaps minus the silly name.

"Tonky's a nickname," she explained to the younger woman, noticing the bemused smirk that flashed across Juliet Parlour's pretty face. "I was christened Antonia. Hate it. I was Tonky or Tonks as a child – Honky Tonk when I soiled my nappy, ha ha."

Bob and Tonky guffawed loudly; Juliet just smiled rather warily.

"So, is this just a social call?" Bob Killington enquired. "Welcome to the village, and watch your backs, my husband's a copper, and all that?"

Juliet ignored him, instead extracting some leaflets from her handbag. "I've come on behalf of Deverton Parish Church. Here are some details of our services, it would be lovely to see you sometime. The vicar, Martin Beauville, is a thoroughly sound guy. Youngish, dishy, not a pair of cords in sight!"

"He's local as well, isn't he?" Tonky Killington enquired.

"Yes," Juliet nodded. "The vicarage is that large red-brick detached house on Upper Deverton Road – you know, the winding road that runs north to south. The church is a couple of hundred yards further on, a modern building with a hall joined on. You can't miss that either."

"Oh yes, we've seen the church," Bob Killington nodded at his wife. There was an uncomfortable pause and Juliet ascertained they were not church-goers.

"Do you share the Christian faith? Juliet enquired nevertheless, making it very clear she did.

Bob shook his head sorrowfully, not for want of partaking in her belief system, but at having to refuse this pretty young woman's invitation to join their congregation.

"We're humanists," he informed Juliet. "We believe in basic human goodness and solving life's problems through reason and rational thought."

Spare me the lecture, Juliet thought to herself.

"We actively campaign to promote the factors that unite us as human beings," Tonky Killington further expounded. "We're members of…"

"Respect and Tolerance UK," Juliet interrupted. "I saw the sticker on your car."

"You've heard of us?" Tonky enquired surprised. Juliet noted the tone of party ownership in Antonia Killington's tone.

"I met your leader the other day. She invited me in for coffee, in fact."

Tonky looked at her husband. "You know Micky?"

Juliet smiled, nodding. "We met in the Post Office. Her daughter is gorgeous, isn't she?"

"She's a poppet," Tonky agreed, pumping Juliet's hand furiously now. "Well, you must stay for a coffee as well, then. Any friend of Micky's is a friend of ours, isn't that right, Bob?"

Bob Killington nodded vigorously. "Indeed. Well, isn't this a coincidence? I was just commenting to Tonky the other morning that that Detective off the telly lives a few streets down, and now I discover his missus knows our Micky!"

Our Micky, Juliet noted, deciding to ignore the repeated reference to her as Parlour's missus. My, they were a close-knit bunch, these RAT-packers.

"I can't stay," Juliet said hastily, raising a hand in the air to stop Tonky in her tracks. "I need to get dinner on. I just dashed up here while I had a minute."

"Well, it was lovely to meet you," Tonky smiled warmly and squeezed her hand in both of hers.

Juliet just looked rather dazed and let them lead her to the door.

Why do I feel rather odd? Juliet wondered, slipping Michaela Brevitt's jacket on as she walked up the driveway. She mused on the sudden appearance of three RAT members in their small community in the space of a month and the almost concurrent arrival of Roy Pedlar, leader of the self-styled opposition - and added to that, the sudden death of Davidson Munroe, vice-chair of Pedlar's baby, the British Alliance of Senior Citizens. It was odd, very odd indeed, and surely no coincidence. She would discuss it with Mark over dinner.

Juliet's thoughts switched to what she could concoct with half a pack of diced chicken, one courgette, half a red onion and a pot of crème-fraiche. Lesley Waters eat your heart out, she smiled to herself, picturing herself finally shutting that gargantuan grinning gob of Ainsley Harriott's as she wowed the Ready Steady Cook team with a brilliant seat-of-the-pants Mediterranean risotto.

16

"If you've come to badger me to join the RATs, you're wasting your time," Nazrul Gani informed Michaela Brevitt at six o'clock that evening. "I just want the dust to settle so that we can all get on with our lives again."

"I've come to talk to you about Salik, actually," Michaela informed him a little frostily. "I'm worried about him."

"You and me both," Naz replied, banging a stack of newspapers down noisily on the counter and removing the paper and string packaging with a pair of scissors.

"He can't stay in that flat of his – not with people slinging shit at the door and chucking bricks through the windows," Michaela continued undaunted.

"He has a perfectly decent family home above the shop where he is more than welcome to stay ad infinitum," Naz said wearily, repeating the exercise with a second batch of Billock Couriers.

"There's not enough room, and you know it," Michaela stated curtly. "You're tripping over each other up there as it is, without Sal and his pot plant collection."

"So what are his options?" Naz asked boredly, carrying the papers over to the floor space below the magazine shelves.

"Well I had half-hoped Alicia Munroe might put him up, she's plenty of room in that grand place of hers. Sal went around there earlier; he was hoping she would offer, out of sympathy for him, but the thought didn't even occur to her."

"There's always the allotments," Naz commented blithely.

"I wouldn't put it past him, you know," Michaela said seriously. "It's hardly the safest option in the world, though, is it?"

Naz shrugged. "My little brother always has a home here, I can't offer more than that."

"Well, I can," Michaela said. Naz turned around and met her face this time.

"He can move in with me."

"You?" Naz spat out.

"Why not?" Michaela shrugged. "I have a spare room and he needs our support at the moment."

"You have a little girl, Micky, who probably won't appreciate you putting up some strange man – or perhaps she's used to it?"

"You're quite safe on that score," Michaela informed him coldly.

Naz ambled back over to the counter. "It won't work, Micky. He'll drive you mad. He's a lazy sod. Never cleans up after himself. And cooks… he cooks all the time. Great big smoky fry-ups at all hours, it'll turn your sophisticated little stomach."

"It's only a temporary arrangement," Michaela shrugged, "until they catch whoever did Davey Munroe in. Then everyone'll get off his back and leave him alone."

"If you're doing this to promote your tin-pot left-wing political party, just forget it," Naz said scathingly. "You should think of your daughter. She won't appreciate a breezeblock through her window or crap through the letterbox. What sort of mother are you?"

"And what sort of brother are you?" Michaela retorted. "More concerned with protecting your precious family business and ingratiating yourself with the local white middle-class hierarchy than standing up against bigotry and racism!"

She stormed out the shop, forgetting her newspaper and roared off in the black Alfa-Romeo.

It was only when she got stuck at the traffic lights beyond Deverton Triangle that the internal storm subsided a little.

Michaela was not overly sensitive, couldn't afford to be in either her profession or her political role, but she had to admit, Naz's comment had got to her. What sort of mother indeed was she, putting the safety of her daughter and herself at risk to protect the life of a casual acquaintance?

Michaela shook her head and dispelled the self-doubt that had crept in. Whoever changed the world by playing safe? No, she was doing the right thing. Anyway, so long as Naz kept his mouth shut, no-one should suspect her of harbouring a fugitive. After all, a posh yuppie pad in Knightsbridge Park on the other side of Deverton was probably the last place anyone would look for Salik Gani.

***

"So how were they, these new neighbours of ours?" Parlour enquired, dishing up a Spaghetti Bolognese he had cracked on with while Juliet had nipped up the road.

"Poaahh! How much red wine did you chuck in here?" his wife enquired, wrinkling her nose in disdain.

"Half a bottle of that Bulgarian grunge someone brought to the barbie last summer," Parlour grinned, draining the penne pasta he favoured to spaghetti. It was typical of Mark Parlour, to favour pasta tubes over the eminently more messy spaghetti pasta that traditionally accompanied the dish bearing its name. He was not one to ruin a good shirt in the name of gastronomic propriety.

It was Parlour's turn to frown as his wife blizzarded her Bolognese with fresh grated Parmesan to offset the alcoholic punch.

Juliet waited for Parlour to give thanks for the food before launching into a narrative on her new acquaintances. Parlour enjoyed the colour and humour with which his wife imbued such meetings; she would make an excellent CID officer in that respect, he thought. However, she was far too idealistic and trenchant by nature to successfully hold down such a profession.

"They're called the Killingtons, believe it or not. They're retired. The husband is called Bob, tall, jovial, a curious mixture of chauvinistic and humanist. Not sure how you would

150

brand that:- chauva-humanist? Huma-chauvinist? Anyway, dark hair greying at the temples, sensible lambs wool v-neck, smart trousers, shiny leather shoes in the house. She – wait for it – is called Tonky."

"Tonky?" Parlour nearly spat out his mouthful of Bolognese.

"Short for Antonia," Juliet continued unabashed. "Tall, horsey, think Lindsay Briscoe in thirty years' time. Bit rah but very friendly. They seemed very … parental, if that makes sense. Went all cooey over me."

"And who wouldn't?" Parlour cooed on demand, reaching across and squidging his wife's cheeks.

"Now this is the interesting bit," Juliet stated, leaning forward in her chair, her green eyes shining a little brighter.

"They're swingers?" Parlour enquired, grinning.

"Mark!" Juliet exclaimed, shuddering at the thought of Bob Killington dangling his Audi keys in her face, a lecherous leer on his lean middle-aged features.

"Sorry, boring day at the station," Parlour apologised.

"A man's been murdered and you have a boring day at the station?" Juliet frowned. It wasn't how police stations were during murder investigations, was it, or had she been watching too much post-watershed television?

Parlour shrugged. "The case is at a standstill, we've been working on other things."

"Anyway, the Killingtons belong to RAT UK, you know, that party my friend Micky is chair of."

Parlour sat up straight. "Really? Now, that is interesting."

Juliet nodded vigorously. "That's what I thought. Don't you think it's a little strange that not long after Pedlar moves into the area, the RAT bunch start taking up property in Deverton, too… and Davidson Munroe gets poisoned?"

"You're not saying your friend Micky or the Killingtons had anything to do with Munroe's murder?" Parlour frowned.

"I don't think for one minute Micky would do a thing like that. You'll see, when you meet her. And the Killingtons didn't really seem the type, either. But you never know, do you, and you have to admit, it does seem a bit of a coincidence."

"Perhaps I should suss out this Respect and Tolerance Party UK a little more," Parlour mused. "I'll get Karen back on the job."

"You've already checked them out?" Juliet enquired.

Parlour nodded. "Of course, you know me, no stone unturned."

"Not even fake front door key receptacles?" Juliet grinned, eyes twinkling. Parlour smiled then his face slowly opened out into Eureka mode.

"What is it?" Juliet enquired.

"Well done, Jules! You just reminded me of something important!"

"What then?"

"Can't tell you yet, need to call Dave Tanner."

Parlour leapt out his chair and grabbed the cordless phone and a scruffy post-it note from the worktop. He hastily punched in a number but put the phone down after a brief exchange with someone who was clearly not retired Detective Chief Inspector David Tanner.

"On the golf course, due back any minute," Parlour informed a bemused Juliet, who was used to his leaping up from the table like a scalded cat every time a potential lead sprang to mind.

"Who's Dave Tanner, when he's at home… or at the golf course, for that matter?" Juliet enquired.

"That retired DCI I sent along to Pedlar's meeting this afternoon," Parlour informed his wife. "I have a feeling Pedlar is up to something and your mother has gone and confirmed that this afternoon."

Juliet frowned. "She just said he didn't seem overly bothered by Davidson Munroe's death, that's all."

"Exactly!" Parlour slapped his pale hand on the table. "And why not? Because his mind's on something else. Of course it matters to him that his henchman's been bumped off, but meanwhile he's got other fish to fry, far bigger fish…"

"Fry or poison?" Juliet enquired.

"Oh, I don't think Pedlar had anything to do with Munroe's death, at least not directly," Parlour qualified. "In any case, he has a watertight alibi, he was definitely in the churchyard throughout that whole period, we have television footage and hundreds of eyewitness accounts to prove it."

Parlour got up as the phone rang. "That'll be Dave."

Juliet clicked in exasperation as Parlour left the room, plate of Bolognese in one hand, cordless phone in the other.

***

"Just call me Gok!" Michaela Brevitt grinned, throwing a Next bag at Salik Gani at 9pm that evening.

Despite his initial misgivings at the safety threat he posed to Michaela and little Sacha, which were little more than perfunctory polite utterances in any case, Gani had taken little persuading in the end to move in with the Brevitts on a temporary basis. Michaela had sent Bob Killington around to the Mini Mart to collect more of Gani's stuff; no-one would suspect a well-spoken, middle-aged stranger of being in any way involved in the whereabouts of Salik Gani, and Nazrul would certainly keep his mouth shut. Meanwhile, she had left Gani alone in the flat while she nipped out for some vital supplies.

And it was these supplies that were absorbing Gani's attention at that moment. He held a lilac Oxford style shirt up to the light and fingered the pure silk purple tie that came with it.

"This is a work shirt, Micks," he commented, puzzlement in his voice as he marvelled over the quality of the neck décor.

"Exactly," Michaela grinned smugly, delighted with the plan she had hatched to house Salik Gani with minimum fuss and threat to the safety of any of them.

"Here," she continued, throwing another bag in his direction, "are your work trousers. And these.." She rummaged around for a third carrier bag, "are your work shoes. Try the whole lot on; if it all fits, I'll get you a spare set tomorrow."

"I don't understand…" Gani mumbled, shaking his head as he considered the expensive black leather brogues in a size eight, his size exactly.

"Think about it, Sal," Michaela grinned, flinging herself down on the sofa and grabbing a cushion to her stomach. "If you start sneaking around the nice end of Deverton with a hoodie on, it'll stand out a mile you're Salik Gani in disguise. However…"

She paused grandly, exceedingly pleased with her ingenuity.

"If I dress you up as a sharp business exec, get you in some smart clobber, give your hair a good trim, get rid of that disgusting facial fluff, no-one will suspect for one moment you're anyone but Veejay Patel, high-flying advertising exec!"

"Veejay Patel?" Salik echoed and groaned. "Couldn't you have come up with something more original than that?"

"Names, schmames," Michaela dismissed his comment with a wave of the hand and continued, "You won't be getting up close and personal with anyone, anyway. You'll be with me most of the time."

"As your up close and personal assistant?" Salik enquired, raising his eyebrows humorously. This could actually be good fun. At least he wouldn't be hiding indoors like some kind of criminal on the run.

His smile turned to a frown as he ran his hand through his, by now, very greasy hair. "I'm not letting you loose on this, though," he warned.

Michaela held her hands up in horror. "Don't worry, Bob's wife Tonky used to cut their boys' hair. She has some clippers; you can get rid of the face fluff yourself."

She stood up and gathered the clothes up in her hand. "Right. Get yourself into the bathroom and try this lot on. There are some smellies in the Boots bag. The Killies are due in ten minutes!"

17

Well, that achieved diddly-squat, Parlour sighed, flopping back on the sofa, hands behind his head. He used his toe to flick shut the leather document file containing his notes on the Munroe investigation. He had read and reread the wad of witness statements and forensic reports, but nothing jumped out to inspire even the mildest tingling sensation between the ears, let alone the mental fireworks display he craved, that Eureka! moment, when the various strands of a murder enquiry converged into one plausible narrative in his brain. Following Parlour's phone call to him, the police pathologist, Nick Hunter, had confirmed that no chemical products excluding the paraquat had been found amid the contents of Munroe's stomach. This scuppered one theory of Parlour's, though in reality, he had expected as much. He might still check up on Alicia Munroe's visit to Utopia's pharmacy on the day of Munroe's murder, all the same.

Time to engage the visual senses, Parlour told himself, refusing to be beaten by the apparently avenueless nature of the information at his disposal. With a characteristic burst of nervous energy, he bounded upstairs to his state of the art PC in its transparent casing.

Parlour clicked it on and inserted a CD-Rom containing thousands of Clip-Art images that Juliet used to brighten up her school worksheets. Within half an hour, he had assembled half a dozen printouts which he hoped would serve as leitmotifs to stir his brain into gear. Clutching the sheaf of papers in his hand, Parlour raked around in his desk drawer for a pair of scissors then returned downstairs.

"And what are the junior staff up to?" Juliet enquired sarcastically, entering the living room to see her husband cutting out pictures of gardening products and rats, amongst other things.

156

"Just trying a different approach," Parlour muttered, spreading the outlined pictures out on the carpet in front of him. So far he had a black rat to represent Michaela Brevitt's Respect & Tolerance Party, a Union Jack to present Roy Pedlar and the BASC organisation, a bottle of weed killer, a church building, a blue square and a magazine.

For some reason, the latter two of these two-dimensional representations of items potentially linked to Munroe's death absorbed Parlour's attention as he tried to conjure up a motive for murder.

As hard as he tried to keep his brain on track, Parlour kept harking back to the mysterious blue note found in his in-laws' spare-key pebble. If the letters and digits stood for what he thought they stood for, how did this relate to Davidson Munroe's murder? And was it a coincidence that a blue note had also been found near the body of Munroe? Suddenly Parlour stood up. Fool! He berated himself, slapping his skinny thigh. Why hadn't he taken the note to compare handwriting?

It was a long shot, but worth a try, Parlour grimaced. He exchanged his chunky loafers for a pair of old trainers, then grabbed his coat and keys and rushed out to his car.

Within twenty minutes, he had pulled up around the corner from 17 Parsley Gardens. Patting the small bulge in his pocket, Parlour satisfied himself that he had remembered his LED mini-torch before gently easing open the Hebbles's front gate with minimal noise.

Parlour scaled around the perimeter hedge to avoid activating the security lights then crouched down underneath the front bay window. Fortunately the blinds were shut and all outside noise overridden by the contemptuously familiar, harsh barking of Deirdre Barlow in full indignant flow, pummelling the front glass.

Parlour got down on his hands and knees and gently stroked the pebbles near the front doorstep until his hand clasped around the impossibly smooth HomeGadget secret key holder.

He shone his LED torch on the grey stone and slid open the secret compartment with the aid of his penknife.

Darn it, Parlour cursed tamely under his breath. The note had gone, as expected, and equally disappointingly, there was no new note contained therein, to provide a sample of the author's handwriting. Parlour stood up and pressed his back against the wall. What next?

His thoughts suddenly turned to the Hebbles' pristinely maintained Billock Borough Council wheelybins. He shook his head. It was a ridiculous notion; it would be easier to find a small needle in a large haystack. Besides, knowing his in-laws as he did, he would be surprised if they were rigorous enough in their recycling efforts to bother consigning a small piece of blue paper to the green bin – assuming they had thrown away the note in the first place.

Botherations, Parlour cursed to himself again, scaling along the side of the house until he reached the bins tucked out of sight around the corner. Sometimes he was a victim of his own obsessive behaviour. Still, as he was always reminding his sergeants, leave no stone unturned. Parlour smiled inwardly at the appropriateness of the expression in the circumstances as he gently lifted the lid of the green bin.

He shone his torch inside, but all that could be seen were a week and a half's worth of the Southern Parishes Express and a couple of editions of The Foxburgh Herald. Parlour turned to the black bin and clicked in disgust as he prodded the kitchen bags contained inside and found as much paper and card as food remains and plastic packaging. What was wrong with these older folks, Parlour wondered, conveniently lumping a whole generation into one category, a habit he was forever ticking Juliet off about.

Parlour snorted. It was typical of his in-laws to be more concerned with personal hygiene than the great big fat hole in the ozone layer. It was a form of extreme selfishness, Parlour thought to himself grimacing. Sod the planet, we won't be here anyway. These self-righteous, middle-aged Foxburgh Herald-reading farts had a lot to learn from the much-maligned youth of today, Parlour thought pompously.

He seized the litter grabber he knew to be concealed behind the two bins and poked around inside the black bin, shining his torch on the contents.

Billocks! Parlour cursed as the torch slipped from his hand into the depths of the plastic container. He fumbled around blindly with one hand but his spindly fingers could not locate the small silver gadget, which was touch operated, and he could not reach right down to the bottom in any case.

Parlour looked around him and noted with a combination of disdain and satisfaction that a totally empty council glass recycling box was propped up against the wall. He turned it upside down and stood on it, able now to delve much deeper into the wheelybin.

Parlour should have known that the bottles box would not have taken even his negligible body mass. He exclaimed out loud as his foot pushed through the black plastic and even louder as, with a loud crash and the shattering of glass, the black wheelybin toppled over, sending Parlour sprawling backwards onto the pathway. He yelled in pain as his head smacked against a fence post then exclaimed in disgust as a mountain of soggy bin bags landed on top of his skinny torso.

Hebble Ten, Parlour Nil, Parlour groaned as Derek Hebble appeared in his dressing gown, bearing a rolling pin in one hand and shining a gargantuan Phillips torch in the other.

Parlour struggled to his feet and brushed his clothes down. He grimaced; some of the bottles inside the plastic bags had smashed from the impact, the shards cutting through the bags, thus enabling some foul-smelling kitchen waste to escape and soil his clothing.

"Why don't you sort your bloody waste properly, Derek?" Parlour moaned to his father-in-law.

***

"To a hassle-free stay!" Michaela Brevitt exclaimed, raising her wine glass aloft at ten pm that evening. The transformation was complete; Salik Gani, scruffy, downtrodden newsagent and murder suspect was now Mashrafe Khan, clean-cut Tommy Hilfiger be-sprayed business exec and Bangladeshi cricket fan.

Gani giggled, still stroking his silk tie. "I can't believe you spent all this cash on me!"

"What are friends for?" Michaela called from the kitchen, omitting to declare that she had taken the cash from party funds, as it could appear that the housing and reinventing of Salik Gani was no more than a publicity stunt. She reappeared with an open bottle of Cloudy Bay and two generous wine glasses of a design more suited to containing Cup-a-Soup than 150ml of expensive wine.

She put them down on the low level coffee table and removed some baby toys, the sole reminder in the dimly lit living room that this was also the residence of a thirteen month old toddler.

"Better just turn the baby monitor on; don't think we'll hear Sacha once we get gassing!"

Michaela got up to flick the switch on the white plastic monitor on the bookshelf.

"Hello, that's not her!" she mumbled, hearing some alien voices on the monitor. She frowned and pressed it to her ear. She didn't have a radio or television on anywhere.

"Come here, Sal, I can hear funny voices through the monitor!"

Salik got up and also pressed his ear to the one-way receiver. "It's one of your neighbours," he informed her. "They work like radios, these things. You can pick someone up over the airwaves, if they've got monitors on as well."

"Really?" Michaela enquired, somewhat dubiously.

"It's true," Gani nodded. "My sister-in-law could hear what next door's kids were watching on telly in the morning through the monitor, when we had the old house in Billock. Don't need the things anymore, not in that pokey flat above the Mini Mart."

Michaela's flat was palatial in comparison.

"But none of my neighbours have small children," Michaela frowned.

Gani picked up the monitor and gave it a good look-over. "These are pretty state of the art monitors you have here. Reckon someone over the road, even, might be able to pick up your signal if they've got their monitors turned on, too."

"Gosh, better not sing Sash to sleep then!" Michaela giggled, reaching for her glass of wine. "How not to win friends and influence people!"

Gani chuckled and resumed his spot on the sofa.

18

Parlour frowned as he knotted his favourite blue paisley silk tie on the morning of Friday 24th March 2006. Loathe as he was to admit it, Juliet may well have had a point whilst ribbing him about his laidback approach to the Munroe case.

It had certain similarities with the Terence Haynes's case a few years back; in both cases, a middle-aged, respectable, but rather self-righteous figure at the centre of community life here in Deverton had been poisoned. In the case of Haynes, someone aware of his severe reaction to peanuts had plopped some crushed peanuts in his coffee. In this recent scenario, a mysterious individual had force-fed Davidson Munroe, by the looks of it, a cupful of liquid paraquat weed-killer. But there ended the similarities. Haynes's murderer could be narrowed down to one of twelve individuals present at the scene of the murder; anyone could have nipped down to the allotments and poisoned Munroe. They had seen a golden opportunity, with most of Deverton's inhabitants absorbed by events up at Deverton Parish Church, to seek personal retribution of some kind by taking the life of Davidson Munroe.

It couldn't be ruled out, unlikely though it seemed in the circumstances, that this was the work of some figure from Munroe's past, an ex-pupil perhaps, who had come knocking at the allotment door. That was one clear difference between Munroe and the late Terence Haynes; Munroe had been a womanizer, Haynes had been devoted to his late wife. Parlour made a mental note to remember to ask Karen if she'd unearthed any useful leads regarding Munroe's love-life. However, Parlour's head told him he should continue to pursue the more obvious links between events at Deverton Church and the murder of one of the main players at the BASC demo in the churchyard. Dave Tanner had had a few interesting snippets of info to report from the BASC gathering, which Parlour would disseminate to the rest of the crew later in the day. Yesterday's excitement concerning the mysterious blue note in his in-law's ersatz pebble had subsided a little; interesting though its contents were, it did not seem to move the actual murder case on. Nevertheless, it could prove relevant and he would be sure to inform the others of the bits of the jigsaw that he had managed to piece together last night by reading through his own notes and touching base with Tanner.

Such thoughts occupied Parlour's mind as he drove the eight-mile journey to the thoroughly modern and entirely soulless urban centre of Billock. He noted to his satisfaction that Goodlove had managed to park legally in an allotted CID bay at the back of the station as he rolled his sleek silver car into his slot between DCI Sewell and DI Leigh Blackman, the most senior female member of Billock CID at that present time, having been transferred from Foxburgh CID to help out with the increase in violent crime in the Billock area. It was Parlour's dearest hope, in the workplace at least, that Preece would pull off some superhuman act of sleuthing very soon and he could at last get her pushed up to DI – vacancy permitting - a status she richly deserved. Then, Parlour thought rather uncharitably, Leigh Blackman could push off back to Foxburgh and Karen could take over the office adjacent to his. Parlour hastily beat down the uncomfortable voice inside that told him it was not only Karen Preece's career advancement he was interested in.

She's not my type, Parlour told his inner demon, wishing his senior officer, DCI Sewell, a good morning in passing. As he set eyes on her across the incident room at Billock CID, he shook his head gently. Broad shoulders, no tits, skinny waist, dark hair, for Cripe's sake… no, definitely not his type. Yet still…. Oh stop it, Parlour admonished the nagging voice and shut himself in his adjoining office. He removed his jacket and loosened his tie, now that he had given a favourable sartorial impression to Brian "The Sewer" Sewell, a nickname accorded

Parlour's boss due to his rather severe expulsions of wind, more often than not in enclosed spaces such as the Station lift.

Parlour rifled through a pile of papers on his desk but there was nothing of major interest. He turned his PC on and made himself a cup of black coffee while he waited for it to boot up.

But there were no interesting emails either. He wandered through to the Incident Room and noted that the white board still bore the same swathe of question marks in red wipe-off marker pen. There was no new information pertaining to the murder of Davidson Munroe, no new information at all.

"Where's Goodlove?" Parlour enquired a mite snappishly of DC Jenkins. The shy Welsh detective constable blushed furiously, a reaction that still befell him every time a senior officer addressed him, despite having spent some four years now at Billock CID, which, despite its inner-city location, boasted a fairly relaxed and easy-going environment. Parlour prided himself on this; to take personal pot-shots at fellow officers, even within the sanctity of the station, was unprofessional, in Parlour's opinion, and he reinforced this view at every opportunity. He wasn't talking about a bit of banter and friendly ribbing, but the sort of niggling petty jealousies and little acts of malice and retribution that threatened the work of the police, and therefore the safety of the general public.

"He's going to be uh.. um.. a little late, Sir," Jenkins stuttered, panicking at the thought of having to grass a senior officer up.

But Ian Jenkins was saved the discomfort by the timely appearance of Goodlove, looking thoroughly dishevelled at ten past nine that morning.

"Don't tell me," Parlour commented sarcastically, walking past him and back into his office. "Dog ate your hair gel."

Goodlove said nothing and disappeared off to the Gents to make himself look more respectable. DC Denton was supposed to waylay Parlour until Goodlove got to his desk, where the hell had he got to? Damn Sean, Goodlove cursed, applying the extra strength gel that he had hastily grabbed from his desk drawer en route to his cropped black hair. You could never rely on Sean when you needed him; Cameron was learning fast. Thank goodness he always kept spare work clothes in the boot of his car; at least he had been able to get changed at the strange house he'd woken up in. It was just a shame he didn't keep a toiletry bag in the boot as well. Had he not still been well over the alcohol limit, Goodlove would have driven home quickly to get showered and changed. However, he couldn't afford to get caught drink-driving in his profession and had left his car, rather fearfully, it had to be said, outside the dilapidated house in downtown Billock, and had walked the one and a half miles to Billock Police Station as fast as his wobbly legs would carry him.

"Bloody hell, Cam," Karen Preece grinned, as Goodlove returned to his desk and hastily plopped a triple X-tra Strong Mint in his mouth. "Giving Parlour a run for his money?"

"Leave it, Kaz," he moaned, brushing his hand over the outcrop of white-heads on his chin that morning. "Late night."

"Late morning as well," Preece commented. "Come on, the boss wants us in his office now. I'd try and look a bit cleverer, if I were you; looks like he got out of bed the wrong side."

"Furrlip!" Goodlove nearly cursed, "that's all I need."

He lumbered after his colleague into the Detective Inspector's Office. But to their surprise, Parlour already had his jacket and overcoat on.

"Grab your winter woollies, you two, we're going to get some fresh air – Cam, you look as though you need it."

He's perked up a bit, Karen Preece thought to herself, following in his wake.

"Sit in the front with him, will you," Goodlove muttered to Preece as they followed the wiry, auburn detective to his car. Preece giggled as she spotted an empty Micro-Noodle tub ill-concealed in the inner pocket of Goodlove's black trench coat.

"At least no-one will taste the difference," she quipped to her ailing colleague as they filed down the steps to the car park. But Goodlove just grunted as he attempted to hold the contents of his stomach in check.

***

"That bugger, Roy Pedlar, has really got it coming to him," Bob Killington remarked acerbically to his wife, as they alighted from the red Audi, their feet crunching on the gravel of Deverton Golf Club's car park.

"Might just take a swing at him with my nine-iron," Killington continued malevolently as he opened the car boot - in rather a loud voice, given the large number of members milling around the arrival area of the recently completed golf course and driving range.

"Bob!" Tonky Killington exclaimed none too discreetly herself. "Don't. Not even in jest. The man's a blight on society, but don't stoop to his level."

"A-ha! So you do think he bumped off the retired headmaster, then?" her husband chortled, hauling the heavy bags of clubs from the boot.

"Reckon he had something to do with it, don't you?" Tonky replied. "We know what an evil waste of space he is; he had the perfect alibi, didn't he? Makes sure he has a full TV crew available to film his every move then gets one of his gullible minions to bump Munroe off."

"Thought we were supposed to espouse the essential goodness of the human race, Tonks," Bob laughed.

"We are," Antonia Killington replied, "but Roy Pedlar is not human."

However, Bob Killington's attention was diverted elsewhere.

"Hello Chas," he smiled brightly at Charles Briscoe as they made their way to the clubhouse to sign in.

"Who's that?" Tonky enquired, as they entered the shiny new club building.

"Charles Briscoe, stockbroker in the City. Met him on the train the other day. Lives the other side of Deverton, on Spud Street."

He grinned; the street-names in Deverton never ceased to bring a smile to his chiselled face, and Maris Piper Way was perhaps one of the more ridiculous examples of Deverton's culinary-themed street-naming policy.

"Aah, let me guess, in one of those thumping great mock-Tudors near the cricket pavilion?"

"Where else?" Bob chuckled.

Charles Briscoe frowned once Killington had passed him. Chas! Bloody cheek... he'd known him all of five minutes. Cripes, please don't say I have to put up with that pretentious old fart every time I enter the clubhouse, he groaned.

19

"Bit early for the ten o'clock communion service, aren't we, Sir?" Karen Preece grinned, reading the notice board in the car park as they pulled up outside Deverton Parish church that morning.

Cameron Goodlove groaned at the thought of supping more red wine as he alighted from the car with Preece.

Parlour just smiled enigmatically and jangled some keys in his hand. He opened the front door to the church building and fiddled with a security system before beckoning his officers inside.

He led them to a small room off the main hall where some easy chairs were housed. Goodlove frowned as his eyes fixed on a wooden crucifix and some purple wall hangings with spangly gold letters on them bearing verses from Scripture. He glanced at Preece, who just shrugged and took a seat.

"Coffee?" Parlour enquired.

"That's the best thing you've said all morning, Sir," Goodlove exhaled in relief, deciding it was blatantly obvious he was well hung-over and adhering to an ethos that had served him well in life thus far; namely, if in doubt, look contrite and suck up to the boss.

Parlour just smiled thinly; he would have words with Goodlove later. Now was not the time, he had to get this case moving forwards again before The Sewer got on his back. If Juliet was making noises about his lack of progress, he could be sure Brian Sewell would be hot on her heels.

"Do you want me to do it, Sir?" Preece asked immediately.

"No, no, Karen; I know where everything is," Parlour smiled and disappeared for a moment to make the refreshments.

"What the bloody hell's he up to?" Goodlove hissed, the moment his senior officer had left the room. "Seeking divine intervention?"

"Less hassle than booking the meeting room at the station,"

Preece grinned, slipping her coat off.

"Who's that?" Goodlove enquired as he heard a velvety smooth baritone voice greet Parlour in the corridor.

"The Reverend Martin Beauville," Preece replied discreetly. Goodlove was such a loudmouth, she thought. He really would have to tone things down to work with Mark and her. Parlour liked his cops smart and subtle, not loud and laddish. "Haven't you met him yet?"

Goodlove shook his head then winced as a searing pain shot across the right side of his brain.

"Nice guy. The ladies like him; the feeling isn't mutual."

Goodlove's ears pricked up at this interesting morsel of local gossip. "Oh yeah?"

Preece shot Goodlove a sidelong glance but the conversation stopped as Parlour re-entered the room.

"That was quick!" Preece commented.

"Beauville's bringing them in," Parlour replied, slipping his suit jacket off. "He's making one for Penny and himself anyway. They just got here; having a confab before the communion service."

"Is that what they call it these days?" Goodlove grinned, his humour returning in anticipation of some much needed caffeine.

Parlour ignored the comment. It was rather tasteless, and not just in terms of its spiritual impropriety. What a thought…

He opened his notebook.

"We are gathered here today…" he began, then stopped and grinned. "Ok guys, change of scenery, that's all. Thought it might stimulate the old grey cells, though in the case of Cam, that would probably take a miracle – still, at least we're in the right place."

"Ha ha," Goodlove grunted.

"Here's the story so far," Parlour began. "On the afternoon of Saturday 18 March 2006, the Reverend Beauville hosts a World Cuisine Festival at Deverton Parish Church.

Participants in the event start appearing around eleven am to set up their tables in the hall. At around noon, Martin Beauville gives a series of interviews in the front of the churchyard to various television and radio crews. The majority of these prove to be bogus and involve media studies students approached by Roy Pedlar to keep Beauville occupied so that Pedlar and his crew can set up shop in the back of the church yard. Pedlar and his organisation, known to us as the BASC, or British Alliance of Senior Citizens, also employ traffic stewards to encourage locals to park in Quail Crescent running behind the church building, thereby enticing them into the event through the back gates so that they stop off at Pedlar's stalls first. Pedlar then proceeds to set up several tables of home-grown produce from Deverton Allotments and begins a sizable demonstration against multicultural and multi-faith Britain, which the national press have clearly been informed of. TV crews from ITN and Sky News amongst others turn up, a melee follows involving Beauville and Pedlar. It is during this demonstration and ensuing scuffle that Davidson Munroe nips off to the allotment to get more supplies in the shape of leeks and spring cabbages. Shortly after the infamous skydive from the church roof by Ordinand Penny Roquet…"

Goodlove and Preece snickered.

"Alicia Munroe appears at around two thirty and breaks the news that she has found her husband's dead body up at Deverton Allotments. At this point, Beauville ushers her away from the press and inside the building. She is then taken to the allotments with Beauville and a police escort. I make my own way there accompanied by my wife, as I felt Alicia would probably be in need of a female presence. At the allotments, the paramedics are in the process of removing the back wall of the shed where Munroe is lying. He appears to have had some kind of fit. I decide to call in the pathologist and the SOCOs when I smell a strong whiff of something chemical in his coffee cup. I also find a little bit of blue paper on the floor, which I will return to later."

Parlour paused for breath as he heard Beauville approaching up the corridor. There was a knock on the door and the tall, silken-haired priest-in-charge of Deverton Parish Church entered with a tray boasting three mugs of steaming coffee and half a packet of Utopia Sugared Butter Squares, aka Nice biscuits.

"I'm just off next door for the Communion Service, Mark," Beauville informed his good friend. "Could I join you all afterwards, perhaps?"

"Why not?" Parlour smiled, noting Goodlove's uncomfortable expression out the corner of his eye.

He waited until Beauville was well out of earshot. "He's a smart cookie, Cam, and the church is pretty central to village life in a place like Deverton, with no pub or community centre to its name yet. He might gain access to some useful information that could help us in our enquiries."

"What, from the confessional?" Goodlove scoffed.

"This is an Anglican Church," Parlour informed him rather coldly; it never ceased to amaze him how seemingly intelligent and well-informed individuals could be so crassly ignorant when it came to denominational matters. Cameron made a handbags gesture at Preece as Parlour looked down at his notes, unaware that Parlour could sense secret gestures through paper. Parlour said nothing; he was used to Sean Denton's clumsy attempts at discreet pee-taking.

"The pathologist's report tells us that Munroe had ingested some liquid paraquat, of a lethal concoction no longer authorised for common or garden use in this country. This paraquat was likely force-fed him, as traces of it were found down his top and in his hair. Fruitcake crumbs were also found down his top, and traces of undigested fruitcake in his stomach, though it is unclear whether the cake was introduced concurrently. However, Munroe did not appear to have been munching on cake prior to meeting his assailant, as there were no traces of cake elsewhere, including in his car. He hadn't eaten any at home that day and his wife hadn't made him any cake either. He wasn't seen eating cake by anyone in the churchyard; however there was plenty of fruitcake on sale inside the church building."

Parlour paused to take another slurp of his coffee. He munched on a biscuit briefly.

"A third-full bottle of 1972 liquid paraquat was subsequently found under the mattress of Salik Gani's bed. Gani works at the Mini Mart owned by his father, Abdul Gani, at Deverton Triangle. This prompted the rather obvious accusation that this was a racially motivated crime and that Gani himself was the perpetrator of it. We were duty-bound to bring him in for questioning, however it soon emerged that Gani, though present at the scene of the crime, had no motive for killing Munroe, other than a dislike for his participation in what he sees as a racist white Supremist movement. And in any case, Munroe, despite his strong pro-British Nationalist views, was by no means the most vociferous of BASC party members and it begs the question anyway, why poison the office junior?"

Parlour paused again and Preece and Goodlove nodded.

"We decided to concentrate our efforts on where the paraquat came from, as it was most likely smuggled into the country some thirty years ago, when customs laws were not so stringent and a more relaxed attitude was prevalent concerning security in general. However, a house to house search yielded no clues and neither did a search of Deverton Allotments, meticulously undertaken by yourself," he nodded in appreciation at Preece, who flushed ever so slightly, "in tandem with Jeff Wilkes and the sniffer dogs."

"We had no choice but to release Gani, as it appeared rather obvious to us that the paraquat had been planted in his bed-sit anyway. A bathroom window that Gani reckons he always kept shut was flapping open and the earth below the window seemed to have been trodden on, though no footprints were found – the suspect probably wore bags over their shoes. In any case, if you want to hide the evidence, you don't hide it under your own mattress, you burn it, or bury it in the woods, or chuck it in the river or something."

"Where is Gani?" Goodlove frowned. "Didn't his brother ring the station last night and said he'd gone AWOL?"

Parlour nodded. "I was coming to that. A Michaela Brevitt – more about her in a minute as well – rang the station late last night to say she had taken him in. This isn't public knowledge; she's got him all dressed up as some yuppie sales exec, he's posing as her business colleague and lodger. She called Nazrul Gani to tell him where Salik was, Nazrul told her she ought to inform the police, lest we send a search party out. Very sensible of him, too."

"So what about Roy Pedlar; where does he fit in to all of this?" Preece frowned.

Parlour made a face. "This is the sixty-four million dollar question," he conceded. "I got Dave Tanner to sit in one of the BASC meetings yesterday. Pedlar was being very coded in his speech; probably realised Tanner was gate-crashing the meeting. Nevertheless, Tanner got the distinct impression that some sort of protest is going to take place in the next few days. Everyone there appeared to be clued in to this. The initials US were bandied about which Tanner believes is the meeting point."

Preece and Goodlove frowned. Parlour could see that they were each trying to work out a plausible long-hand fit for the initials and decided to put them out of their misery. Time was of the essence, after all; Parlour was anticipating a terse phone call from Detective Chief Inspector Brian Sewell any moment now concerning the lack of progress on the case.

"I have strong reason to believe that US stands for Utopia Supermarket," Parlour informed his two sergeants. Goodlove and Preece looked rather non-plussed, Parlour thought. "A few weeks back, I came across a note left in one of those fake spare key-holder pebbles outside my in-laws' house. It contained a rather cryptic message on blue paper. I made a note of it; it seemed somehow significant. The note read US2730900 and was signed Inspector Gadget. My mind immediately made a link between its sender, our mysterious Inspector Gadget, and a really naff homewares magazine that my in-laws get posted through the door once a month. I decided that the deliverer of the magazine must go by the name of Inspector Gadget, ridiculous but seemingly true. The magazine in question is called HomeGadget – hence Inspector Gadget – and is full of the usual potty labour-saving devices for the anally retentive."

Goodlove sucked in his breath in an exaggerated manner.

"Ooh, you can't beat their microwave baked bean saucepan!"

"Would that be for the anally loose, then?" Preece grinned.

"Don't talk to me on that subject this morning, please," Goodlove frowned.

"Moving swiftly on," Parlour chided them and turned a page of his notebook. "At the time I simply thought it was some item code; that the deliverer of the magazine was passing on an order code or something to my in-laws. It didn't occur to me at that point that some kind of coded message was being communicated. However, since this person clearly didn't want their identity to be known, it was logical to assume that some kind of clandestine activity was afoot. Whatsmore, I couldn't find an item in the magazine with a vaguely similar code. It was then that I realised that this had nothing to do with ordering products from the catalogue."

"The catalogue is being used as a means of passing on information!" Preece exclaimed, grabbing the arms of her chair.

"Exactly," Parlour smiled at his favourite colleague. "It provides a means by which individuals can be contacted without others at home, who may be privy to telephone messages or email communications, knowing the score. My guess is, all those who receive HomeGadget also have a secret door-key pebble outside their front door where Inspector Gadget leaves messages for them. This was probably provided when they signed up for the magazine. The actual magazine is probably just a red herring."

"And these messages are written on blue squares of paper," Preece filled in. Parlour nodded.

Goodlove frowned, sharp little darts of pain acupuncturing his skull as he racked his brains. "Wasn't there a scrap of blue paper among the bagged items from Munroe's shed?"

Parlour nodded keenly. "I was coming to that, Cam. On this occasion, though, the note wasn't written in code. It contained a request, apparently to Munroe, to meet the person at the allotments at two pm."

"So if we find out who delivers HomeGadget magazine, we've worked out our killer?" Goodlove frowned. It seemed far too simplistic.

"Oh, I know who Inspector Gadget is," Parlour informed the others, waving his hand matter-of-factly. Preece clicked in irritation; Mark Parlour was such a condescending smartarse at times. Parlour reached inside his coat pocket and withdrew a white plastic item about six inches long. He flicked it in front of him and it immediately extended into a long eighteen inch rod with a slightly curved white plastic scoop at the end.

"Recognise this?" Parlour enquired of Preece and Goodlove. They shook their heads slowly. In the manner of a magician producing his next trick, Parlour deftly clicked open his briefcase and pulled out a report from Forensics. He handed them a black and white photocopy of items retrieved from Davidson Munroe's potting shed and drew their attention to item number thirteen.

"Long-armed shoe-horn," Goodlove read. He shook his head. "I don't get it."

Parlour smiled irritatingly and pulled another sheet from his briefcase. This contained a list of items found in Derek Hebble's garage. Preece read down the now-legendary list of competition winnings then suddenly looked up as she got to the miscellaneous items towards the bottom.

"One hundred extendable shoe-horns, delivered not by HomeGadget, but by Superware magazine!"

"Jesus!" Goodlove blasphemed, incurring a filthy look from his superior, "Your pa-in-law is Inspector Gadget!"

"Whoa!" Parlour held up his hand. "Not so fast! This list only states that he was housing a large quantity of these shoe-horns. The invoice inside was addressed to a Mr …"

"R Pedlar!" Preece gasped, slapping her skinny thigh. "I knew he was involved somehow."

Parlour smiled. "Indeed. My gullible father-in-law, it seems, is being taken for a ride by our friend Pedlar. Pedlar probably uses these as some kind of weapons at these demos of theirs and quickly stashed them in Derek's garage when he discovered the police were doing a house-to-house to find the paraquat. He probably thought it was the safest place to hide them, as well, with Derek being my father-in-law. Of course, he wasn't to know that Cam had no idea who Derek was, and that Derek's garage would invite suspicion on account of his hoard of electronic toys!"

"So Pedlar uses a bogus homewares magazine delivered to select individuals as a means of disseminating information to party members," Goodlove surmised. He frowned. "But it couldn't have been Pedlar at the allotments that Saturday afternoon; he was at the church the whole time."

"No, it couldn't have been," Parlour agreed.

"He could have got someone to do his dirty work for him, he's pretty good at that," Preece chipped in.

"But why kill his sidekick?" Goodlove frowned. "It doesn't make sense."

"I've done some behind the scenes questioning," Parlour informed them, "and I've discovered no hint of jealousy or rivalry between Pedlar and Munroe."

"It wasn't you father-in-law?" Preece asked slyly.

"They did leave early, I grant you that," Parlour grinned, "after a tongue-lashing from Jules, but I can't see a motive. I don't think Derek's after the vice-chair position, if that's what you're angling at, Karen! Far too busy ringing 0870 numbers!"

"So back to Utopia Supermarket," Preece frowned.

"They're up to something on Monday, aren't they?" Parlour replied rather impatiently, hoping they would have worked it out by now. "273 – it's twenty-seventh of March. Meet outside Utopia on Monday 27th March at zero nine hundred hours."

"Of course!" Karen groaned, feeling rather foolish. What would Parlour think of her?

"That's this Monday," Goodlove stated. "But…"

"But what?" Parlour interrupted, hoping Goodlove was going to ask the right question.

"But how does this move our case on?" He did.

"This is the problem," Parlour conceded. "I got all excited last night when I worked out how Pedlar ran his nasty little Pensioner Army. But then I thought, so what? We've pieced some pieces of one jigsaw together, that's for sure. But where does it fit into the puzzle of who murdered Davidson Munroe - if indeed it belongs to that picture at all?"

"It must do," Preece frowned. "It seems too much of a coincidence that the moment Roy Pedlar gets his machinery up and running in this neck of the woods, somebody pops their clogs."

"Hold on," Goodlove interrupted. "Didn't you mention some woman who's put Gani up in her house? What role does she play in all of this?"

Parlour nodded. "Michaela Brevitt. I've not met her, but my wife knows her, they've met in the village a few times. Micky Brevitt runs a pressure movement called RAT UK. You might have seen a few cars around with a bumper sticker or rear windscreen sticker bearing their logo. It has a black rat with a web address on it. If you go onto their website, you'll find this."

Parlour pulled another sheaf of papers from his Tardis-like briefcase and handed them to Goodlove this time.

"Respect and Tolerance Party UK," Goodlove read. "Rallying against Racism and Beating Out Bigotry around the Regions." He looked up. "Rolls off the tongue quite beautifully."

"Mm," Parlour agreed.

Preece scanned down the document quickly. She read the editorial blurb from Michaela Brevitt.

"You've not met Brevitt yet, you say?" she checked.

"Not yet," Parlour conceded, though a plan was rapidly forming in his head.

"So Pedlar has recently moved here and fronts a nationalist over-sixty party. Michaela Brevitt has been here how long?"

"A couple of months," Parlour replied.

"And chairs a Club 18-30 anti-racism group," Goodlove surmised.

"Actually, they do have some older members," Parlour informed them, Bob and Antonia Killington and their shiny red Audi springing to mind. "And they are anti-violence. Not a shoe-horn in sight!"

There was a brief pause as they digested the information available to them so far.

"So to surmise," Preece said finally, "Deverton is currently the national headquarters of two amateur pressure groups in political opposition to one another. The vice-chair of one of these parties has recently been murdered, which may or may not have something to do with political affiliations. A non-white, non-politically active British national has been suspected of the crime but appears to have no clear motive."

"Full-house," Parlour grinned at her, but his smile soon subsided. "Really this doesn't move us any further on, except that Pedlar needs a close eye kept on him. Hopefully we can unearth that missing piece that provides a link between Munroe's murder and political allegiances in these parts."

"And meanwhile?" Karen enquired.

"Meanwhile we need to keep an open mind and continue to pursue all lines of enquiry," Parlour replied functionally. "Karen – did your investigations into Munroe's past throw up any new leads?"

"They just made me throw up," Preece groaned, opening her notebook. Parlour grinned.

"Alicia Munroe furnished me with a long list of names which I had checked out. Those I could get hold of confirmed they'd had a fling with Munroe in the past, but that it had just been kids' stuff, Munroe hadn't got it up with any them."

"Hadn't or couldn't?" Parlour enquired, his thoughts harking back to the original pathologist's report on Munroe.

"Hadn't even attempted to, with any of them," Preece said, shaking her head rather incredulously. "In each case, he'd done the protective Sugar Daddy thing with some young bit of skirt which had turned to kisses and cuddles, but he'd always broken it off when the girl got too keen or demanded more. Seems he was a serial flirter, but not a serial adulterer. Obviously loved his wife deeply, underneath it all."

Parlour snorted. He didn't subscribe to that point of view.

"There was one interesting bit of info, though, Sir," Preece continued.

"Oh yes?" Parlour's ears pricked up.

"We did find one woman from his past who didn't quite fit the mould. A games teacher from his school – a Miss Jayne Wainwright. They had a bit of a thing for a while, but he broke it off when she got too amorous. She didn't take it too well, and took up a teaching post at another school soon after."

"She wasn't young and flighty, then?" Parlour queried.

"Anything but," Preece replied, shaking her head. "Forty something; as tall as Munroe himself, shoulders like barn doors, a former England Ladies rugby player."

Goodlove sucked in his breath. "Tasty!"

"Did you actually meet her, then?" Parlour asked.

Preece shook her head again. "She refused to talk to us, I got the description and low-down on her from Munroe's former secretary at Foxburgh High School."

"Hmm." Parlour furrowed his brow and made some notes in his pocket book. At that point Martin Beauville entered the room, cup of fresh tea in his hand.

"So what now?" Goodlove enquired.

"Pray?" Parlour grinned, as Beauville slid his clerical collar from his shirt and took a seat opposite him.

"What an excellent idea!" Beauville grinned and shoved a Sugared Butter Square in his mouth.

Cape Cod, Parlour groaned inwardly as Beauville shut his eyes and spread his palms upwards on his knees. He's going to, as well.

He shot an embarrassed glance at Preece and a visibly uncomfortable Goodlove then closed his own eyes, feeling a pink onslaught rise up his neck, the curse of the fair complexioned person.

20

Why did I find that so hard? Parlour berated himself later, once he had revisited the scene of the crime at Deverton Allotments with Goodlove and Preece and had safely deposited them all back at Billock Station. What was that passage from Luke's Gospel that Penny Roquet had preached on the other week? Something about not being shifty in one's faith, wasn't it?

Parlour rooted around in the top drawer of his office desk and pulled out the dog-eared pocket Bible he kept at work for the sadly rather sporadic moments of personal prayer time during working hours. His fingers soon located the ninth chapter of Luke's Gospel, for despite his rather non-existent prayer life at this point in time, the ability to locate Books of Scripture promptly from years of attending Bible-based church gatherings had not left him.

If anyone is ashamed of me and my words, the Son of Man will be ashamed of him… Parlour read. The tips of his ears burned, in conviction perhaps.

Damn it, Parlour cursed, I was embarrassed! Yes, he had been ashamed when Beauville had started beseeching the Lord to help in their quest to find the killer of Davidson Munroe lest he or she strike again. Suddenly Parlour knew what he should take up for Lent, and it wasn't soggy lettuce sandwiches. It was time to stop relying on his own mental strength the whole time – he knew it was a weakness of his and perhaps endemic in a profession such as policing. Parlour shut his eyes and bowed his head, trying to ignore the nagging deterrent that all eyes were on him though the Perspex glass, mocking him and his Maker. But it was no good; he just couldn't relax and focus on the spiritual, all trussed up as he was in the straightjacket of his own self-consciousness. It would have to wait until later.

***

"And you really can't remember seeing a soul at the allotments that afternoon?" Michaela Brevitt frowned at Salik Gani over a coffee early that afternoon. With Sacha safely dispatched at nursery, Brevitt had dedicated the afternoon to helping Gani in his attempts to prove his innocence. Though the police were leaving him alone, mud stuck as firmly as the waste matter hurled at Gani's maisonette and sales were noticeably down at Deverton Mini Mart as well. It was a matter of family pride now, to find out who actually did Davidson Munroe in; hence a trip to the county town of Foxburgh where they could chat in obscurity. In addition, they would be able to pay a visit to the expansive county library, to conduct some research into Davidson Munroe.

Gani shook his head. "Leesh and me… we were pretty much out of it. I can't even remember what we were saying to each other, except that it seemed hilariously funny at the time. Bloody vodka!"

"But even in your drunken stupor, you might have noticed someone slinking around the allotments," Brevitt persevered.

Gani frowned, shaking his head slowly again. "I don't recall seeing anyone. But I wasn't paying attention."

He slapped the table. "If only I hadn't shut up the shop. I've never done it before. I wouldn't have been at the blimmin' allotments!"

"Munroe would still have been killed," Brevitt shrugged. "Who's to say the village idiots wouldn't have put the blame on you anyway? You weren't at the Cuisine Festival, after all."

"True," Gani conceded. "But pissed, brown-skinned and at the scene of the murder…"

"You couldn't have planned it better!" Brevitt grinned. Gani's tense expression relaxed into a smile and he tossed a couple of Demerara sugar sachets at his friend.

"Come on," Brevitt stood up and gathered her things together. "Let's go to the library and get the low-down on our friend Davey Munroe. See if we can dig some dirt that might point us to our killer – and find some quality mud to sling at Roy Pedlar, while we're at it. It's not long until the RAT Race in London. Pedlar's sure to try and sabotage that."

Gani followed her obediently from the coffee bar in the direction of the County Library, which housed newspaper archives and local information not always available on the worldwide web.

But their search for ammo on Pedlar was in vain. It seemed that Roy Pedlar, whilst succeeding in offending many with his right-wing rantings, had, bar a few minor warnings for breaching the peace, done nothing to significantly sully his public standing. They had found absolutely no dirt on Davidson Munroe, just endless articles on his prize vegetables and historical items pertaining to his stint as headmaster of Foxburgh High School. There was no documentation of under-age sexual relations with schoolgirls. It appeared that Alicia had been right concerning Munroe's flings with ex-pupils; he had not been guilty of the eminently more serious charge of seducing under-age pupils in his charge. Michaela had trawled though public school alumni and details of professional organisations on various websites, but no historical links had been found between Pedlar and Munroe or between Munroe and any current Deverton residents. Whilst Gani had been occupied elsewhere, Michaela had also entered details concerning the Gani family into the search engine, but this had thrown up no leads, either – at least in the articles she could understand. She had to confess, she wasn't exactly sure what she was looking for, in any case. But she just felt sure that Munroe's death was in some way politically motivated.

"Watch it!" an upper-class voice bellowed at Salik Gani, as he ambled across the busy main road behind Michaela Brevitt. Gani looked up briefly into a pair of cold pale blue eyes, shrouded by a fur-lined hat. Their eyes locked for a brief second, long enough for both to register mutual recognition.

"Sorry," Salik mumbled and got out the way of the figure carrying a battered briefcase.

"Come here, Space Cadet," Michaela grabbed his arm impatiently and dragged him across the busy road.

***

A place for everything, and nothing in its place, Parlour grumbled to himself, tidying up the remote controls that Juliet had left scattered around the living room as he returned home at five-thirty that evening. He put his briefcase down then wandered into the kitchen in search of his wife.

"Make any headway today?" Juliet Parlour enquired as Parlour wrapped his arms around her from behind and kissed her neck. She tipped her head back in pleasure and the pairing knife slipped from her hand. She turned in her husband's arms and attacked his mouth with her own.

"Whoa – where did that come from?" Parlour laughed, pulling apart a moment later.

"Decided I've been a little … functional … towards you lately," Juliet admitted.

"Aah, you mean making mass withdrawals from the Sperm Bank?" Parlour grinned wickedly.

"I'm sorry," Juliet smiled ruefully and cuddled her head in at Parlour's chest. "Has it been too awful?"

"Oh, I've coped," Parlour chuckled and pulled away to rifle through the day's post. But there was nothing of interest.

"Jules, I've had an idea."

"It really was the vicar this time?" Juliet teased.

"Penny Roquet," Parlour grinned. Juliet giggled. It was a ridiculous notion. Penny Roquet couldn't kill a flea, even with a flea-comb and some conditioner!

"I was thinking, how about having one of our little dinner parties again? We haven't had one for a year or so. We've

184

been so consumed with the whole baby thing. Perhaps we need to chill out a bit, let nature takes its course."

"The course has taken a detour with us, or hadn't you noticed?" Juliet frowned.

"Just a couple of people," Parlour persevered.

Juliet groaned. Parlour, like many men, had that unfortunate habit of dropping invites to dinner into conversation with every new acquaintance he made, with no intention of being the one to tidy the house and prepare a three course meal. Poncing around with his latest hi-tech corkscrew and jiggling the buttons on his sound-system to impress male friends hardly constituted a major contribution to entertainment proceedings, in her book.

"Whom did you have in mind?" she queried, returning to her carrot batons.

"Cam and perhaps your new friend… Michaela, was it?" Parlour feigned casualness - badly, Juliet thought.

She frowned. "Cameron and Micky? Bit of an odd combination, isn't it?"

Parlour shrugged. "Not really. Both young, free, single, newish to the area. Cam's pretty talkative, as is your Micky, by the sounds of it."

"She's not my Micky," Juliet bristled, sensing that her husband was mocking her obvious admiration for the smart young new addition to the Deverton community.

"Whatever," Parlour shrugged. "It was just an idea, that's all." Best feign nonchalance, Parlour decided, unaware of quite just how transparent he was to his wife.

"You're just dying to see what Micky's like, that's all," Juliet scoffed.

"And you're not gagging to suss out Cam either?" Parlour grinned, squeezing her shapely bottom.

"I have to confess, I am rather curious to see what sort of person belongs to a name like Cameron Goodlove," Juliet conceded, giggling.

Parlour consulted the kitchen calendar then tapped into his PDA. "How about this Saturday? We're booked up the next few."

"Bit short notice, isn't it?"

Parlour shrugged. "It's worth a shot." He handed his wife the cordless phone and called up DS Goodlove's number on his mobile.

"Cam's free. Well, he adjusted his plans to brown-nose to the boss, at any rate," Parlour grinned as Juliet returned a few minutes later. "Any joy with Micky?"

Juliet made a so-so face. "She has some guest staying with her at the moment."

I know who that is, Parlour thought to himself.

"So I said she was welcome to bring him along, but she didn't sound keen."

I can imagine, Parlour mused.

"Micky said she would let me know, he might not be with her by Saturday, she wasn't sure."

"What about her little girl?" Parlour enquired.

"She has friends who could baby-sit, it isn't a problem."

"So was that a yes or a no?"

"A maybe," Juliet replied, frowning. Michaela hadn't sounded that keen, especially when she'd told her a young police sergeant was coming, too.

Parlour made a face. It wasn't a very satisfactory outcome; he wasn't used to being kept dangling like this. He attempted to quell the rather arrogant coda to this, especially not by some jumped up single mother.

***

I'll kick your skinny arse to the Bloody Republic of Congo, Roy Pedlar grimaced nastily, gnawing, not for the first time, on the bone of rejection tossed to him by the Fresh Produce

Manager of Utopia Supermarket, Mr Trevor Tolt. Just you wait until Monday!

Pedlar couldn't wait to eek revenge on Tolt via the pro-British food demo outside the snooty supermarket on Monday morning. The press had already been informed and Pedlar was expecting a large turnout of party members, with extra help from outside the county, too. Hopefully no-one had tipped off that blasted Brevitt woman and her Vermin Party. He had succeeded in keeping her away from the Cuisine Festival; he couldn't afford for her to steal his thunder with her clever-clever London PA talk and cocky New University status sidekicks. At least he didn't have to keep an eagle-eye on that parochial oik Munroe anymore.

Pedlar rummaged around in the box of shoe-horns lifted from Derek Hebble's garage. He tipped them out on the floor and sorted them into batches of ten, which he grouped together with thick rubber bands. Hold on, Pedlar frowned. There was one missing. He checked the invoice; yes he had ordered a hundred. Bloody idiots can't even count! Pedlar muttered out loud. Probably have half a GCSE between them, he fumed. The alleged illiteracy of the current young generation was another of Pedlar's unattractive party pieces, guaranteed like some almighty windsock to suck in dozens of like-minded greying judgemental souls every time it was espoused down his red megaphone.

Pedlar carried the shoe-horns out to his car along with a brown box of concertina flyers advertising the antics of the British Alliance of Senior Citizens. You couldn't leave anything lying around in your garage at the moment with the local plod sniffing around, he snorted to himself. Good job I have trusty Derek to keep hold of Party supplies, Pedlar congratulated himself smugly. It did not occur to Roy Pedlar for one moment that he was perhaps taking matters just a little too far beyond the pale in his desire to whitewash the British Isles.

21

"Best not mention Pedlar's demo outside Utopia on Monday," Parlour warned Cameron as they awaited the arrival of Michaela Brevitt to Spatchcock Drive that Saturday evening. "She'll probably organise some RAT counter-attack; we could have a free-for-all on our hands. In one way, I'd welcome that; might throw up some interesting clues. However, she'll probably get wind of it anyway. Just can't be at our instigation!"

"The thought had already occurred to me," Goodlove replied a little tersely. He had been warned about Parlour's fondness for educating grandmothers in the art of sucking chicken produce, and Parlour had not failed to live up to expectations on that score.

"Good," Parlour nodded, Goodlove's tone escaping him as he watched out of the window for Michaela Brevitt, opening a bottle of Chilean red as he did so.

"Cam, why don't you join me in the living room?" Juliet called, fed up of being left alone while the men talked shop in the kitchen. The Moroccan stew was cooking nicely and the Italian roasted tomato soup had been prepared earlier; there was nothing to do now but wait for Michaela to show.

Goodlove obliged, grateful for the chance to escape to the comfy seats and away from the rather anal Parlour. His wife was an entirely different proposition, Goodlove thought. Far more of a goer, though it was probably all tease and no tickle, given her Bible-bashing tendencies. Hopefully old Pizza features would relax, once the fermented grape juice was flowing.

He took a seat opposite Juliet and flopped back in the rather squishy sofa, his legs wide open, every inch the cocky young man about town.

"What's Mark up to?" Juliet enquired.

"Watching out for Micky Brevitt," Goodlove replied. "Eyes glued to the kitchen window!"

Juliet chuckled. "He's dying to meet her, you know."

"Hence the dinner party," Goodlove grinned. The only flies on him are on his trousers, Juliet thought to herself.

"Actually, I was pretty nosy about you as well," she grinned, the bravado that came with the second glass of wine well and truly kicking in. "Keen to see what sits inside the clothes of a man called Cameron Goodlove!"

She was flirting outrageously, and she knew it. Juliet went a little pink, self-admonishment always swift to follow a loss of self-control, however slight.

"Don't," he groaned. "That name is the bane of my life! Hot-love, Lovejoy, Speed-cam… I've heard it all."

"Can't be as bad as Parlour," Juliet giggled, "I guess you're aware the guys all call him Pizza!"

Goodlove felt a little embarrassed and just nodded. He didn't quite have his feet under the table far enough yet to take pot-shots at the boss, and it was a little unfair of Parlour's wife to put him on the spot like that – spot being the operative word! Fortunately, he was saved from steering the conversation in another direction by the doorbell.

Juliet grinned at Cameron as Parlour rushed to the front door.

"Hello!" Parlour greeted the lady on the doorstep rather over-jovially. "You must be …Micky." He stuttered somewhat as he took in the young woman before him. She brushed past his taken-aback face and into the hallway. She had seen that look before. Michaela smirked to herself, hanging her cream designer raincoat on the peg.

She turned and grinned at the visibly embarrassed Parlour. "Jules didn't tell me you were quite so ginger!"

Parlour was left blushing furiously as the impossibly self-confident Michaela Brevitt strode into the living room to greet Juliet and Cameron.

You idiot! He berated himself. But why hadn't Jules told him? But why should she? Michaela just wasn't what he had expected, that was all. It was unusual to see a coloured person in Deverton, after all, he consoled himself. He wouldn't have batted an eyelid in Billock. But here in Deverton, with just the Ganis to add some local colour to the middle-class white hegemony, Michaela Brevitt was practically exotic.

Parlour went into the kitchen, took a hefty swig from his wineglass, inhaled deeply then joined the other three in the living room.

***

There's nothing to this babysitting lark, Salik Gani thought to himself, kicking his shoes off and sitting back on the sofa at Michaela Brevitt's flat, remote control in hand. Sacha was sound asleep, Michaela having read to her and tucked her up in bed prior to leaving for the Parlours. Gani had been quite willing to baby-sit; he was pretty used to caring for his nephews and nieces. At least Michaela was in the right place, should anything untoward happen to them back at the flat. But he felt quite safe there, anyway. No-one had twigged that the smart young marketing professional going by the name of Mashrafe Khan was in fact the prime suspect in a murder case.

He flicked onto ITV and noted with satisfaction that Millionaire was just starting. That was always good value for money – especially if you were one of the lucky sods who got in the hot seat. Gani pulled his newly acquired mobile phone from his pocket and turned it on; might need it to text in an answer to a question before the next ad break. He could do with a grand to get his flat sorted out and pay Michaela back for all this posh clobber she'd bought him.

'Spose I ought to turn the baby monitors on, Gani thought to himself, as the sequence music from the popular quiz show boomed out of the surround sound. He rose reluctantly from the corner of the sofa. Won't hear Sacha crying above this racket!

Well well, Gani exclaimed, as he adjusted the volume and frequency settings, it's the mysterious voices from across the airwaves again! Inquisitive by nature, Gani turned down the television volume; you could still see the questions and play the game without it, and it was boring in the early stages, anyway.

Oh my goodness, someone's getting a right old-ticking off, Gani grinned gleefully, pressing his ear to the dotted front-piece. He turned the volume right up; the voices were too distant to be distinguishable otherwise. Gani pulled his ear away and frowned as the word harlot was uttered in a flurry of expletives which questioned the moral fibre of their recipient in no uncertain terms. His jaw dropped as he heard the unmistakeable thwack of a slap administered to the face followed by a woman's screams.

Murder in Deverton, and now domestic violence, Gani thought, a little shaken by the raw anger he had just been privy to. If you're going to have a marital, at least be smart enough to turn off the blinking baby monitor!

Gani shook his head and sat back down. The male voice on the monitor had sounded familiar for some reason. He shook his head again, and turned his attention back to the television. Which of these is a kind of weed killer? Tarrant read from his screen. Paraquat? Parakeet? Paragraph? Or Parachute?

Parakeet! Gani shouted at the television for the hell of it and opened his bottle of beer.

***

Cameron Goodlove poured Michaela Brevitt another glass of red wine and she smiled her thanks across the table. Parlour winked at Juliet; their two guests had taken to one another like a match to paraffin, after the rather awkward start to proceedings.

191

"Just call me Cilla!" Parlour whispered in Juliet's ear as they began to clear the main course plates away.

"Would that be Cilla Black?" Juliet teased him.

"Shut it," Parlour hissed then smiled broadly as he returned to the dining room.

"Oh, if you haven't been to The Filling Station on a Friday night, you haven't lived!" Goodlove informed Michaela, both of them leaning forward, faces close together, quite oblivious to Parlour's attempts to clear their plates.

"My, I feel quite ancient!" he grinned as he realised his junior was discussing the Billock nightlife with Brevitt. He hadn't even heard of the entertainment venue in question; clearly CID hadn't found an occasion to visit their premises yet. Probably one of those nasty student clubs near the station that were forever changing management and with it, name.

"I've only been there on a Tuesday," Michaela replied.

"Oh, but everyone's there on Friday," Cameron enthused.

"So that's your top recommendation, then?" Brevitt enquired, sitting back in her chair, finally registering that one of the Parlours had been attempting to whisk her dirty plate from in front of her for the last five minutes.

Cameron put his head to one side to contemplate this weighty question.

"There's a new wine bar just opened on Billock Broadway. Indigo Honey I think it's called. That might be up your street. I couldn't say. They have a live jazz thing on a Monday night, I believe. For the more discriminating…"

"Ethnically inclusive chocolate brownie or thoroughly British cherries and cream!" Juliet Parlour announced in her best drunken impression of Roy Pedlar to drown out Brevitt and Goodlove's exchange.

"I'll have a bite of your cherry, if I may," Cameron grinned at Juliet Parlour, inhibitions downed along with four glasses of red wine.

"Mm, that sounds good," Michaela smiled broadly at her hostess and placed her tongue firmly inside her cheek as Goodlove kicked her under the table.

***

Parlour exchanged hi-fives with his wife as they shut the front door behind them at one am that Sunday morning.

"She's taken his arm!" Juliet giggled, dashing to the kitchen window and watching the tall broad-shouldered figure of Cameron Goodlove stride confidently down Spatchcock Drive with the designer clad Michaela at his side, his gait somewhat affected by the copious amounts of alcohol he had consumed at the Parlours.'

Juliet la-ed the Wedding March rather pre-emptively, it had to be said, waltzing drunkenly around the kitchen with Parlour.

Parlour, far less the worse for wear, pulled away and sank down on the sofa, hands behind his head. Juliet flopped down and lay across him.

"That's what I call a successful evening," he said, in a self-satisfied manner. "Got to know your friend Michaela a little better, you get to meet Cam, and best of all – we hook them up together too! Hey, Jules, you don't think she's going to invite him back to her place, do you?"

"I wouldn't have thought so," his wife replied. "She's got Gani staying there as well as her kid, hasn't she? I don't think he'll be too pleased to face one of your lot across the breakfast bar, do you?"

"True," Parlour conceded.

"So what did you think of Micky – suntan aside, that is," Juliet grinned wickedly.

Parlour swatted her arm. "Shut it. I'm so embarrassed about that. You might have said…"

"It wasn't relevant," Juliet shrugged.

193

"I beg to differ in the present circumstances," Parlour disagreed, trying to save at least a little face.

"Oh come on," Juliet protested, "you don't seriously think she had anything to do with Munroe's murder, do you?"

Parlour shrugged and frowned slightly. "We can't entirely rule out she had some involvement in Munroe's death. After all, it does appear to be a racially motivated crime in the present circumstances, and she is the chairperson of an anti-racism pressure group."

"A passive pressure group," Juliet defended her friend stoutly, not admitting to her husband at this point that she had already made noises to Michaela Brevitt in the kitchen, albeit rather alcohol-laced noises, about joining RAT UK.

Parlour just snorted at his wife, who had a curiously naïve side to her nature for all her intelligence and intuition.

"Even Roy Pedlar probably purports to run a passive pressure group. Incitement to violence is taken almost as seriously by the police as …"

"Wielding long-armed shoe-horns at non-indigenous members of the community?" Juliet grinned.

Parlour chuckled, a ridiculous picture of his father-in-law in his brown machine-knit tank top brandishing HomeGadget's bestseller along Whitehall springing to mind.

"Time for bed, I think." He got up. Tomorrow he planned to take a complete mental break from Roy Pedlar, Michaela Brevitt and co and have an unashamedly veggy day. There was some golf on the telly; he'd do his duty and go along to church in the morning then return home with a stack of newspapers and turn the box on.

22

But Parlour never made it through the doors of Deverton Parish Church that Sunday morning; in fact, he didn't even make it out the bedroom door of 5 Spatchcock Drive. The previous evening's festivities had entirely wiped out Parlour's skinny 5ft 9" frame, and it was to the dulcet tones of her husband's post-indulgence chesty snores that Juliet Parlour got dressed for church that Sunday morning.

***

"Afternoon!" Salik Gani grinned at Michaela Brevitt at one minute after midday.

"Don't even ask," Michaela grinned, kissing her daughter on the head. To her pleasant surprise, she noted that Sacha was not still weighed down by a heaving night nappy, but was sat at the breakfast bar eating some little squares of cheese on toast, sporting vaguely matching clothes and a fresh nappy.

"Well done, you," she smiled, swatting Gani on the arm. "Go to the top of the babysitting class!"

"I think I've just about paid my keep now," Gani laughed, pouring Brevitt a black coffee.

"I should say so, thanks Sal, you're a brick. She was no trouble, was she?"

"She's been an angel," Gani lied, having been woken up at 5.07am, when Sacha got no response from a near-comatose Michaela. He must have watched every programme on CBeebies at least twice through and could just about have strangled Miss Hoolie by now.

He grabbed his newly acquired soft leather jacket and wallet. "Just off for the paper. Don't worry, I'll stay this side of the tracks!"

"Very wise," Michaela nodded, sipping at her giant mug of black filter coffee.

***

Meanwhile, on the other side of Deverton, Bob and Antonia Killington were firmly ensconced around the farmhouse table, sporting his'n'hers half frame reading glasses, the Sunday papers spread about them.

"Grr!" rumbled Antonia Killington behind the *Foxburgh Chronicle*.

"You growled?" Bob enquired humorously, reading a hyperbole ridden over-inflated piece of tosh espousing the certainty with which England were going to win the next football World Cup.

It was part and parcel of the whole Sunday Paper experience to read aloud articles from the section under perusal to the other person, whether they were interested in its contents or not.

Antonia put the paper flat on the table and stabbed the leading article on the page with her forefinger. Bob Killington angled his head to consider the headline.

Fears mount for right-wing grey uprising

Below the headline was a picture of Roy Pedlar in full flow behind a lectern at a BASC rally in London the previous week.

"It makes me so cross!" Antonia exclaimed.

"What does?" Bob enquired, though he knew full well what had put the steam up his wife.

"This…" she stabbed the offending article once more, "this assumption that everyone over the age of fifty-five is right-wing and racist!"

Killington frowned and picked up the Foxburgh Chronicle. He considered the article in question, brows knitted above his scanty eye-gear.

"I must say, it does paint a rather unflattering picture of the whole senior generation. The BASC represents only a small minority, after all."

"You can't deny he's gaining influence though," Antonia conceded ruefully.

Bob Killington stood up and paced the floor, hands in pockets in a gesture rather reminiscent of Richard Briers in *The Good Life*.

"We need to get hold of Micky," he said finally. "We need to get the balance redressed. She's the one with all the press contacts. Get an opposing view across."

"But she's just a whippersnapper," Antonia protested. "She's not a figurehead for pensioners in the parishes."

"Well that's where *we* come in, darling," Bob grinned, slapping the table in his enthusiasm, his dwindling supplies of testosterone suddenly finding a new lease of life. "We could even set up a separate RAT division specifically aimed at senior citizens; I'm sure Micky would go for that!"

He gesticulated with his hands, in the manner of one holding aloft a banner.

"Vote Killington for a Kinder Britain!"

Antonia's eyes lit up, temporarily seizing the baton. "Don't be a donkey! Vote Bob'n'Tonky!"

Killington chuckled then sat back down at the table. He grabbed his wife's hands and looked fondly into her eyes. "Let's just approach Micky about this article for now."

"Yes, dear," Antonia replied in the measured tone required of her. But inside, a little flame of excitement was performing a *Riverdance* in her heart.

***

"How was it, then?" Parlour enquired, who had made the initial transfer from bedroom to breakfast table, though it was, in fact, lunchtime.

"Quiet, very quiet," Juliet frowned, throwing her keys on the worktop and slipping her jacket off. "No Sheltons, No Briscoes, not a single Mogridge-Winstanley. Mind you, Martin *did* let Penny lead the whole service, perhaps that's why. Someone obviously tipped off the congregation – all except me, worse luck!"

"Well, people should go along and support her, not stay at home," Parlour frowned.

"What, like you?" Juliet scoffed, cutting herself some bread to make some toast. She couldn't face anything more adventurous after the culinary voyage of the previous evening.

"That's different, I wasn't staying away, I was just…"

"Hung-over?"

"Jules, I'm not getting anywhere with this Munroe business," Parlour stated, deciding a change of subject was in order. Unknown to his wife, he had been sat brooding over a mug of coffee for some time now.

It was quite an admission from Parlour, who hated admitting defeat. Juliet took a seat opposite him at the kitchen table. She squeezed his hands. "No new leads, then?"

Parlour shook his head miserably. "Rang the station this morning. Not a bean; not even the merest whiff of a lead. I'll just have to hope this shindig outside Utopia tomorrow throws up something. It's hard to believe Pedlar isn't involved in some way."

"Mm," Juliet nodded. "You don't seriously think Micky has anything to do with Munroe's death, though? You sounded doubtful last night."

Parlour shrugged. "I was just playing devil's advocate as usual. I can't deny she threw me a bit when she first arrived; I wasn't expecting her to be quite so …."

Juliet refrained from teasing him this time.

".. forceful. But she had a lot of integrity, I could sense that. She seemed genuine enough, and we've had RAT checked out and they're pretty well respected. However, she could have fooled us all; there's no room for naivety in our profession."

"I guess not," Juliet replied quietly.

Parlour perked up. "So, what did you make of our new Detective Sergeant then?"

Juliet grinned. "*Gel*-boy? He'll give you a run for your money in the hair product department!"

"Mm!" Parlour frowned, running his hand through his, as yet, un-Brylcreemed auburn locks. "Talking of which…"

He stood up, stretched, and made upstairs for the shower.

***

It was such a beautiful spring day, Salik thought to himself, sauntering back from Utopia, where he had purchased a paper from the kiosk in store. He couldn't risk walking the extra half mile to the Mini Mart and blowing his cover. The sun had finally managed to beat out the chill in the late March air, and it was really quite pleasant walking along with just his lightweight leather jacket over his shirt.

There was no hurry to get back to Michaela's flat. He had more than done his stint with little Sacha this morning, and he could do with some fresh air and exercise, having been cooped up in the apartment since early yesterday evening. He cut across the esplanade and onto the main road that dissected Deverton into east and west. Spotting a play park in the distance that Naz and he had occasionally taken the kids to, Salik crossed over and took a short cut past the cricket pavilion until he came to some chunky wooden benches. He found one bathed in sunlight, overlooking the swing park, and read the paper from the back pages in, as was his custom, being an armchair sports fan of the highest calibre.

A couple of dads were already at the park, pushing designer-clad children in black rubber harnesses that bore more resemblance to Sumo-wrestling pants than swings. *Divorcees let out with the kids for the day,* Gani thought a mite presumptively, forgetting that Naz often took the kids to the play park of a weekend to give Zoreena a break, and there was nothing wrong with their marriage. Far from it, they were disgustingly happy together, Gani thought.

He returned to the report on Southampton's home game and rued once more how they had let a crucial lead slip in the dying seconds of their Championship encounter at St Mary's.

It was pleasantly warm sat there in the sun, with just the gentlest of breezes lightly teasing the pages of Gani's paper back and fore. Before he knew it, nearly an hour had elapsed. He looked up; the dads had all left, doubtlessly off to *La Rotisserie*, as Deverton rather fancifully called its burger bar, to treat themselves as much as the kids.

It was just at that moment, as he lifted his head from the sports pages, that a lightweight blue football flew over the perimeter fence of the play park and pinged off his forehead.

"Oh I am sorry!" a lady's voice exclaimed, running hastily in the direction of Gani.

"Don't worry about it," he said graciously, handing the ball to her over the red railings. Their eyes briefly met, long enough for Gani to spot that the woman in question bore an absolute shiner around her right eye, and long enough for him to register that he'd met her some place before.

***

By the time Salik Gani had mounted the stairs to Michaela Brevitt's apartment, he had it all worked out. It was funny how simply being at the right place at the right time – twice – could give him all the information he needed. Being at the wrong place at the wrong time didn't seem so terribly frightening anymore; now he had the opportunity to eek revenge on the evil toe-rag who'd framed him and bumped off Alicia's old man.

23

Parlour groaned as his alarm sounded at the unsavoury time of seven am on the morning of Monday 27 March 2006.

He looked across to the wrinkled indentation in the bed-sheet where his wife's body had lain and brushed it absent-mindedly with his hand. It had been nice having Jules there in the morning, whilst Billock Community School was shut for emergency repair and maintenance works. But with the exploding boiler replaced and the school environment rendered healthy and safe once more, it was back to the grindstone - for the staff at least. Coincidentally, the 27 March was a staff INSET day, enabling the pupils to enjoy another lie-in.

Parlour registered the sound of water pelting against the walls of the shower cubicle in the ensuite. There was no need for him to encroach on Juliet's morning routine; he could stay in bed a little longer. The beauty of mainly working the Deverton side of the tracks, was there was rarely any action that required a crack of dawn response – or earlier, perish the thought. The poisoning of Terence Haynes nearly four years ago had been the last murder to have taken place in Deverton prior to the discovery of Davidson Munroe's body. And he hadn't even officially been on the case for that, Blackman had been. And DI Leigh Blackman seemed to be getting most of the nasty stuff at the moment, as DCI Sewell tried to bring her up to scratch by consistently throwing her in at the deep end, knowing he could always call on Parlour to assist if he sensed she was in over her head.

Parlour sat up and rubbed the sleep from his eyes. He must follow through; he didn't want to be caught out as they had all been at the World Cuisine Festival, where Pedlar had had his troops organised and mobilised well before the official start of proceedings. Parlour wanted a heavy police presence, both uniformed and plain-clothed, well before Pedlar and his ageing gang of Grey Priders turned up. Utopia opened at 8am; Parlour wanted to make sure that he had at least half a dozen plain-clothed officers subtly placed in and around the store, ready to radio for uniformed help once Pedlar got underway. Parlour didn't want the protest stopped; far from it, he wanted a good look at Pedlar and his gang, to see if anything, or indeed anyone, could provide any clues to the curious murder of Davidson Munroe. Perhaps the RATs would turn up as well; Parlour hoped so, though he might have a riot on his hands. But it would be interesting to observe the dynamics of a verbal dual involving the bombastic, old-school Roy Pedlar and the cool, professional Michaela Brevitt.

He stared at his wife appreciatively as she ambled naked across the bedroom, rubbing her thick, shoulder-length dark blonde hair furiously with a blue hand-towel.

"Come on yet?" he enquired. Juliet's period was due and as usual, there was the anxious wait to see if their frantic attempts at conception had been successful this time.

Juliet shook her head. "The signs are there, though." She patted her rather swollen belly and Parlour noted indeed that she had retained a little fluid in that area.

"Could just be our little over-indulgence at the weekend!" he grinned hopefully.

"If that was a little over-indulgence on our part, I'd hate to see a full-scale banquet."

"Mark and Jules's *beastly feast*," Parlour mimicked a well-known TV dietician, attempting her mid-Atlantic Scottish accent and failing dismally.

"Talking of beastly, you're off to watch Pedlar in action this morning, aren't you?" Juliet enquired.

"Indeed I am." Parlour grabbed a toilet brush from the ensuite and proceeded to march around the room brandishing the said article in the air and advocating the purchase of British foodstuffs.

"Stop it!" Juliet giggled, pushing him in the direction of the shower. "You're spraying pooey droplets everywhere!"

***

"Thanks for that, Bob." Michaela Brevitt put the phone down at ten past seven that morning.

"Who was that?" Salik yawned, stumbling into the living room in a threadbare blue dressing gown that belonged to his old, pre-Knightsbridge Park existence.

"The Killies," she informed him, brushing past him en-route to the shower. Why did she think of The Krankies every time their name was uttered? "Need to get our gorgeous butts in gear, Sal. Bob rang the Foxburgh Chronicle for some reason, they let slip they'd had a fax from Pedlar, inviting them to cover a demo outside Utopia this morning. Bob'n'Tonks are on their way here now; need to get the rest of the gang mobilised, if they're out their pits yet! Hey, perhaps you could do that for me."

She threw a contacts list and the cordless phone at a bleary-eyed Salik.

"But I need to talk to you about the voices on the monitor!" Gani protested. "I've worked out who they are… Micks?"

"Can't chat now, sorry!" Brevitt cut him short, shutting the bathroom door in his face.

***

"Morning Karen, Morning Cam," Parlour greeted his two sergeants, as arranged, in the deliveries bay behind Utopia Supermarket. "What's the crack?"

"Nothing suspicious so far, Sir," Preece replied. "The manager says he's heard nothing about any protests taking place; wasn't too keen that we were prepared to let it go ahead, explained about the murder investigation, blah blah. He's cool – for now."

203

"However," Goodlove continued, "Denton radioed me from King Eddie Mews. He saw Pedlar pack his car with a load of placards and boxes. He had someone with him." Goodlove read from his notepad. "A slightly-built gentleman of around sixty-five years, bald on top, dressed in smart grey slacks, a barber jacket *and a brown tank-top*" He looked up at Parlour, grinning.

"My bloody father-in-law – God bless his soul," Parlour groaned. He shook his head in displeasure. "This is not good. I'd get mother-in-law to go and talk some sense into him, if it didn't give the game away that we're onto them."

What would Juliet do, if her father got himself arrested – or worse? It was a sobering thought. Parlour shook his head; he couldn't afford to get side-tracked by what-ifs concerning his father-in-law's welfare.

***

"Sal – you need to stay here, person the phones," Michaela commanded Gani as the RAT UK committee prepared to stage a counter demonstration outside Utopia. It was eight-thirty and six of the seven local committee members had already managed to assemble at Michaela's flat, including Bob and Antonia Killington.

Gani feigned a crestfallen expression which succeeded in duping a rather distracted Michaela.

"Sorry, just too risky, Sal," she consoled him.

I'll divert the phone to my mobile, Gani thought to himself. *I've got business to attend to.*

"Will – have you got the party banner?" Michaela enquired of mature Law Student, Will Entwhistle, who was her Higher Education party rep.

"It's in the car," Will replied.

"Right, I have some of the new flyers with the date of the *RAT RACE* in Hyde Park," Michaela informed them all.

"Tonky's going to go on ahead of us and do a pseudo shop at Utopia. She'll call us and give us the lie of the land. Now remember…"

She eyeballed every one of them. "*No* stooping to Pedlar's level. We are a professional, pacifist – and above all – *intelligent* political pressure group, not a bunch of amateur vigilantes providing fodder for the tabloids."

"Yes, Ma'am," Bob saluted her. Michaela grimaced as his wife enveloped her in a maternal hug.

*****

With all attention focused on Roy Pedlar and events outside Utopia Supermarket, the coast was clear for Alicia Munroe to make the forty mile drive to her sister's house in West Sussex. There she could pick up Margot Eltringham's passport and car, and travel on to Gatwick, where she would board an Iberia flight to Málaga Airport. Alicia Munroe had been requested to stay on home soil until the identity of her husband's murderer had been established; Margot Eltringham had no such restrictions placed on her.

From Málaga Airport, it was just a short drive to Marbella, where Margot owned a holiday apartment. No-one would suspect a thing; with just eighteen months separating them and sporting the same tawny blonde hairstyles and green eyes, there was not a lot to choose between them.   She would leave her car on the driveway of Margot's house. To all intents and purposes, she was enjoying a well-deserved break at her sister's house – it wasn't an out-an-out lie, after all.

It should take a few days for the police to register that she wasn't at home. Doubtlessly they would soon uncover the scam instigated by Margot and herself and would send the local *gendarmería* pronto to the villa. She would plead extreme stress and request that the local police keep her under surveillance instead. They should be quite understanding in the circumstances, shouldn't they? Her husband of thirty-one years *had* just been murdered, after all. In any case, it was worth the risk to escape from the prison that was her home in Deverton these past few weeks, where the only faces she saw were those of the Utopia delivery driver and that sweet but rather simple Police Family Liaison Officer. Alicia still couldn't bring herself to make even a simple trip to the local supermarket, for fear of the soppy sympathetic stares her presence alone would attract. Far easier to deal with were the "street-crossers", who had no conception of what to offer by way of condolence, verbal or otherwise, so simply abstained from the exercise altogether. No, she was best off making a run for it. At least the travelling and subterfuge should keep her mind occupied lest she become entirely eaten up with hate and bitterness towards her late husband.

Alicia peered through the front nets; there were no fastidious neighbours to be seen polishing the car or tending their front gardens at 9am that Monday morning. She considered the vista from the back of the house as well; no, not a soul around. The elderly neighbours to the left of her, fed up of constant police and press attention, had temporarily upped sticks to their daughter's house in Billock. The Morgans to the right of her were never in anyway, using the house as no more than a weekend base; true to form, his blue saloon car and her red hatchback were not on the driveway.

Alicia put the answer-phone on, then immediately thought better of it and turned it off again. She shut the internal doors, flicked the burglar alarm on, then picked up her handbag and slung an inconspicuous black shoulder bag over her shoulder. There were plenty of cheap markets in the locality where she could pick up essentials and cheap clothing once she arrived in Marbella.

24

"Right, prepare for action," Parlour instructed Goodlove, flipping his mobile shut. Karen Preece had just rung from her position across the Esplanade, overlooking the entrance to Utopia.

"Do you want me to call the cavalry?" Goodlove enquired.

Parlour shook his head. "Not yet. Let's see what he's up to, first. It might just be a calm, low-key demonstration…"

"And Utopia pork sausages will fly…" Goodlove chuckled.

Parlour grimaced and followed his junior around to the front of the shop. He instructed Goodlove to buy them a couple of coffees and took a seat by the window in the supermarket café.

He cursed as he spotted his father-in-law trotting along obediently behind a strident Roy Pedlar, carrying a bundle of placards. Behind Pedlar and Hebble were a further two dozen or so members of the BASC, carrying an assortment of signs and banners.

"Here comes the Pedlar Youth," Goodlove quipped. Parlour just frowned; it would have been comical, no more than a minor social nuisance, were events not tinged with tragedy following the murder of Davidson Munroe. The concurrence of Munroe's murder with the last BASC demonstration justified, in Parlour's eyes, employing so many officers in Deverton that Monday morning.

"Looks like the Guv'nor's arrived," Goodlove informed his superior, nodding in the direction of Lionel Bunt, the Utopia Store Manager with his distinctive Sue Pollard style bright large-framed glasses.

"Could you go and have a word with him, Cam?" Parlour requested. "I don't want Pedlar to catch sight of me through the doors. You're less distinctive than me."

Goodlove nodded and ambled over to Bunt, trying not to draw attention to himself.

Parlour focused back on events outside. The BASC were now arranged in two rows, the front row holding a banner that read *Buy British, Buy back our National Heritage.*

The back row held placards bearing various slogans, all carrying the BASC logo on the bottom right hand corner and all advocating in no uncertain terms the necessity of buying British products to keep the foreign wolf from the door. Derek Hebble was engaged in handing out leaflets to customers entering the shop. Another member of the party, whom Parlour recognised to be the mother-in-law of Constable Paul Tucker, himself a resident of Deverton, was darting around the Esplanade handing out leaflets to unsuspecting members of the public.

Roy Pedlar, meanwhile, was blasting rhetoric down the megaphone along similar lines to that espoused at the Cuisine Festival just over a week ago.

In accordance with police instructions to keep a low profile and avoid confrontation of any sort, as, following the example of events at Deverton Parish Church, this would only further ignite the flame of Pedlar's passion, Lionel Bunt did not venture outside to have words with Pedlar. Instead, he issued a message across the in-store Tannoy to staff and shoppers alike, advising them to pay no heed to the ignorant rabble outside and continue to enjoy the variety of fresh produce brought to them by Utopia's ethically sound global purchasing policy.

It was this announcement that greeted Michaela Brevitt as she received a phone-call from Antonia Killington, live from the frozen sausages section.

But national news channels and the local independent news channel arrived before RAT UK, much to Parlour's consternation.

"Marvellous," he groaned to Goodlove as Pedlar led his troops in a rousing rendition of *Ten British Sausages, Sizzling in a Pan.*

"There's Micky, Sir," Cameron nodded to the right of the Esplanade where Brevitt was approaching, flanked on either side by a Killington. Half a dozen or so local RAT members were marching purposefully behind, carrying just one solitary banner. Immediately several journalists dispersed in the direction of Brevitt and co, cameramen scurrying after them. Pedlar decided to step up his efforts, putting down his megaphone to conduct the makeshift BASC choir.

Ten British Sausages, sizzling in a pan,
Ten British Sausages, sizzling in a pan,
Utopia replaced them with Sushi from Japan,
Now there's eight British sausages, sizzling in a pan!

"Give me strength!" Parlour groaned, venturing to the foyer of the store, now it was apparent a visible police presence would be required. He issued the command for uniformed officers to make their way to the front of Utopia.

Eight British Sausages, sizzling in a pan,
Eight British Sausages, sizzling in a pan,
Utopia bought in lamb shanks from Uzbekistan,
Now there's six British sausages, sizzling in a pan!

In his very best impression of a Premiership football manager, Parlour used a variety of hand signals to convey to Michaela Brevitt that she should use her brain and keep things calm. But Brevitt, who was frantically issuing well-rehearsed and highly polished sound-bites to the local and national media, studiously ignored him, preferring to focus the corner of her eye on her arch-rival, Pedlar.

It was hard for Brevitt to make herself heard over the booming tones of Roy Pedlar, amplified through his ever-present, yet not altogether necessary, megaphone. Bob Killington was becoming more and more agitated with their impotence, outnumbered and out-blasted as they were by the vastly more impressive BASC presence. It was just as the television crew panned over to their counter-demonstration that Killington decided to inject some Viagra into proceedings. Surprising Pedlar from behind, he snatched the megaphone from his opponent's grasp and instructed the good people of Deverton to wash their hands of Roy Pedlar's racist nonsense and support RAT UK, for a fairer and more tolerant Britain.

Pedlar attempted to snatch the megaphone back but in doing so, tripped over a box of his own flyers. Farce turned to fracas as the burly Pedlar crashed into the towering figure of Bob Killington and the two men ended up in a heap on the concrete floor. A mass of journalists, cameramen, uniformed and plain clothes officers and BASC and RAT members all converged in the middle and absolute pandemonium broke out.

Suddenly there was a blood curdling yell as Roy Pedlar pulled a small plastic object from his pocket, flicked it into a long white stick and proceeded to slash wildly at Killington with it.

It's a bloomin' long-armed shoe-horn! Parlour registered incredulously. He noted that a number of BASC members also sported hard objects in their front pockets which presumably extended into shoe-horns as well. A number of uniformed officers entered the scrum and successfully removed the weapon from Pedlar.

The colour drained from Parlour's face as he suddenly realised, to his great dismay, that his own wife was at the centre of the melee, dressed in that hideous biker jacket, attempting to drag her father out of the dogfight. Margaret must have called her at school – how on earth had Juliet managed to convince the Head of Billock Community School to release her for the morning, especially after all the recent shenanigans? She'd probably pleaded some family emergency, Parlour thought grimly to himself, and it could yet prove to be a prophetic statement. Margaret was clearly deeply worried about the potential consequences of Pedlar's demo outside *Utopia*, enough to contact her daughter directly at work.

However, Derek Hebble, confidence bolstered in the presence of like-minded souls, was not to be thwarted and resisted Juliet's desperate attempts to remove him from the scene. Parlour groaned as a blitz of flashlights went off, doubtlessly capturing images of his own wife seemingly engaged in fisticuffs with an OAP. The damage was already done; Parlour knew better than to make matters a thousand times worse by muscling in himself, or at least insofar as his skinny frame would allow him. That *would* make front page news, that was for sure, Parlour could see the headline now:- *SENIOR CID OFFICER IN PUNCH UP WITH WIFE AND FATHER-IN-LAW AT POLITICAL RALLY*. Perhaps the local press wouldn't recognise her in that out-of-character leather garment, Parlour thought hopefully.

As Parlour turned to locate Goodlove amid the furore, he spotted the desolate figure of Michaela Brevitt, stood back from the crowd, leaning against the glass frontage of the supermarket. She looked quite disgusted, Parlour thought, as members of her own Respect and Tolerance Party engaged in a slanging match with the local BASC movement.

"I've requested more officers," Parlour informed her, trying to sound positive and in control, though inwardly he was berating himself furiously for underestimating the depth of feeling on both sides of the multicultural debate.

"How about zookeepers?" Brevitt remarked sarcastically, shaking her head. "That man's an animal."

"I can't say your Mr Killington's exactly covered himself in glory this morning, either," Parlour replied dryly.

"Oh, don't you worry," Michaela frowned darkly, "Bob's just got himself removed permanently from the Party. Strong views I can tolerate, physical retaliation is never acceptable."

A disturbing thought suddenly crossed Parlour's mind. "Where's Mr Gani?"

"Salik?" Brevitt frowned. "At home babysitting for me, why?"

"Shouldn't we check on him? Given what happened last time Pedlar and co staged a demo, it might be wise…"

"But Sal had nothing to do with Munroe's death…" Brevitt began, hackles rising.

"I meant for *his* safety," Parlour interjected hastily. "Perhaps he shouldn't be left alone."

Sacha! Brevitt's thoughts turned to her daughter's wellbeing for the first time that morning. She fished her mobile out of her jacket pocket and hastily called up her home number.

Parlour watched as she frowned then relaxed into a smile as she talked to Gani and was reassured of her daughter's safety.

"Sash is fine," Brevitt smiled, flipping the lid down on her mobile phone.

"He's at your place still?" Parlour checked.

The frown returned to Brevitt's face. "I'm a bit confused, to be honest. My phone was ringing then seemed to divert to another number."

She fished her phone out again and selected last number called. But it registered her home number. Brevitt's confusion turned to irritation as she realised what Gani had done.

"He's diverted my landline to his mobile!" She stared crossly into Parlour's blue eyes as he nodded slowly in concurrence. "He must have sneaked out, thought I wouldn't realise what he'd done…"

"But he had Sacha with him?" Parlour checked.

"He just said Sacha was fine," Brevitt said slowly. She looked up at Parlour, concern flecking her brown eyes. "Those were his exact words:- don't worry, she's fine."

"Try him again," Parlour commanded.

Michaela hit the redial button on her mobile. She shook her head at Parlour. "He's not even answering now, it's diverting to his mobile and it's just ringing."

"It's not then diverting to voice-mail?" Parlour frowned.

Michaela shook her head.

"Try again."

She obliged, but there was still no answer.

"I'll get an officer sent around there immediately," Parlour said briskly and radioed for help. It was reassuring at least to see that an additional two dozen or so uniformed officers were now present at the scene of the riot and were succeeding in dispersing the angry crowd. Juliet and Margaret Hebble appeared to be giving Derek Hebble a real dressing down, his bravado somewhat dissipated now that Pedlar had been frogmarched into the back of a secure police van, where doubtlessly he would be taken to Billock Police Station for a severe ticking off. He'd probably get off with an ASBO or something; a scuffle outside a supermarket with no serious injuries would hardly set the civil court alight, Parlour thought to himself, infinitely more concerned about the whereabouts of Salik Gani and the safety of little Sacha Brevitt.

"Why don't you get your lot rounded up and help tidy up this mess, before Utopia decide to take action against you?" Parlour suggested not unkindly to an anxious Brevitt. "It'll pass five minutes while we get your house checked out."

For once, Brevitt obeyed meekly and returned to the RAT party members she had shunned for the past half hour on account of their boorish and unprofessional conduct.

The call came through in a matter of minutes and Parlour walked soberly over to the thirty-something woman, her aloof air of extreme professionalism now replaced by the natural anxiety of a mother fearful for the safety of her child.

He put a comforting arm on her shoulder. "Michaela – Micky – there's nobody at your flat. Can you think where else Salik may have gone?"

"His brother's…" Michaela began.

Parlour shook his head. "We've checked that out. His father is manning the shop. The family have gone out for the day; they left at the crack of dawn. Abdul Gani hasn't seen hide nor hair of Salik, or Sacha for that matter."

Michaela uttered a mild swear word and put a stressed hand to her forehead. "This is serious, isn't it?" she stated slowly, unaccustomed to panicking about such everyday practical issues as her daughter's safety.

"It could be," Parlour conceded, trying to work out what implications a missing Salik Gani had on the murder inquiry. He was fairly sure Gani was innocent of Davidson Munroe's murder, and in any case, there was probably a perfectly innocent reason as to why Gani had decided to go out that morning. He was not a parent; it may not have occurred to him that Michaela would worry about Sacha. She didn't strike Parlour as the precious type when it came to childcare, in any case. Michaela's world did not revolve around her offspring; rather Sacha had to fit in with an already existing lifestyle, as far as was possible. To Michaela, who had yet to experience the terrible twos, Sacha was just a rather messy portable item to be shoved in the hatchback along with her shoulder bag and electronic notebook - up until that point, that was. Suddenly Roy Pedlar and co paled into insignificance, confronted with the more pressing issue of Sacha's safety.

"Come on, Sal, answer," Michaela hissed, frantically pressing redial on her mobile, but to no avail.

Parlour felt a cold sweat break out across his pale forehead. It was that same panicky feeling he had experienced the other day at the station; the sense that he had no sense of direction, and therefore no control over, this investigation. In addition, he had an errant wife to deal with.

25

Despite her anxiety concerning Sacha's whereabouts, Michaela Brevitt had still succeeded in delivering a withering tongue-lashing to Bob Killington for becoming embroiled in the supermarket scuffle. It was left to a contrite Tonky to lead the RAT pack back to the Killingtons' house for coffee and a slice of fruitcake.

Without their charismatic leader, the BASC pensioners soon dispersed as well. Derek Hebble was no Davidson Munroe in the vice-chair hot seat, and submitted weakly to a command issued by his own son-in-law, to beat it before the riot police were summoned.

With the rival forces removed from the scene and a smarting Juliet ordered back to school by a furious Parlour, efforts could now be concentrated on locating Salik Gani and Sacha Brevitt.

Parlour sent Goodlove and Preece to do a recky of the local area, while he drove Michaela and himself to her flat. He followed her up the stairs to the first floor apartment, nodding in approval at the electronic secure entry system as they entered the building from the underground car park. Also favouring the minimalist look, Parlour was impressed with just how uncluttered and spacious Brevitt's two bedroom apartment was, especially given it was also home to a toddler, with all the paraphernalia that involved in the way of toys and essential living equipment. It was a look to which he could only aspire, however, given the sheer volume of paperwork he and Juliet accrued, in their respective professions of Police Inspector and Secondary School Teacher.

"Any messages?" Parlour enquired from the cream leather sofa, as Michaela checked the answer-phone. She shook her head as she walked into the living room, hands on hips.

"No note?"

Brevitt shook her head. "Absolutely nothing. There's no clues at all, except that Sacha's coat and shoes have gone, so he must have taken her out somewhere. The buggy's kept in my car, and he doesn't have the keys. He must have carried her, she can't walk very far."

"I've got my officers scouring the area, they'll soon pick him up if he's just taken her to the park or something," Parlour attempted to reassure her, though he thought it far more likely Gani had got bored of hiding out in Brevitt's flat and had jumped on a bus. He had probably headed for the anonymity of Billock, Sacha in tow. Odd that he didn't leave a note, or contact Michaela, though.

"Perhaps he went up to the allotments for a spot of gardening!" Parlour laughed, trying to lighten the atmosphere with a bit of black humour, but it failed dismally.

"Don't," Brevitt shuddered. "Sal hasn't been near that place since Munroe died, in any case."

"Don't blame him," Parlour admitted. "It can't have been pleasant stumbling upon the body like he did, let alone what followed."

"He's had a hell of a time," Brevitt nodded. "It's disgusting, what people have been saying about him, purely because of his skin colour…"

Parlour held his hand up. "Let's save that debate for later," he said hastily. "We need to focus our minds on where they could have got to."

***

Goodlove and Preece drew a blank in their search for Gani and his young charge in the Deverton area and discreet enquiries were made at the bus and train stations within the Billock-Foxburgh conurbation for sightings of a forty-one year old Asian man and a thirteen month old baby girl of mixed race.

Time was ticking on; it was now three hours since Brevitt had made telephone contact with Gani outside Utopia

Supermarket and fears were mounting for the safety of the odd duo, and naturally more so for the toddler.

Meanwhile, Michaela Brevitt paced the floor of her apartment, beside herself with worry and self-admonishment for leaving Sacha alone in the flat with Gani that morning – though no such fears had entered her head the previous Saturday night whilst enjoying dinner at the Parlours'.

So fraught was she, that she almost ripped the phone of the wall when her landline rang early that Monday afternoon.

Parlour exhaled in relief, seeing a palpable expression of joy flood across Brevitt's cheeks as she engaged with the caller.

"Good news, I take it?" he asked as she sat down slowly. Brevitt buried her head in her hands and Parlour gave her a couple of moments, as she wept in relief. Perhaps he had been a little hard on Juliet, after all. She would have been very handy to have had around these past couple of hours. She was strong and kind in a useful, non blousy kind of way, when she had her sensible head on.

Brevitt raised her head finally. She apologised, as surprised as Parlour was at her own spontaneous reaction to news of her daughter's safety. She couldn't remember the last time she had wept in private, let alone in public. Crying was a luxury the hard-nosed Michaela Brevitt rarely indulged in.

She stood up and grabbed her house keys. "Come on, we need to go. That was some crèche in the shopping centre in Foxburgh. Salik plonked her in there at 10 am so he could go shopping for an hour. But he didn't turn up at 11 to collect her. They've been ringing and ringing his mobile with no reply."

"So how come they got this number?" Parlour wondered.

"He gave them this number as a default," Michaela explained. "But the person who took the call wrote it down badly and they've been calling Deverton 788788 instead of 788783. When they kept getting no response, they realised their mistake. Oh, the stupid idiot… why didn't he just tell me?"

"He thought you'd say no?" Parlour shrugged. "He was fed up of being holed up at your apartment, decided at the last minute to give you the slip. He probably thought he'd be back before you."

"If he'd gone to Billock, maybe," Brevitt replied. "But not Foxburgh… it's a bit of a trek."

"I agree," Parlour nodded. "It does seem a bit odd, I have to say. Why go all the way over there? If it was just a spot of chain store shopping, Billock's got it all, and far closer to home."

"What are you saying?" Brevitt frowned, putting her jacket on.

"Well I know you've tarted him up a bit, but all the same, Salik Gani doesn't strike me as the sort to go window shopping," Parlour commented, following her down the stairs to his car.

"Ah, but Mashrafe Khan is a fashion junkie!" Michaela grinned, confidence returning now her daughter's life was not in danger.

"But seriously…" Parlour persevered.

"I agree," Brevitt said more soberly this time, climbing in the passenger seat of Parlour's SLK. "He hasn't gone for a browse around the *Burgh Centre*. He may have gone to the library, however."

She informed Parlour of their little trip to the county library the previous week, and their futile attempts to unearth some dirt on Roy Pedlar.

"It would explain why he put Sash in the crèche," Brevitt added. "He could hardly expect her to sit quietly in Foxburgh Library for an hour. They're so frightfully uptight in there. I don't think the Head Librarian has emptied her bowels in twenty years."

"Yes, they are," Parlour agreed, who had often had recourse to visit the county library to research various aspects of cases he had been working on. However, their strictly enforced library etiquette was what made Foxburgh library such a revered local institution, unlike Billock Library, which was more like a teenage drop in centre, especially on a rainy day. It was the recent addition of a fizzy drinks machine with its thumping and clunking invitation to young people to hang around indefinitely which had proved to be the final nail in the coffin of Billock Central Lending Library's attempts to be taken seriously as a retreat for quiet study and intellectual stimulation.

Half an hour later, Parlour had parked his car free of charge in County Police HQ. They made their way towards the Burgh Centre to pick up little Sacha from *Beetles*, the crèche facility run by a private company housed within Foxburgh's expensive indoor shopping complex.

As Michaela engaged in a long embrace with a rather bemused Sacha, who had been well supplied with healthy, organic snacks from the supermarket downstairs, Parlour proceeded to question the staff about Salik Gani/Mashrafe Khan.

But nothing in his behaviour had given rise to suspicion, as least at the time of "check-in" as they rather functionally described the depositing of small human beings within their childcare establishment. To all intents and purposes, he appeared a very pleasant and well-dressed older Dad, who, like most men, did not have any patience with very small children who were past the initial sleepy baby stage, and chose to offload them as soon as a suitable opportunity presented itself.

A more observant younger employee, however, did comment that Gani had a very sweaty hand when he handed over his six pounds ninety-five at the till.

Parlour made a note of this information and passed it on to a bemused Michaela, all sweetness and light now that Sacha was safe and her guilty conscience assuaged.

"All those flipping fry-ups," she commented flippantly. "Wouldn't lay too much store by that. Cholesterol's probably through the ceiling."

Parlour grinned. It had to be said, Gani wasn't the most well-ventilated of men. Like a well-known reindeer associated with Christmas, one could even say he *glowed.*

"Do you mind if I just pop into County HQ for two minutes?" Parlour enquired as they headed back towards his car. "I just want to check Goodlove's done his job and they're keeping an eye out for Gani in the town centre. Might see if I can get my hands on some CCTV footage as well; they've got enough blinking cameras in Foxburgh town centre."

"Sure," Brevitt smiled, who would have agreed to anything now that she was reunited with her beautiful baby daughter.

"Oh, and Micky…" Parlour called out as he left her by his car. "You might want to nip across to Parentcare and get a car seat. We should have gone in your car. Shouldn't really be driving an infant without legal restraints. I can probably charge it to expenses."

Or I could just keep it for when Jules and I have a nipper, Parlour thought fancifully, and a mite optimistically in the circumstances.

What sort of mother am I? Michaela groaned. *Why didn't I think of that?* She scooped Sacha back up in her arms and headed for the baby store across the road.

***

Foxburgh Police reported no sightings of Salik Gani in the city centre that Monday morning. Parlour snorted. This wasn't Billock, for Cripe's sake. How difficult could it be to spot an Asian man in a Pedlarian white utopia like Foxburgh? Shame Gani had deposited Sacha in the shopping centre crèche, Parlour thought; a cute young thing like Sacha tottering along the pavement would have been far more likely to have caught the attention of passers-by than a lone Salik Gani.

Parlour bemoaned, not for the first time, the arrogance and lack of cooperation of Foxburgh Police. The snottiness that was rife in the county town seemed to have pervaded County Police HQ as well. It was with a tone entirely devoid of deference for rank that Parlour was dispatched to a small room in the basement that took a feed from the CCTV control room managed by Foxburgh City Council.

Grudgingly, the young constable agreed to keep an eye out for Gani and if necessary, to provide Parlour with tapes from that morning should the riddle of Gani's whereabouts not be resolved later that day.

Parlour returned to his car, where Sacha was now snugly strapped into what was clearly *not* a serviceable infant car restraint towards the bottom of the range available at *Parentcare*. Parlour gave a little smile – he would expect no less from Brevitt. Leave your child with a semi-stranger and murder suspect while you stage a political protest with your mates, then insist on a top of the range car seat to make a one off journey back home. He saw right through her; she was the archetypal modern professional mum with ambition. No patience to spend quality time with her child, yet all the money (and guilt) in the world to furnish her with the latest products of the global merchandising kingdom, an entity that she herself well and truly bought into. And Sacha, the child, was simply an extension of this material kingdom, an allegedly must-have product to be picked up and disposed of as and when required. Well it would only work for so long, Parlour thought to himself, greeting her and starting the engine. There were only so many benevolent friends and casual acquaintances able to help her out with childcare, and soon Sacha would become a whole lot more demanding. For all her rhetoric on human rights, it seemed to Parlour that Michaela Brevitt didn't afford her daughter much of the basic nurturing required by a very young child.

Like a great many individuals, Parlour was prone to making moral judgements about others with little knowledge or personal experience of their circumstances.

However Jules and I handle having kids, Parlour thought to himself self-righteously as he joined the ring road leading out of Foxburgh, *we won't have trophy children. We'll spend quality time with them; we won't shove them in front of satellite channels or leave them with strangers. They'll eat healthy organic snacks and we'll **never** take them to McDonalds.*

He smiled to himself as he remembered a conversation Jules had had with him the other week. Apparently the Chudders had spent over two thousand pounds getting some fancy black and white photos done of their children, to be displayed around the home and office in gigantic chunky dark-wood photo frames. Jules had commented that it was to remind Marina and Nigel Chudder what their children looked like!

Yet despite her transparency, there was something about Michaela Brevitt that he liked and admired. Perhaps it was her flagrant ambition, and the clever way she managed to stay on the right side of the moral divide with her cunning ethical spin on the RAT Party's antics. And political stunt or otherwise, taking Salik Gani in, clothing him, offering him protection - political asylum of a sort – was a worthy course of action in Parlour's eyes.

The call came through on Parlour's mobile five minutes later. He decided not to impart the information to Brevitt just yet.

26

"Hill's Bills!" Parlour *ersatz*-cursed, punching the side of his car after alighting from it at the entrance to Deverton Allotments. "How could I be so bloody dim?"

"You can't blame yourself," Karen Preece consoled him in vain. "No-one could have expected to find Gani here. It seemed too… well… obvious."

"The blinking obvious is the first place to start. Basic rule of thumb, Karen," Parlour groaned in anguish. He looked up at his junior colleague. "When did you find him?"

"It wasn't me, Sir, it was Goodlove," Karen conceded. "We split up; I did the north side, Cam went down to the new estate. We had no joy so swapped over. I hadn't bothered with the allotments, it never occurred to me to drive up there. Cam, fortunately, used some logic and thought if Munroe was done in during one of Pedlar's demos, it may well follow that Gani was here."

"And it looks like suicide?" Parlour frowned, traipsing down the hill to the white tent surrounding the body, where Scenes of Crime Officers were busy gathering forensic evidence.

"Seems that way," Preece replied. "There was a half empty cup of the same liquid paraquat next to him; it's been taken off to the lab for safety's sake. Obviously the stuff we found at Gani's flat wasn't the job lot. No sign of a struggle, no drip marks down his clothes to indicate it was force fed him. Oh, and there's a note, as well."

"A suicide letter?" Parlour made a face. This was getting cornier by the minute.

"More of a suicide snippet, actually," Preece laughed. "*I can't go on living like this*, or something of the sort."

"His hand-writing?"

"Jenkins has gone to the Mini Mart to fetch a sample of his writing."

"He's not telling Abdul Gani about Salik yet, is he?" Parlour exclaimed, visibly wincing. Jenkins was far too junior an officer to impart to elderly Mr Gani that his son had potentially taken his own life, especially given the absence of his family that day.

"We weren't authorised to pass on that information, so no," Preece replied rather coldly. It did annoy her that despite many years of working together, Parlour still questioned her common sense and obedience to protocol at times. Though she deeply admired his intellect and professionalism, she found his unconscious arrogance and rather controlling nature difficult to let wash over her at times.

"Good," Parlour nodded. He took a deep breath then stepped inside the tent. As with Davidson Munroe, one side of the shed had been dismantled to enable a proper investigation of the body. Parlour could see that the local police pathologist, Peter Obermann, was busily engaged in a thorough examination of the body and opted not to disturb him for a few moments yet.

This time, the body was not slumped on the floor; rather the victim was sat on a rickety wooden chair, arms floppy at his side, head lolled back with mouth gaping open foolishly.

"New clothes, same old body," Parlour muttered, considering Gani's skinny wrists poking out of his casual shirt, fresh from the packet. It wouldn't have surprised Parlour, had there still been pins lurking within the lilac fabric. He turned to one of the Scenes of Crime Officers. "Where's this alleged suicide note, then?"

A female SOCO handed Parlour a bagged item. Parlour considered the scrap of paper which bore the words, written in spidery black handwriting:- *I can't go on living like this.* He frowned, turning the cellophane bag over in his hand. The note was written on some kind of business flyer. Parlour peered at it more closely then beckoned Preece over.

"Karen, have a look at this, will you?"

DS Preece turned the item over in her hand. She looked up at Parlour. "It seems to be details for a property, Sir. Estate Agent blurb."

"That's what I thought," Parlour nodded. He looked into Karen Preece's cool blue eyes. "If you were going to do yourself in, would you write a scrappy little note like this on the back of some house particulars?"

"If it was the only piece of paper I could find, maybe," Preece frowned, struggling to place herself in that situation.

"Exactly, which suggests the note was written here in the shed – if it is indeed a suicide note - as he would have ample access to paper both at Brevitt's flat and in the middle of Foxburgh."

Preece nodded thoughtfully.

"If Gani did commit suicide," Parlour continued, "then we are to believe that he came here to his allotment, rooted around for something to write a note on, then drunk some of his own lethal liquid paraquat. Why on earth would he have property particulars in his potting shed anyway?"

"He was thinking of moving house – to escape the nutters outside his front door?" But Karen Preece didn't sound at all convincing.

"Well, he'd have to move out of Deverton, and I can't see him doing that with all his family here – they're a close-knit bunch. And where would he get the cash from to move house? He rents that maisonette of his opposite the Mini Mart."

"Blackmail money?"

"Still doesn't explain why he wrote that note on some ripped up house particulars," Parlour replied, brain cells doing furious gymnastics as he tried to find an explanation for the scenario before him. The Estate Agents would need to be traced. Most agents these days kept records of individuals to whom they had sent property details.

Preece's mobile went off.

"That was Jenkins," she informed Parlour a moment later. "He's bringing a sample of Gani's writing over, but he reckons it's his on the note all right, from what he's seen."

Parlour frowned and raked his fingers through his Brylcreemed ginger locks.

"Afternoon, Mark," Peter Obermann greeted Parlour, standing up finally and removing his sterile gloves.

"Well?"

"He's been dead no more than two hours. The body was placed here, it's not suicide."

Parlour took a sharp intake of breath, though the latter verdict was not entirely unexpected.

"Are you sure?"

"Absolutely positive," Obermann nodded firmly. "Look at the way he's sitting. If you were to drink some lethal weed-killer of a type to cause instant death, unless you happened to have tipped your head back and gargled it, your body wouldn't flop back in this way. You would slump forward, and in this case, fall to the floor."

"Like Davidson Munroe?" Parlour enquired.

"Like Davidson Munroe," Obermann repeated.

"But it was paraquat that killed him?" Preece checked.

"Oh yes," Obermann nodded. "I can smell it in his mouth. However, there are no obvious traces of it on his clothes or hair. If it was force-fed him, as in the case of Davidson Munroe, then the victim's been cleaned up. Perhaps he wore a bib or something!"

"But it didn't take place here in the shed?" Preece frowned.

Obermann twitched his nose. "I would say he was poisoned beforehand and his body was placed on this chair; it would explain the unnatural position of it."

Parlour looked perplexed. "But Gani was last seen at 10 am. His murderer must have acted very quickly, to have killed him then driven him all the way over here from Foxburgh."

"This was someone ruthless who knew exactly what they wanted to do and didn't baulk at following through."

"Like with Davidson Munroe," Parlour nodded. "His killer struck while the iron was hot… most of the village was busy at the church, Munroe nipped off to the allotments briefly for some leeks. The killer seized his chance. Bam, Munroe was dead."

Preece shuddered. "This is one very cold-blooded individual."

"You'd say it was the same murderer?" Parlour checked with Obermann.

"That's your department, Mark," the pathologist replied. "But on the balance of evidence, I'd have to say it looks likely."

Parlour felt the little colour he had in his pale cheeks drain away. He was gutted, absolutely gutted. Guilt at his own ineptitude flooded through his veins; on numerous occasions, a little nagging voice inside had told him he needed to stop and examine the evidence, reflect on the case so far, ask Sewell for advice, even ask for some divine input if necessary. But instead he had ploughed ahead, acting in his own feeble strength and his own limited perspective. And this was the result – another tragic loss of life that could have, and should have, been prevented.

Parlour turned away, disgusted at himself, and disgusted at humankind in general.

He left Preece to consult with the pathologist and made his way back to his car. He would make the necessary phone calls then lock himself away from the world for a few hours to try and get his head around events. His two sergeants were more than capable of taking over for the rest of the afternoon; perhaps Goodlove could zap over to Foxburgh CID and pick up those CCTV tapes for him. It was a very long shot, but they might just provide a glimpse of Gani about his business in the county town that morning and supply a clue to the identity of his killer.

That's the last time I hanker after an allotment, Parlour thought grimly, as he made his way up the hill to his car, remembering his earlier desire to escape from Juliet's sexual advances into the quiet haven of Deverton Allotments. Some safe haven, he groaned inwardly. He never wanted to set foot in the place again, if he could help it.

***

Gordon Brown! Juliet exclaimed to herself, catching sight of the final edition of the Billock Courier at the filling station, as she went to pay for her petrol on the way home from school late that afternoon.

She had made the front page, engaged in what appeared to be a scuffle with her own father, though in truth she had been attempting to wrestle him away from the riot unfolding.

Phuket! She groaned. Mark would kill her. The picture bore the caption:- *Juliet Parlour, schoolteacher and wife of DCI Mark Parlour of Billock Police, tussles with Deverton pensioner Derek Hebble.*

Of course, the journalist who had unearthed her professional and marital identity had refused to disclose her relationship to Derek, preferring instead to depict her as a pensioner beating harridan.

Mark was in a foul enough mood concerning his lack of progress in the Munroe case without her adding to his burden. And the powers that be at Billock Community School, ever mindful of the establishment's rather rough reputation, would not be best pleased with her either, for drawing attention to the school yet again for all the wrong reasons. To add fuel to the fire, she was supposed to have been present at a staff training day between the hours of nine and three pm, not at the centre of a political row outside Utopia supermarket. There *were* mitigating circumstances; she had been fearful for her father's life on quite reasonable grounds, and it was this fear that had

228

prompted her to drive to Deverton like a woman possessed in the middle of a working day. Nevertheless, it was hardly the behaviour expected of a reasonably senior member of staff. *Now it's my life at stake*, Juliet groaned, anticipating with dread the inevitable showdown with Barry Hewson, the Head of Billock Community School and the even scarier Miriam Philpot, chair of the Board of Governors. *Next time Mum can sort out her own problems*, Juliet thought to herself. It was the last time she was muscling in to save family face; it had achieved the precise opposite.

***

Parlour lifted his head from his folded arms at his desk at home and stretched back in his chair. He felt better for taking a few hours out, his head clearer and his heart a great deal lighter. Had he been faced with the unenviable task of breaking the news of Salik's death to the Gani family and to a lesser extent, to Michaela Brevitt, he would perhaps not be feeling quite as chipper. But that job had gone to the ultra-professional and generally unflappable Karen Preece, in tandem with Cuddles Cadley.

The doorbell rang. As Parlour went downstairs to answer the front door, he saw the bulky silhouette of Cameron Goodlove through the semi-opaque glass.

"Got those videos for you," Goodlove grunted, following Parlour through to the kitchen. "Had them sent over, been helping Blackman out with that smack raid in Billock."

"Nice for you," Parlour commented, who found neither Leigh Blackman nor drugs raids very interesting.

"Foxburgh got one of their DCs to whiz through them briefly, but they couldn't see Gani on there, at least no-one resembling the photo we gave them."

"I'll go through them anyway," Parlour replied as expected, knowing full well, and with justification, it had to be said, that nobody was as painstaking as himself when it came to sifting through evidence. "How did Karen get on with the Ganis?"

"They're absolutely distraught," Goodlove conceded soberly. "I don't know if Mr Gani senior will ever get over it. He's a bit of an old knacker, isn't he?"

"He's rather frail," Parlour agreed. He frowned, hating the line of enquiry he must inevitably pursue. "I hate to say this, but do we have an alibi for them all?"

Goodlove frowned. "You surely don't think…"

Parlour held his hand up. "No. But we can't rule out some family tiff, can we?"

"You didn't take that line with Alicia Munroe," Goodlove commented.

"True," Parlour conceded. He really should touch base with Munroe's widow, he'd kind of forgotten about her.

"I'll get onto it," Goodlove sighed, sensing his Monday club night was about to be interrupted by some uncomfortable home visits.

"Thanks, Cam."

"But it's definitely murder?" Goodlove enquired, who had been sent off to help out with the drugs bust in Billock shortly after stumbling on Salik Gani's body at Deverton Allotments and hadn't been privy to Parlour's discussions with Preece and Peter Obermann.

"Pathologist reckons Gani was fed some 72 vintage paraquat then driven to Deverton Allotments and planted – pardon the pun – in his potting shed."

"No witnesses?" Goodlove frowned.

"Not as yet," Parlour shook his head, leading Goodlove to the front door. He had a long night's CCTV viewing ahead of him.

27

"Good Lord," Antonia Killington remarked, and not in appreciation of the Son of God. "This doesn't do our cause much good, does it?"

She shook her head at the large double spread in the Foxburgh Herald on the fracas outside Utopia, which bore the headline:- *White on White* in screaming bold capitals. Below the main headline was the disparaging sub-header:- *Yuppie Yobs Wage War on Neo-Nazi Geris!*

"There you are, Bob, in all your glory," Antonia commented sarcastically, drumming her finger boldly on a shot of Pedlar and Killington rolling around on the ground outside Utopia.

Bob groaned; the photo was neither flattering to himself nor the cause. "I'm going to be further in the doghouse with Micky after this," he grimaced.

"Mm, and she's going to be in an even fouler mood when she sees this!" Antonia said slowly, turning the page to the continuation of the article. She gasped then put her hand over her mouth.

"Oh dear, it *is* kind of funny…"

"Give me a look!" Bob commanded, snatching the paper from his wife. He took a sharp intake of breath then broke into a loud, belly-stretching guffaw.

"Good God in heaven, I *do* hope she has a sense of humour!"

***

"Mark, you're going to kill me," Juliet Parlour said meekly, contrition written all over her face as she entered the living room at six pm that evening, having stayed on at school to complete some reports and getting caught in the rush-hour traffic for her exertions.

"Ay?" Parlour said absent-mindedly, eyes glazed from peering at CCTV footage that past half hour. He flicked the VCR on pause and gazed up at his wife.

Juliet handed him the paper, awaiting that familiar look of calm disappointment that would cross her husband's face, an expression that she feared more than any verbal thunder bolt. It was the look that magnified her impulsiveness and immaturity more than anything he could say and reduced her to an internal storm of self-loathing.

But nothing. He studied the front page and the double spread bearing his wife's monochrome image, but no reaction.

"Aren't you cross with me? It's got your name on it and everything."

"So I see," Parlour remarked quietly.

"I thought you'd be mad at me!" Juliet exhaled with a combination of relief and bewilderment.

"Jules," Parlour responded soberly. "Salik Gani was found dead in his potting shed this afternoon."

"What?!"

Parlour looked balefully at his wife. "The murderer tried to cover it up as suicide but it's murder alright. Almost a carbon copy of the first, by all accounts, except Gani was killed beforehand and his body dumped there."

"Oh my goodness!" Juliet exclaimed.

"I feel terrible," Parlour conceded, shaking his head. He stopped the tape and joined his wife.

"Why? It's hardly your fault!" Juliet exclaimed. "You were doing all you could to catch the killer."

Parlour shook his head slowly. "I've been too busy sniffing around Roy Pedlar and co… and meanwhile someone else has paid with their life."

"Oh Mark!" Juliet exclaimed fondly, clasping his hand. She hugged his skinny frame with her rather chunkier, full-breasted top half. He held on tightly; he'd missed those little touches. They'd been so wrapped up in the act of intercourse in their desire to produce mini-Parlours, they'd lost the emotional support and friendship part of their marriage, that had always played such a prominent role.

"But surely Pedlar *does* have something to do with this," Juliet protested. "Albeit indirectly. Both times he's staged some protest, a man has died. And in very similar circumstances. That's too much of a coincidence, surely?"

"The coast was clear, that's all," Parlour shrugged. "Our murderer saw a good opportunity to bump Munroe and Gani off, with the police and the public distracted by Pedlar's demos."

"You think it was the same murderer?"

"I think Gani was sniffing around to try and clear his name and worked out who the murderer was," Parlour replied. "Instead of coming to me, the stupid fool decided to play vigilante and approach the killer. The killer decided to silence him for good – and attempt to cover it up as suicide."

Juliet screwed up her nose dubiously. "I can't believe Pedlar isn't involved in some way. He's a thoroughly nasty piece of work, and all these things have started happening since he moved to Deverton. We haven't had a suspicious death in the area since Terence Haynes was murdered four years ago."

Parlour looked up at his wife. "I'm not saying Pedlar had *nothing* to do with the murders, but I have to consider the possibility that the two are entirely unrelated and widen the net. I thought you'd be glad; it takes the attention off your old man, after all."

"True," Juliet conceded, picking up the paper again. She spread it out across her knee and they considered the salacious article together.

"I bought the *Herald* as well," she informed him, "there's a picture of that Bob Killington chap on the front."

"Let's have a look."

Juliet fished it out of her shoulder bag and handed it to her husband.

She looked up from the Courier as Parlour began to chuckle, increasingly louder.

"What?"

Parlour smacked her in the stomach with the rolled up paper.

"Take a look at the Page 3 girl!"

28

If you think of anything, however trivial, that might help us with our enquiries into Salik's death, please don't hesitate to contact us.

Michaela Brevitt shuddered at 9pm that evening, drawing her knees up to her chest and replaying Cameron Goodlove's parting words to her from earlier on. He'd had his professional head on, which nevertheless still bore copious amounts of Wella's finest out-on-the-lash-proof hair gel.

Her dark eyes wandered across to the purple silk tie she had purchased just a few days ago for Salik, slung lazily across the leather tub chair in one corner of the living room.

I can't spend the night here, with all his stuff lying around, Michaela thought. On cue, the phone rang.

It was Juliet Parlour, offering Michaela and Sacha a bed for the night. Michaela gratefully accepted and began the now familiar process of gathering overnight supplies for Mother and Toddler into a holdall. Her fingers hesitated on the baby monitor. Should she bother with them? She would probably be sharing a spare room with Sacha... but on the other hand, she might stay up chatting to Juliet and wouldn't hear Sacha stir. Michaela unplugged the monitor and wrapped the cable around the parent unit before going through to the nursery to fetch the baby unit as well.

She stopped in her tracks halfway down the hallway; that was it. That was what had been bugging her and had kept her awake for ages the previous night. Salik reckoned he had worked out the identity of the mysterious yelling woman on the baby monitors and was just about to tell her when the call had come through from The Killies about the demo at Utopia. They'd never finished the conversation, and now they never would. Michaela felt hot tears spring up behind her eyelids; it was an unfamiliar sensation.

Was it relevant? Michaela frowned. She couldn't see that it was; surely Davidson Munroe and Salik Gani's deaths were linked, and given that both took place during one of Pedlar's crazy demos, it was logical to assume there was some link with the BASC movement.

If anything springs to mind, however trivial…

Michaela resolved to inform Parlour as she gathered up a sleepy Sacha in a cotton waffle blanket and carried her down to the car.

Unaware that she was being watched by the owner of a dark saloon car from the far side of the residents' car-park, Michaela started the engine of her black Alfa Romeo and exited the basement of the apartment block.

She put Classic FM on quietly as Sacha slumbered on, but the Mendelssohn overture was too melancholy given the circumstances and Brevitt flicked to the local community radio which was playing a trite, but soothing, medley of easy listening love songs.

Had Brevitt paid a little less attention to the car stereo and a little more to the fuel gage, she might have spotted the petrol light blinking furiously at her.

Bugger! she exhaled as the car kangarooed then juddered to a halt halfway along Upper Foxburgh Road. Michaela thumped the dashboard furiously, as if it might magically shift the fuel gauge arrow back into the black. She was sure she'd only filled up the other day.

Michaela zipped her jacket up and alighted from the car. She opened the boot and grappled around for the plastic jerry can, but no joy.

Fudge! She had emptied the boot this morning, hadn't she, to get all the counter-demo flyers and the banner in. All that remained was Sacha's buggy and the overnight bag.

Fool! Brevitt berated herself, which was futile in the circumstances. How could she have possibly predicted this scenario? She rummaged around again, to make sure, which was her undoing.

Her body slumped to the ground with a gentle thud. Her assailant returned to the dark saloon car and pulled off noiselessly with no lights on until a safe distance away. There was nobody around as far as the driver of the car could see; and in any case, the false plates should throw the police off the scent.

***

Roy Pedlar kissed his wife tenderly mid-forehead and switched off her bedside lamp at nine fifteen that evening. As was her custom, she had retired upstairs to read whilst he busied himself with party matters downstairs. As was also her custom, she had fallen asleep on the job, her book splayed open in her outstretched hand, her reading glasses, dangling on their chain, resting on the slightly wrinkled bit of cleavage exposed by her pink button down nightshirt.

Like Mark Parlour, Roy Pedlar also felt the need for some time of quiet meditation and reflection. It wasn't as if Lucinda would notice his absence; Pedlar was one of those bundles of nervous energy who burnt the candle at both ends with relative ease.

Pedlar stepped into the annexe and into the little white box room Lucinda termed his chapel. He bowed in front of a black and white photo of his late father, receiving his Second World War Defence Medal, then took a seat at the chair and rested his head on his hands, as if in prayer.

Dearest Father, Pedlar began. *Give me boldness to fight for our country like you did. Help me defend our island against foreign infiltrators; make Britain great again and help me play a role in this. Forgive me my lily-livered placard-waving and find me a more effective way of protecting our land. For the sake of Queen and Country and in your name, dear Father.*

Pedlar rose his head and as was *his* custom, stood up and stared long and hard at each photo of his father in turn, in the same clockwise sequence he always followed.

***

"Cape Cod!" Parlour exclaimed, suddenly jumping up from his perch in front of the VCR. He flicked it off and grabbed his jacket and car-keys. The same gut-feeling that had caused his wife to call Michaela Brevitt and offer her a bed for the night was propelling him down the driveway to his car.

"What is it?" Juliet called, chasing after him.

"Micky!" Parlour shouted back. "She said she'd be around in ten minutes. That was half an hour ago!"

"I'm coming with you!" Juliet yelled and hastily grabbed her coat before banging the front door shut and joining him in the passenger seat.

Sheep! Sheep! Sheep! Parlour exclaimed, well and truly breaking the speed limit for a built up area as he pulled onto the main road that led to the far side of Deverton.

"That'll be her," Parlour said quietly as they spotted a huddle of people gathered around a black car on the other side of Upper Foxburgh Road. He noted with satisfaction that WPC Wendy Fullerton was already at the scene of the crime with PC Nick Rossi.

Juliet put her head in her hands and had to be dragged out of the car by the hand as Parlour walked grim-faced across the road to the small crowd that had formed around the black Alfa Romeo.

"Ambulance is on its way," Fullerton informed him.

Parlour looked puzzled; Rossi was bent down and murmuring words of comfort to the prone figure of Michaela Brevitt.

"She's alive?" he queried, hardly daring to believe it. He had been so sure she'd fallen prey to the ice-cool opportunist who'd taken the lives of Davidson Munroe and Salik Gani.

"Blow to the back of the head, by the looks of it. She's drifting in and out of consciousness, Sir," Rossi replied.

Parlour bent down to utter some of his own words of comfort to Brevitt, his skinny knees cracking as he did so. But she didn't respond. He stood up and noted with satisfaction that Juliet had climbed inside the back of the car to sit with little Sacha Brevitt, who had now stirred and was beginning to whimper for her mother.

The ambulance arrived within five minutes of Parlour's arrival on the scene and he elected to travel to Billock General with Michaela while Juliet took Sacha back to Spatchcock Drive along with Brevitt's belongings. Forensic scientists would be along soon to check the black car for clues to her assailant's identity.

<h1 style="text-align:center">29</h1>

"How is she?" Juliet Parlour asked anxiously, rushing to the front door as Parlour returned just after midnight that evening.

Parlour shut the door behind him and hugged his wife tightly. She pulled back, fearing the worst, but Parlour did not have bad news, he was simply feeling glad, very glad, to be alive.

"She'll be fine," he informed Juliet. "She's had a nasty blow to the back of the head, but preliminary scans reveal no brain damage and she's come around. They'll do more tests tomorrow – later on today, I mean – then transfer her to the private unit. She's got private medical insurance, it won't surprise you."

"Was she able to…" Juliet began.

Parlour shook his head. "The doctors wouldn't let us near her. I've got Goodlove stationed there overnight in case she decides to talk – and for her safety, in case our murderer finds out they didn't succeed in their mission."

"They definitely wanted her dead?" Juliet checked.

"I'd say so," Parlour nodded. "Gani had obviously got some information on Munroe's killer and they were afraid he'd spilt the beans to Michaela. So she had to go as well - as a precautionary measure, you understand."

Juliet shuddered; it was too cool and calculated for words.

"How's the baby?" Parlour enquired, wandering into the downstairs loo. He'd drunk enough tea to sink the Titanic.

"Gave her one of the bottles of milk Micky had packed then put her in bed. She whinged for ages so I picked her up and she did a big burp and fell asleep. Haven't heard from her since."

"You're supposed to wind them after a bottle, aren't you?" Parlour called to her. "Even I know that."

"How do you do that?" Juliet asked in all innocence. Though she had heard the expression, she had no idea how it worked in practice. Boy, she had a lot to learn.

"Pat them on the back until they belch, I think," Parlour replied. "Or throw up over you – one of the two."

"What a criminal waste of milk," Juliet commented, fetching herself a glass of water for bedtime.

"So what's on the agenda for tomorrow – I mean today?" she yawned, wandering upstairs to brush her teeth.

Parlour shrugged. "Can't do much until Micky's allowed to talk. They said she has to rest for at least twelve hours. Guess I should go through those blessed CCTV tapes again, in case I missed something. I was so hoping to spot Gani on them. I know it was a long shot, but I had a gut feeling they would come up trumps – looks like I was wrong again."

Parlour frowned; it was bad news if his spookily accurate intuition was malfunctioning. Perhaps it was the Maker's way of humbling him; making him trust in Him more and think a little less of himself.

He let out a huge yawn to rival his wife's, then flicked off the light and closed his eyes, already heavy from fatigue. Before Juliet had returned from checking one more time on Sacha, he had fallen asleep.

***

The telephone pre-empted Parlour's radio alarm at 7.29 that morning. Parlour raised a sleepy hand from under the duvet to grab the handset; it was sure to be for him.

"Parlour," he grunted.

It was Karen Preece. Apparently, Alicia Munroe had gone AWOL leaving no trace of her whereabouts.

"Great," Parlour groaned. "Get hold of her family. There's a sister in Bognor."

"We're already onto it," Preece replied tersely and put the phone down.

Parlour's brain creaked slowly into gear as he contemplated this worrying new snippet of information. But he was distracted a moment later by the unfamiliar bleating of a waking infant.

"What the…" Parlour groaned, then remembered. "Jules?"

But Juliet had already left for work that Tuesday morning, having suddenly found a pile of prep that could only be done at school.

Parlour uttered a swear word of a slightly less tame nature than usual and got out of bed. Surely she hadn't left him in charge of that baby all day, knowing he was knee deep in a double murder investigation?

He gathered up the squalling child in his arms, wrinkling his nose in disdain as he felt a soggy sensation on his left forearm. He looked down; hadn't Jules bothered to change Sacha's nappy before she left for work?

He carried the toddler tentatively downstairs and into the kitchen. There was a note from Jules stuck to the Golden Flakes box.

Micky's Mum coming to collect baby at 9am. May the Force be with you!

Great! Parlour groaned. He didn't know which was worse; caring for a soggy, bad-tempered and undoubtedly hungry baby for over two hours, or facing Ms Brevitt senior. Hardened criminals he could handle; the awesome and undoubtedly frightening creature that had mothered Michaela Brevitt was quite another kettle of fish. She would be sure to fire questions at him - probably down the barrel of a large verbal shotgun - concerning her daughter's safety and the lack of police protection afforded her.

But Parlour's thoughts were taken elsewhere as a vile odour began to invade his nasal cavity. He looked down and to his abject horror, saw that Brevitt junior was turning a bizarre shade of purple as she performed her morning glory.

***

"I gather you've requested a transfer to our Private Patient Unit?" a smiling blonde junior doctor inquired of a turbaned Michaela Brevitt at 9am that Tuesday morning.

Too bloody right! Brevitt thought, but nodded curtly in acquiescence instead.

"Well, they'll need to keep you in a few days for observation," the Registrar informed Brevitt. "The CT scan was clear, but you've sustained a nasty blow to the head. There should be no lasting damage, but the Consultant at the PPU would like to keep an eye on you all the same. Meanwhile, you can expect the usual symptoms of concussion, a little dizziness and perhaps nausea."

"Fab!" Brevitt groaned.

"You may also experience some blurred vision," the doctor continued in a matter-of-fact tone. "But no, and I repeat *no*, involvement in political rallies."

"You heard about that?" Michaela groaned, considering the Registrar, who was attractive in a kind of delicate, sleepless kind of way. What was it about lying incapacitated in a hospital bed that made you seize up the physical attraction of anything that moved?

"You're all over the local papers!" Dr Paltrowski chuckled, leaving the room to continue the morning round.

Fantastic! Michaela rang the bell; perhaps Jolly Bran Flake Lady could find her some copies of the Courier and Herald.

I'm not your bloody servant! Corinne Drewery felt like shouting at the bossy black woman in Spinnaker Ward, but thought better of it. She'd only get done for racial harassment. She beamed at Brevitt instead and tottered over to the bed by the window.

"I was after a copy of…"

"Yesterday's papers?" Drewery beamed. "Your Detective friend left some at the nursing station for you. You can look at the pictures, if you like, the doc says you shouldn't strain your eyes at present."

"Nice one, Cam!" Michaela exclaimed, ignoring the instruction as usual and grabbing the papers.

Drewery returned to the nursing station outside of the room and wickedly summoned her colleagues over to watch Brevitt's reaction through the glass.

***

It could have been worse, Parlour kidded himself as Delphine Brevitt pulled out of his driveway in a smart electric blue Mercedes A-Class. At least he'd been able to furnish her with a child-seat for the car, as she'd blotted her Super Gran copybook by forgetting this rather vital bit of baby kit. Like Mother, like Daughter, Parlour had thought, considering the fifty-something lady's pristine appearance and spotless car. He'd failed on every other front, though. How was he to know that if you didn't put the nappy on tight enough, wee would leak out the sides? Or that the vest thing with poppers went *under* the t-shirt. And apparently thirteen month babies didn't have skimmed milk and bio-active yoghurts for breakfast, either. In her haste, Michaela had only packed enough milk for the previous night's feed.

Still, it was all good practice, wasn't it? Parlour groaned. He was beginning to realise that babies, however cute and winsome they may appear, could also be quite gross and disgusting at the same time, with their diverse range of unappealing smells and anti-social physical functions.

He sniffed his arm; yuck, he could still smell that sickly sweet yoghurty goo that had seeped out of Sacha's nappy. Delphine Brevitt had informed him that Sacha had been suffering from a stomach bug that week and really shouldn't have been taken out of the home environment. Parlour couldn't have agreed more.

Parlour returned upstairs and stood under a fiercely hot shower before scrubbing at his pink skin and furiously massaging shampoo into his fine auburn hair.

Suddenly three hours of CCTV footage seemed like the premier showing of the latest Star Wars prequel as Parlour left baby care for the world of work once more.

He wandered through to the fridge to gather some supplies, cursing as he attempted to find some cheese to nibble on. Finally he spotted it right in front of him. Hopefully his peripheral vision would serve him better with those CCTV tapes. Somewhere, somehow, they held a clue to Gani's murder; hopefully viewing the tapes with fresh eyes that morning would highlight some vital clue that had escaped his notice yesterday.

Inserting the first tape again, Parlour sat cross-legged in front of his 32" plasma television screen, slurping his bowl of own brand Corn Flakes, putting them down every so often to pause the picture.

The footage covered a selection of views of Foxburgh City Centre. The first tape, which Parlour had watched first of all the previous day, covered the main town square in Foxburgh and the roads leading off it. The second tape contained comings and goings at Foxburgh train station; a third contained footage of Foxburgh's busy bus and coach station just behind the main square. The final tape contained views of the County Library, Courts of Justice and County Council headquarters, which were housed in a large white building in an administrative square to the north of the main town square.

Parlour decided to watch the last tape first, as he had watched that tape with less fresh eyes the night before. He smiled as he spotted a couple of constables known to him from Foxburgh County Police Headquarters on city centre patrol.

Parlour paid particular attention when the camera panned around to the County Library; Michaela Brevitt had mentioned yesterday that a potential reason for Gani travelling to Foxburgh that morning could have been to visit the lending library, and had admitted to a spot of dirt-digging on Roy Pedlar. That had come as no surprise to Parlour; he would have expected no less of Michaela Brevitt in the circumstances. He was not naïve enough to think that her hospitality towards Gani was entirely altruistic. It did the Respect & Tolerance Party UK no harm at all to make a stand on Salik Gani's behalf. Unfortunately, Brevitt had failed in her bold mission to attain political protection for him – if indeed Gani's murder *was* political, which was likely, but not a dead cert.

Parlour paused the picture as he thought he saw somebody he knew enter the Courts of Justice. The shot only lasted a couple of seconds, but he was fairly sure it was an acquaintance of his.

Some two hours later, and with still no evidence of Gani's whereabouts the previous day to show for his diligence, Parlour saw the same figure emerge from the Courts and walk briskly to a car parked in a bay outside. Parlour frowned, tilting his head to consider the image before him. There was something odd about it. He rewound the tape and watched again, then once more, pausing the image at set points this time.

He felt a sudden rush of blood to the head and stood up. He had absolutely no idea of the relevance, if indeed there was any, of the peculiar scenario on tape before him. But the tingling of blood in his veins told him that somehow, crazy though it seemed, he was onto something.

The telephone rang.

Parlour took a second or two to register the sound then grabbed the cordless phone from the coffee table.

It was Cameron Goodlove. Michaela Brevitt had been given the all clear after a second scan and was fit to take questions following transferral to a private unit.

Parlour grabbed his jacket, mobile and car-keys and rushed out of the front door.

30

"Thought you were off-duty," Parlour commented snidely as he entered the rather soulless single occupancy room in the private wing of Billock General Hospital with Karen Preece at quarter to twelve that morning.

Goodlove hastily broke off the deep conversation he appeared to be sharing with Michaela Brevitt, and stood up to greet his superior.

"I asked the Hossie to give me a call when Micky was fit to talk," he admitted. Parlour grimaced; he detested the influence of Australian soap operas on the English language. The Queen's English was one aspect of Britishness he preferred not to share with the rest of the Commonwealth.

Parlour exchanged the pleasantries expected of him concerning Brevitt's health and her daughter's welfare before getting down to the serious business of ascertaining what had happened the previous evening.

Unfortunately, as the blow to the back of Brevitt's head indicated, she'd had no idea of what was about to befall her when rummaging in the boot of her car. Hence she had no information to give Parlour as to the identity or appearance of her would-be killer. She had not been aware of having been followed by anyone and no, she had no idea who should want to take her life. She was able to remember leaving the flat and driving to Parlour's house; there were certainly no worries regarding her short-term memory.

"It seems rather obvious to us that Salik knew something, and his killer was terrified he'd already spilt the beans to you," Parlour commented.

Brevitt just shrugged. "I hardly saw Sal the day he died. He was there when I briefed the Party at my flat before the demo at Utopia. Then he stayed behind to person the phones and take care of Sash - or so I thought."

"He wasn't acting strangely in any way?" Parlour persevered. "Did he appear either excitable or evasive – as if he was up to something?"

"I didn't notice anything in particular," Brevitt replied, shaking her bandaged head slowly.

"You mentioned yesterday that you paid Foxburgh Library a visit the other day with Gani – to carry out some research on Roy Pedlar."

"Sal wanted to clear his name with all the nasty rumours going on about Munroe's murder," Brevitt replied. "He felt he needed some ammo on Pedlar. Despite the lack of evidence, it's hard to believe he hasn't got something to do with Munroe's – and now Salik's – death."

"I still don't get it, though," Karen Preece commented to Parlour, as they nipped outside on the pretext of fetching some coffee. "Why would Pedlar get one of his own bumped off?"

"Petty jealousy?" Parlour suggested. "Munroe wanted Pedlar's job and had dug some dirt on him himself. Pedlar decided to get Munroe removed, so to speak. Gani saw something, perhaps he wasn't that blotto at the allotments after all, so he had to go as well. Pedlar thought Gani probably told Micky here, so she had to be taken care of… do we have an alibi for Pedlar for last night?"

"He said he was in all evening working on the computer and went to bed around midnight," Preece replied, staring at her notepad. "His wife corroborated his story, though admittedly she went up to bed about nine o'clock to read and fell asleep soon after."

Preece's bleeper went. "Excuse me, boss."

She returned two minutes later. "That was Denton. They've traced Alicia Munroe; she's staying at her sister's apartment in Marbella!"

"Marvellous!" Parlour groaned.

"Can't we just order her back?" Preece wondered.

"Extradite her on what grounds?" her senior colleague replied. "There's no evidence to link her with the murder of Munroe beyond the purely circumstantial. We can't drag her all the way back just because she disobeyed a request from us to stay in the country. She'd probably contest extradition in any case; she's no shrinking violet."

"So what do you want to do?" Preece frowned.

"Fancy a jolly to the South of Spain?" Parlour grinned. Preece broke into a smile.

"Is that my reward for digging up Deverton Allotments?"

"Call it payment in kind," Parlour winked rather flirtatiously at her, as she left him standing at the vending machine. He cleared his throat then returned to Michaela's single room, lips twitching as Goodlove hastily ended a private conversation with Brevitt.

"When precisely did you leave for our house?" Parlour enquired of the bandaged woman, flicking open his PDA. "I know Jules rang you about nine."

Brevitt considered her movements the previous evening. "I guess I took about fifteen, twenty minutes all in all, from phone to car. I'd say about twenty past nine, to err on the side of caution."

Goodlove glanced at Parlour. Roy Pedlar could easily have slipped out that evening if his wife had nodded off early. It was a shame there hadn't been a soul around that evening. But it had been dark and there were no amenities on that particular stretch of Upper Foxburgh Road to cause people to be milling around at that time of night. The houses that ran along the bendy road that wound its way in an east-west direction from one side of Deverton to the other were mostly set back from the road, their occupants enjoying the privacy afforded them by a wall of leylandii planted by the developers at the time of construction. It would also have been pretty easy to siphon off the contents of Brevitt's fuel tank in the dark, private, underground car park.

"And you saw absolutely nothing?" Parlour checked.

Brevitt shook her head. "Sorry."

"Nobody acting strangely?" Goodlove persisted.

"I was thinking of Salik," Brevitt said, shaking her head sadly. "My head was full of all that's happened these last few days."

"That's understandable," Parlour nodded in sympathy. He looked across to Cameron Goodlove. "Can you pull Pedlar in for questioning?"

Goodlove sighed. He was wrecked, having spent half the evening with Michaela Brevitt at the hospital. Another altercation with that pompous waste of space was not an appealing proposition at that exact moment in time. He rose slowly to his feet.

"See you later, Micks," he winked at her, before vacating the room, his inappropriate familiarity with Brevitt causing Parlour to cringe. Mind you, it would cheer Jules up no end to know she'd instigated romantic proceedings between his new Detective Sergeant and her new friend.

It was a blow that Brevitt could offer nothing in the way of information concerning her assailant, Parlour thought ruefully, his thoughts turning back to the perplexing murder inquiry once more. He was not satisfied, however, that Gani had not provided at least one clue to explain his mysterious visit to Foxburgh that Monday morning. He did not believe for one minute Gani had travelled twenty odd miles to Foxburgh by public transport with a small toddler in tow simply to carry out further research at the public library. Gani clearly had a desperate need to be in the county town that morning, to have gone to so much grief.

"Is there anything, however insignificant it may seem to you, that struck you as odd about Salik's behaviour these past few days?" Parlour tried again. "Or has anything strange happened?"

"What, beyond two murders and an attempt on my life?" Brevitt enquired archly.

"Has anything out of the ordinary taken place – even something quite trivial?" Parlour persevered.

Brevitt made a face, deciding whether the monitor thing was worth mentioning.

"We had some interference on the baby monitors," Brevitt replied finally. "Sal was listening in on it, out of curiosity."

"Go on," Parlour leaned forward in his chair.

"He heard some woman having a barny with a man over the airwaves. Presumably someone with a baby who had their monitors on at the same time. I was there the first time it happened. She was pretty hysterical. When I was around your place for dinner, they started up again, apparently. Only this time, it got violent. Sal said it sounded as if the woman was being beaten."

Parlour frowned. "Any ideas who it was? Are there any other mums with young children in the flats around you?"

Brevitt shook her head. "Well this is it, no. These apartments aren't designed for families with kids."

"Was Salik snooping around, trying to work out who the woman was?" Goodlove enquired.

"He said he'd worked it out," Brevitt replied.

"What?!" Parlour leant even further forward. His heart was thumping; as with the video footage earlier, he had the feeling this was highly relevant, though again, it was unclear precisely why.

"He was going to tell me," Brevitt said miserably. "He said he'd worked out who was talking on the monitors. He tried to tell me yesterday morning, but I was too busy organising the counter-demo. If only I'd paid more attention…"

But Parlour was no longer listening. He stood up, turned this way then that, his suit jacket swinging from side to side as the pixels of the picture began to form a mosaic in his mind.

Parlour sat down as more and more pieces of the puzzle began to fly towards a central meeting point in his brain, propelled by a force seemingly independent of him. He put his head in his hands, dizzied by the frenetic activity going on between his ears. It couldn't be, could it? No, surely not! But it fitted...

"What is it, boss?" Goodlove enquired, but Parlour was in far too much of a rush to explain.

"Can you take Sean with you to visit Pedlar...oh, and try and get hold of Alicia Munroe by telephone – I need to ask her a few things urgently, Karen won't get there till early evening, I expect. Here – I've made a list of questions we need to ask her." Parlour tore a leaf of paper from a spiral bound notebook and thrust it in Goodlove's huge right hand.

"Right-o," Goodlove replied, stuffing the list in his pocket and giving Brevitt a bewildered glance as Parlour nearly sent a porter flying in his haste to leave the hospital.

***

C'mon c'mon c'mon! Parlour growled, slapping the middle of the steering wheel impatiently as he got held up at yet another red light on the road out of Billock.

Some ten minutes later, he had emerged from the dense lunchtime traffic and was out onto the open road. Parlour put his foot down, deciding he could justify the excess speed in the circumstances. Within fifteen minutes, he had parked up at the entrance to Deverton Allotments and was sprinting down the hill to the plot where Salik Gani's shed still stood, the side panel re-attached following forensic investigations.

Fuchsia! Parlour cursed, seeing the padlock was locked. He got a safety pin from his pocket and after a bit of tinkering, succeeded in manipulating the lock. He didn't anticipate finding the main item he was searching for within the shed itself, but perhaps a clue that he was on the right track. But there was no evidence. Parlour took a deep breath and stood outside the shed. He looked around him, then spotted one of those large black bins with the holes in the sides, for burning garden waste in. Donning some latex gloves, Parlour began to sift through the contents of the nearest one, cursing at intervals as thorny branches pierced through the filmy material of the protective hand wear.

But he still couldn't find the evidence he required. Parlour debated calling in the Police Dog Control Unit. But that would be expensive in the circumstances, and he was still operating on a hunch, albeit a very strong one. Parlour returned to the top of the hill and looked down on the allotments. He considered the black bins dotted around the site. If he were the killer, trying to bury evidence, where would he stash it? At home, or in the boot of one's car was too obvious. He'd burn it, for sure. Perhaps it was naïve to think the killer would perform this deed in close proximity to Gani and Munroe's sheds.

Parlour meandered back down to a bin at the opposite end of the allotments to Gani's shed. He paused briefly before rummaging inside once more, this time hauling all the contents out onto the ground, trying to ignore the constant jabbing of thorns in flesh. Juliet would have a field day removing all those thorns from his hands that evening. It didn't occur to Parlour that she may just have something better to do.

Once he had finished that task, he bent down and poured over the contents of the bin, separating the rubbish with gloved fingers.

Hello, what have we here? Parlour pulled up some ragged material in his hand and felt his heart thump against his ribcage. He paused for a moment before bagging it and placing it in his inside pocket. A quick trip to the forensic lab should confirm his suspicions.

Meanwhile, he needed to ensure his quarry didn't escape.

***

"So you're sure you saw absolutely no-one at the allotments the day your husband died?" Cameron Goodlove double-checked with Alicia Munroe on the remarkably clear phone-line to Southern Spain. He had connected the telephone up to a recording device, so that Parlour could hear the interview for himself later if required.

"I'm not proud of the fact, but as I've told your lot on several occasions already, I was pretty far gone, as was Salik. As far as I can recollect, the place was deserted. I can't remember seeing anyone around, but I *was* larking around with Mr Gani at the time and could have missed something."

"Were there any cars parked nearby?"

"There were no cars parked at the top of the allotments and there's no way of getting a vehicle down to the actual sheds. It's a sharp descent."

"Yes, we know," Goodlove conceded. The steep gradient of the large plot had caused many a grumble during both murder investigations so far. "And were there any cars parked up on the road outside, close to the allotments?"

"There aren't any houses up there, are there?" Munroe replied. "You would park in the allotments if…" her voice broke off and Goodlove sensed she was recollecting some piece of information.

"Mrs Munroe?" Goodlove prodded her gently. He uttered her name again. Finally she emerged from her reverie and broke the silence.

"There is something," she began slowly. "Again, it's all rather embarrassing. We were very tipsy, Salik and me."

"We've gathered that, Mrs Munroe," Goodlove chuckled, trying to put her at ease. He could tell her many a tale of drunken escapades featuring his good self, but it was probably taking his empathic skills a little far.

"I do recall walking up Upper Foxburgh Road and stumbling a little. Sal said something funny, or at least, it seemed hilariously funny in the way everything does when you've been drinking…"

"Yes yes," Goodlove said with less patience this time, as a note was thrust under his nose by a junior colleague, informing him that Parlour was anxious for news from Spain.

"Well, I sort of slapped him on the back as I was laughing and he pushed me in the arm. I wobbled and fell against this car that was parked on the side of the road, oh, about fifty yards down from the entrance to the allotments. I bent the wing mirror right back; Sal tried to ping it into place for me but I think I'd broken something inside the casing. It wouldn't go back on as it was. In the end we just gave up and carried on going. I thought about writing a note to plop under the wipers, but I guess I just forgot about it, with what happened afterwards."

"Of course," Goodlove muttered, but his heart was thumping. He wasn't sure if this was important or not, but it was the best evidential offering they'd had for a while.

"What sort of car was it?" Goodlove asked, trying not to sound too animated too soon.

There was a pause on the line. "That I couldn't say," Munroe replied finally. "But it was dark coloured, dark blue or grey or green… those dark metallic colours all kind of look the same to me. And big… Sal made some comment about me choosing that car of all cars to trash…" Munroe's voice tailed off. "Much more than that, I can't recall, I'm sorry. Could it be important?"

"Possibly," Goodlove replied, smiling to himself and slapping the table victoriously. She could have made it all up, of course, to deflect attention away from someone, possibly even herself. It couldn't be entirely ruled out that she had nothing to do with either murder, unlikely though it was in the circumstances, especially now that her best friend had been killed as well. In any case, her story seemed plausible enough.

Goodlove tied up the interview with Munroe's widow, barely able to contain the excitement burbling up inside. *Pedlar* had a big dark saloon car and had been potentially free to chase Michaela through the streets of Deverton. Who was to say he didn't lend his car to someone to murder Davidson Munroe during the World Cuisine Festival – the event gave him the perfect alibi with all the media coverage. What's more, Pedlar had been very busy, very busy indeed, in ensuring he gained maximum exposure at the event.

He would make a quick call to Parlour before returning to Roy Pedlar in Interview Room One.

31

"Blimey, Roy Pedlar hasn't beaten us to it, has he?" Parlour groaned, stepping out of his car and noting the heavy media presence outside Foxburgh Crown Court at 1.30 that afternoon.

"Cam's still plying him with tea and biscuits, no worries there, boss," Darren Keough grinned, alighting from his own car parked next to Parlour's outside the imposing white building. "Did you get hold of Alicia Munroe?"

"Cam talked to her on the phone about an hour ago, she was most helpful," Parlour replied enigmatically. Keough stared at him quizzically, but Parlour was giving nothing away.

"Why are we attending the trial of the Bingo Butcher?" Keough frowned, watching some reporters interfacing with fellow journalists in the television studio, under the misguided impression that viewers found this tedious inter-journalistic speculation on the outcome of a trial vaguely interesting.

"Wait and see, Darren, wait and see!" Parlour replied mysteriously, walking briskly towards the back of the Chambers.

"Haven't they got some big-wig judge in from London?" Keough enquired.

"One of the very biggest wigs," Parlour said darkly. He had not yet informed his staff as to the nature of his visit to the Crown Courts. There was just one vital piece of evidence to check out before he ran in, all guns blazing.

"Hi Stu, glad you could make it," Parlour smiled, slapping the back of his good friend, Forensic scientist Stuart Beattie.

Keough frowned, annoyed at being kept in the dark by Parlour. He skipped to keep up with the other two men as they pushed through the agitated throng of journalists, flashing their police badges to ease their passage into the building.

"Phew," Parlour exhaled, brushing the sleeves of his suit jacket once safely inside. After a consultation with a security guard and a bit more badge-waving, the threesome from

Billock CID made their way downstairs and through a labyrinth of corridors.

"Sir, I don't understand," Keough grumbled, as Parlour exclaimed in delight at what appeared to be some sort of cloakroom.

"Just need to check something out first, Darren," Parlour smiled smoothly, though his heart was thumping against his chest wall once more as the adrenalin pumped furiously around his skinny body. If he was right, this was some coup… and a bit of a shocker, to boot. Not least for him. He would certainly need to revisit his own judgement.

Keough sat inwardly fuming in the corner as Parlour and Beattie began searching coat pockets for a set of car keys.

***

Beattie's team had just located the suspect's car and begun their initial inspections, when the call came through from Goodlove. The condition of the wing mirror was duly noted along with some other interesting findings from the inside of the dark coloured vehicle. Parlour hadn't batted an eyelid at authorising one of his officers to essentially break into the private vehicle; the end would justify the means, he was sure. For along with the evidence located in the recesses of Foxburgh Crown Court, Parlour now had more than enough ammunition to arrest his suspect. But did he have the genital equipment to do so at this precise moment?

Two innocent people have lost their lives, and a further attempt was made on a young woman's life, Parlour told himself firmly.

He took a deep breath then put the call through to DCI Brian Sewell. He would need to be informed before he requested reinforcements and a secure vehicle. This case was proving to be politically sensitive in quite a different way than he had first imagined.

***

After a thorough inspection of the evidence presented to him by Parlour and Beattie, Brian Sewell had no choice but to authorise the immediate arrest of Parlour's prime suspect.

"Ooh, I feel like I'm waiting to take the stage in the school play!" Parlour laughed rather effeminately, butterflies doing acrobatics in his empty stomach. He'd forgone lunch that day in his excitement at piecing the murder puzzle together.

"Shame we're not over the pond, Sir," a fully-informed Darren Keough grinned jovially at Mark Parlour, visibly excited now the finishing post was near. "Or you'd be on live telly!"

"I know," Parlour replied, feigning disappointment. "I'll miss my fifteen minutes of fame."

"Perhaps they'll do one of those naff court-drawings of you, boss," Goodlove laughed, who'd made the breakneck journey with DCI Sewell and DC Jenkins to the county town of Foxburgh. "Want to borrow some of my ultra firm hold gel?"

Parlour laughed nervously and ran his fingers through his Brylcreemed hair. This was the most controversial arrest he'd ever had call to make in his seven years as Detective Inspector with Billock CID.

"Bloody cameras in the court-room, like some kind of Channel Four reality show!" Sewell grunted.

A visibly nervous DC Jenkins slipped out of the courtroom.

"The defence lawyer's just winding up now," he informed Parlour, stuttering slightly. "I'll bang on the door in a sec."

Parlour nodded to his junior, and took several deep breaths as Sewell patted him on the back in encouragement.

This would make or break his career; in any case, it was certainly a career defining moment. He was sure he was right; the motive was now clear and the evidence now apparent. It

260

didn't stop a little nagging voice inside querying his judgement at this, the final hour.

The knock came just moments later. It was too late to turn back now.

Help me, God, Parlour muttered, stared at the ceiling one last time, then marched into the packed courtroom.

A sea of well-known legal correspondents and an even better-known officiate of the law turned Parlour's way as he strode across the chamber to the judge's seat.

"Farquahar Ralph Briscoe:- I arrest you on suspicion of the murders of Davidson Munroe and Salik Gani, and the attempted murder of Michaela Brevitt. You do not have to say anything. But it may harm your defence if you do not mention when questioned something which you later rely on in court. Anything you do say may be given in evidence."

Oh the irony of it, Parlour thought to himself, almost feeling the air being sucked from his skinny frame as the court-room took a collective intake of breath.

Farque Briscoe gave Parlour a steely-eyed glance that spoke of revenge as two strapping young constables from Foxburgh police headquarters escorted him, handcuffed, to a waiting police van. Parlour gave his acquaintance a long hard look.

Don't you think you can trash my career, Mr So-Called Dispenser of Justice, Parlour's stare said. *You're going to die at Her Majesty's pleasure.*

32

"Front page of *The Times*!" Juliet Parlour exclaimed, prodding proudly at the crayon portrayal of her husband's entry to the packed court-room the previous day.

"Beat that, Black Pudding!" Cameron Goodlove grinned, squishing Michaela Brevitt's rather cherubic cheeks.

Only he could get away with that, Juliet thought to herself, considering both the physical gesture and the reference to the rather unflattering photo from the Foxburgh Herald of Michaela standing disconsolately and unwittingly before a poster advertising Utopia Finest Black Pudding at the demo the other day. Brevitt had been very good-natured about the whole thing in the end.

"They've skimped on the carotene," Brevitt joked, considering the grainy court-room artwork that straddled the front pages of most of the daily papers that day, and which had even made it to several international publications.

"And the crow's feet," Juliet giggled, slapping her husband fondly on the back. "You look about twenty-five in it!"

"I must concede, it is rather flattering," Parlour chuckled. "More tea, vicar?"

"Please," Martin Beauville smiled, offering his mug up to his friend and parishioner late that Wednesday afternoon.

"I'll be saying that to you, soon," Parlour smiled at Penny Roquet, who had also joined them for the unofficial friends and family debriefing in the Parlours' conservatory that afternoon.

"I do hope so," Roquet quivered in reply. Despite her rather public fall from grace, that had also enjoyed some media coverage, she had thoroughly enjoyed her time as ordinand at Deverton Parish Church.

Parlour relaxed back into one of the director's chairs Juliet and he had chosen to furnish their conservatory with instead of the standard wicker fare Parlour so detested. Around him sat his new colleague, Cameron Goodlove; Karen Preece, freshly arrived from Spain; Martin Beauville and Penny Roquet from Deverton Parish Church; Juliet of course, and Michaela Brevitt. Nazrul Gani had already been put completely in the picture regarding his brother's murder, as had Alicia Munroe in a telephone conversation with Parlour himself. Parlour had also invited DCI Sewell to join their little soiree, but he had declined, having a prior invitation to a golf tournament in Chave.

"Please, Mark, put us out of our misery!" Juliet exclaimed, cutting through the niceties. Following an intense period of press activity followed by numerous debriefings and finally the dreaded paperwork, Parlour had not arrived home until the early hours that morning. There he had been met on the doorstep by yet more journalists from the national and local press, which he had successfully dispersed with the promise of a photo-shoot the following day, once he'd caught up on his sleep.

Though Juliet had heard of Parlour's daring arrest of Farquahar Briscoe in the middle of the Bingo Butcher trial at Foxburgh Crown Court, she had as yet, like the others present at the little gathering, no idea of the ins and outs of the double murder case. Preece and Goodlove had been filled in as regards the identity and motive of the killer, but Parlour had kept the finer details of his investigation and personal triumph to himself thus far.

"What do you want to know?" Parlour asked infuriatingly, though in truth, he hardly knew where to start. "Farque Briscoe murdered Davidson Munroe, as he discovered Munroe was having an affair with his daughter-in-law…"

"With Lins?" Juliet exclaimed, completely shocked.

"He decided to take his chance while the whole village was at the church for the World Cuisine Festival," continued Parlour unabashed as his wife sat open-mouthed. "Briscoe Senior sent Munroe a note purportedly from his daughter-in-law, asking him to meet her at the allotments, their usual meeting place, at two pm. Only he didn't bargain on Salik Gani and Alicia Munroe making an unexpected trip to the allotments to continue their boozy afternoon. Unknown to him, Alicia Munroe had stumbled on the main road up to the allotments where he had discreetly left his car, and had a close encounter with the wing mirror of his Rolls. She forgot all about it until questioned yesterday; Gani hadn't forgotten about the car incident though and along with some other evidence, put two and two together and worked out the identity of the mysterious visitor to the allotments – Munroe's killer."

"What other evidence?" Juliet frowned.

"The baby monitors!" Michaela Brevitt exclaimed.

The others looked mystified as Parlour nodded, smiling.

"Micky here had some interference on her baby monitors. If someone nearby also has baby monitors on, it's possible to pick up conversation and other background noise over the airwaves."

"Well I never!" Juliet exclaimed. They would have to be careful, in their respective professions, if and when the Petit Parlour arrived.

"Salik heard a woman arguing with a man on Sacha's monitor," Parlour continued. "It seemed pretty nasty stuff. He never got around to telling Micky the whole story, as they got sidetracked by the demo outside Utopia. But he had obviously worked out the identity of both parties. Unfortunately, Gani decided to take matters into his own hands and pursue Briscoe himself, with a view to getting revenge for framing him over Davidson Munroe's murder. It was clear Gani had witnessed something or someone the day before he died. My guess is that he discovered the identity of the woman on the monitors and realised this was an argument over a man. Lindsay Briscoe lives just around the corner from Michaela Brevitt, in Maris Piper Way, *and* has young children; Gani realised it was her voice on the monitor and presumably recognised Farque Briscoe's, too. He delivers papers – though not to them - it's my guess that he'd overheard them talking on one of his rounds and knew their voices. A police officer is with Lindsay Briscoe at the moment, and I gather she has substantial bruising to the left cheek."

Penny Roquet subconsciously brushed her hand across her own cheek.

"The vicious bastard!" Juliet exclaimed. "So that's why she wasn't at church on Sunday… we thought it was odd. She makes a point of attending whenever possible – and informing us of the fact as well."

"Gani went to see The Honourable Mr Justice Briscoe at Foxburgh Crown Court the morning he died. He knew from the television coverage of the Bingo Butcher case that Briscoe was in Foxburgh that morning; his family told me he had a bit of a fixation with the local news, my guess is he saw Briscoe enter the Courts of Justice on *Southern Aspect* or something, when they do their pointless reports outside empty buildings. At a guess, Briscoe went in to attend to some administrative matter prior to the trial. Gani presumably accosted Briscoe in a downstairs chamber. He was no match for Farque Briscoe, though. Briscoe force-fed him a cup of our favourite 70s weed killer. However, unlike in the case of Davidson Munroe, there were no bruises to the face, so it initially appeared to be suicide. However, Gani was a very slight figure; there wouldn't be much force required on Briscoe's part to restrain Gani. Indeed, slight bruising to the wrists tell us Briscoe held Gani's hands behind his back with one hand and administered the paraquat with the other. He then bundled Gani into the back of the Rolls."

"What?" Preece exclaimed. "How on earth…."

Parlour waggled a video tape in the air. "This held the clue to it, the boring old CCTV footage I trawled through not once but twice! It was only on the second viewing that I spotted something rather odd. Farque Briscoe emerges from the rear of the courts holding what appears to be a very packed suit carrier over his arm.”

There was a collective intake of breath at the chilling and rather gruesome explanation of how Gani’s body was removed by the killer from the scene of the crime.

“As I zoomed in on the image, I could see that Briscoe was grimacing, as if he was carrying a very heavy load, not just a couple of legal gowns. At this point, Gani’s body was still floppy. He was a slight man; nevertheless, his body would have still been a considerable weight to bear over one’s arm. But Briscoe had to give the appearance of carrying clothes. His car was parked up right next to the entrance, as visiting High Court Judge and big noise. It was fortunate for him that it was only a short journey from the back of the Crown Court to his car, thereby providing only the briefest of excerpts of CCTV footage.”

“He dumped the body in the boot then drove to the allotments and made it look like suicide,” Goodlove surmised.

Parlour nodded. “We’ve now questioned Briscoe, and it transpires that Gani had approached Briscoe for money, saying he needed to buy himself a new flat after what the local thugs had done to his place. He banked on the fact that Briscoe would want to save public face at all costs and would give into his demands. But Farque Briscoe isn’t the type of man to be controlled by anyone, and decided to nip the Gani issue in the bud. I guess he figured Gani would continue to blackmail him for infinity, which may well have been the case – we’ll never know now – but he didn’t bank on getting caught on camera.”

“I guess he knew there was a risk of being spotted,” Preece mused, “hence the impromptu body-bag.” She smiled warmly at her boss. “Just his bad luck *you* happened to be trawling through the CCTV footage. Can’t imagine many of us would have spotted that little cameo by Briscoe.”

“And Gani,” Goodlove added macabrely.

"But what on earth would someone Lindsay's age want with an old sleaze like Davidson Munroe?" Juliet interrupted, unable to contain her curiosity any longer.

Parlour shrugged. "Charles isn't at home much these days, is he? And he has let himself go a bit…"

"It's no excuse for adultery!" Penny Roquet commented, surprising them all with the vehemence of her tone. Martin Beauville shot her a sidelong glance. Perhaps there was some history of family break-up in Penny's past; that might go some way to explaining her lack of social confidence. The sudden removal of a much loved parental figure from the family equation could have devastating effects on some individuals that carried through to their adult life. Perhaps he should be a little more tolerant of her less than dynamic demeanour.

"So Munroe did go – pardon the schoolgirl language – *all the way* with Lindsay?" Preece queried, looking confused.

"Apparently so," Parlour confirmed.

"But…" Preece stuttered.

"He never did with his previous bits on the side? I thought Alicia was just deluding herself at first, but then the women in his past confirmed he'd stopped at amber. Alicia seemed so sure he hadn't cheated on her; I then thought, maybe she knows something we don't. Immediately I jumped to the conclusion that he was impotent, hence her confidence that he'd never had an affair in the full sense of the word. Yet if this was a crime of passion, it didn't really make sense that Munroe would be killed over a bit of slap and tickle in the shed. I felt sure he must have committed the final act this time – which made me wonder whether he'd taken something for his *problem*."

"What, Viagra?" Juliet snickered.

Parlour nodded. "Precisely. But there had been no traces of it in his system, when Hunter opened him up. A chap preparing for a bit of action would have to take a Viagra pill about 45 minutes before performing the.. erm.. deed. Munroe obviously hadn't, so bang went my theory, pardon the pun."

Juliet giggled.

"So why *was* Alicia so trusting?" Preece wondered.

Parlour grinned. "Do you really want to know?"

He subconsciously slouched back in his chair, opening his legs a little wider.

"Mark! Don't be such a tease!" Juliet exclaimed.

"He was hung like a dachshund!" Parlour guffawed.

"No!" Beauville exclaimed. "But Munroe was such a …

"Stud?" Parlour chuckled, enjoying watching Penny Roquet squirm in the corner.

"So he didn't do it with all those girls because he…" Beauville faltered.

"Was more gherkin than courgette!" Juliet hooted. Roquet frowned, less from embarrassment than from discomfort at their mirth over another's perceived misfortune.

"He was ashamed of his small penis," Parlour confirmed. "But then along came Lindsay, who's…"

"Married to Charles!" Juliet guffawed.

"Who's kind and understanding and very different from the more shallow women he'd been involved with in the past." Parlour stated.

"And an adulteress," Preece interjected dryly.

"They made each other feel good," Parlour shrugged.

"Munroe was having a bit of a midlife crisis; Lindsay was lonely and desperate for affection."

"If you don't mind me asking, Sir," Goodlove began, "how do you know about Mr Munroe's tackle?"

Parlour grinned. "When I first viewed the body, Hunter had covered up the lower half with a white sheet. I had no reason to look down below - the man was poisoned with weed killer, after all. But when I shot a blank with the impotence theory, I decided to pay our little friend a visit!"

"It's not really a laughing matter, Mark," Beauville chided him, his conscience suddenly pricking him.

"I just can't see how they got together in the first place, though," Juliet stated, eventually. "Where did their paths cross? It's not as if Munroe was a churchgoer, or Lins was involved in the BASC party…"

"I asked myself the very same question," Parlour conceded. "So I ploughed back through my notes on the various interviews. I then reread the forensic report on Munroe, and something struck me as odd. I had a substance found on his clothing further investigated. The results of these findings, coupled with an item of interest in Lindsay Briscoe's kitchen, gave me the answer."

Juliet snorted, as only she had liberty to do so. "Well that's as clear as mud, Mark!"

"Elucidate, my dear friend," Beauville grinned.

"Cakes brought them together," Parlour smiled.

"They rendezvoused at the potting shed to scoff Battenberg?" Juliet frowned.

"Lends a whole new meaning to waiting for the sponge to rise!" Goodlove guffawed. Parlour shot him a warning glare; they were in the presence of female clergy after all. But the comment was entirely lost on Roquet.

"Do you remember that when Munroe's body was found, they discovered fruitcake crumbs down his front and traces of fruitcake in his stomach?" Parlour began.

"But we decided it was no big deal, since you couldn't move for grannies with fruitcakes at the BASC stall that Saturday," Preece added, looking puzzled.

"We dismissed the fruitcake crumbs initially," Parlour nodded. "But when I reread my initial interviews with Alicia Munroe, I picked up on a snippet of information. Some fried food was found among the contents of her husband's stomach when our forensic team examined him. As we were naturally keen to establish what precisely he had eaten and drunk that day, we asked his wife to confirm what he had had for breakfast that Saturday morning. Alicia Munroe informed our constable that Davidson had cooked a fry-up as usual, consisting of bacon, tomatoes, mushrooms, sausages and fried bread. He *hadn't* fried any eggs, as he was intolerant of them."

"You're not telling me someone force-fed him a boiled egg, are you?" Juliet scoffed incredulously.

"Oh no, it was the paraquat that killed him alright," Parlour replied, "there were no traces of egg in his stomach at all."

"So what are you getting at?" Juliet frowned.

Preece snapped her slender fingers. "The fruitcake! It would have contained eggs.."

"Three or four of the blighters," Goodlove chipped in.

"But it didn't," Parlour stated enigmatically.

"I'm confused," Juliet frowned.

"The fruitcake contained no traces of eggs at all."

"A fruitcake *without* eggs?" Martin Beauville exclaimed, palpably shocked at the concept. "Mrs Simpson's prize fruitcake at the World Cuisine Festival was egg-free?"

Parlour shook his head. "Oh, Audrey Simpson's fruitcake contained eggs alright, as did the other offerings from Deverton WI."

"So what are you saying, boss?" Karen Preece frowned. "Munroe was fed some kind of brown substance masquerading as fruitcake?"

"Fruitfake!" Cameron giggled but nobody laughed.

"Take a look at this," Parlour grinned, tossing a glossy brochure at his two Detective Sergeants. It was advertising literature for Lindsay Briscoe's home-baking business, *Tumtations*.

"Your attention is drawn to the penultimate page," he instructed his rapt audience.

"Dairy-free products," Goodlove read out.

"Oh my goodness!" Preece exclaimed, prodding her forefinger on an item half way down the page. "Molly Cake:- sample our *egg-free* fruitcake, an exquisitely moist, dairy-free fruit fest, to rival the very finest of traditional recipes!"

"I still don't get it," Juliet moaned.

"That's the link between Lindsay Briscoe and Munroe," Preece continued excitedly. "She baked him egg-free products, didn't she?"

Parlour nodded. "That's how they were introduced. A friend of a friend knew of Munroe's intolerance to eggs and suggested Lindsay Briscoe, the local speciality baker. She came up with some recipes for him and an acquaintance was made. She was bored, lonely, fed up of Charles drinking himself silly with his golf cronies. Davidson Munroe was local, interested in her – it probably wasn't that hard to get his way with her after some initial resistance."

Juliet shuddered at the thought of anyone getting close and personal with the ageing sunbed god, least of all her good friend and solid churchwoman, Lindsay Briscoe.

"But surely Alicia could have baked his special fruitcakes?" Karen Preece frowned. "She worked for Lindsay, didn't she?"

"I wondered that," Parlour conceded, "and when I spotted the fruitcake issue in my notes, I initially thought the evidence pointed to his wife. So I questioned Alicia Munroe about it. It transpires that Lindsay Briscoe enlisted Alicia Munroe's help to help out with traditional fare, Victoria Sponges, scones etcetera, leaving her free to bake the speciality stuff. It was during their initial introduction that Lindsay discovered Alicia was a half decent cook herself, and decided to take her on as an extra pair of hands. It may well be the case that Salik Gani had bumped into Lindsay at Alicia's house, too, which helped him put two and two together. In any case, it was Lindsay who concocted the dairy free delicacies for Munroe."

"So he'd been eating one of her cakes on the day he was murdered?" Preece looked baffled.

"Or more likely, given the quantity of cake crumbs down the front of his shirt, he was force-fed them by Farquahar Briscoe along with the killer cuppa," Parlour stated. "It would account for the finger marks on Munroe's cheeks, where

Briscoe presumably held his face in his hands. Briscoe knew the Molly cake was Munroe's favourite delicacy of Lindsay's, and decided to ram the stuff down his throat."

"As a payback for sticking his tongue down his daughter-in-law's throat," Juliet grinned.

"Please!" Michaela protested.

"The Briscoes weren't at the Cuisine Festival," Beauville mused.

"They had a birthday bash at home," Parlour nodded. "I dropped by on the way back from the church that day; I had a book to lend to Charles.   Charlie Boy was well sozzled, I thought I'd look out for his old man for a chinwag instead, but he was nowhere to be seen. We now know he nipped off to Deverton Allotments."

Juliet whistled. "So Farque Briscoe bumped off Salik Gani because Gani saw him up there?"

"Gani only saw his car, actually," Parlour corrected his wife. "It wasn't until he heard the argument on the baby monitors and saw Lindsay Briscoe at the play park with a black eye that he sussed it all out. I guess, as well, that he recognised Farquahar Briscoe's voice from television or from a chance encounter. Briscoe does have quite a distinct, upper-class snarly voice."

"And it was Briscoe who tried to kill *me*?" Michaela wondered.

Parlour nodded soberly. "The evidence pointed to Pedlar, of course – the dark saloon car, the inability of his wife to provide a cast-iron alibi for him. But of course Briscoe has a dark green Rolls, which, under the influence of alcohol, wouldn't necessarily stand out above any other dark coloured expensive saloon car."

"So all the political stuff…" Preece began.

"Complete red herring," Parlour replied swiftly. "This was to do with one man's furious desire to protect the family property."

"But why resort to murder?" Juliet enquired. "I mean, he is a High Court Judge… *was,* I should say. You'd think that he, of all people, would know not to take the law into his own hands."

"You would think so, wouldn't you," Parlour agreed. "I guess he thought he was above the law, and in a manner of speaking, he was. A judge of his fellow men, sat high above them in the Courts of Justice, with the power to send others down to their fate. His arrogance was his downfall, of course."

There was a moment of sober silence.

"He tried to reason with both Lindsay and with Munroe, from what I can gather from Mrs Briscoe. He begged her to stop the liaison with Munroe, and became more and more agitated when she refused to stop meeting him. In the end he decided there was nothing for it but to put a final stop to matters himself."

"Why didn't he just tell Charles?" Juliet wondered.

Parlour shrugged. "I guess he thought it would break him. Charles's career is on the slide by all accounts, none of us realised he was in trouble, though the signs were there. Whatever you think of a man who kills two of his fellow men and threatens the life of an innocent woman and mother of a young child, you can't deny his fierce loyalty to his son and his love for his family."

"But Farque Briscoe!" Juliet still gasped incredulously.

"So where did he get the 1970s paraquat from?" Beauville enquired.

"Briscoe Senior worked in South Africa for some ten years back in the late sixties, early seventies," Parlour explained. "He must have brought some of the nasty stuff back with him. It didn't occur to us to look for some kind of colonial link to the paraquat."

"And the blue note?" Goodlove enquired, anxious to tie up all the loose ends so that he could relax once more.

"Briscoe mimicked Lindsay's handwriting. It wasn't hard, she wrote in tiny capital letters. He used the blue paper favoured by Roy Pedlar in his key-pebble notes as a ruse to point the finger at Pedlar."

"Did he have it in for Pedlar, then?" Beauville enquired.

"Pedlar had had several run-ins with our esteemed friend in the past, court appearances for breach of the peace etc. Pedlar moved here from…."

"Surrey!" Preece realised, clicking her fingers.

"I don't think Briscoe had any personal grievance against Pedlar," Parlour continued. "At a guess, he just thought it a good wheeze to point the finger at Pedlar. It was highly convenient in the circumstances."

"What a bloody waste of police time!" Goodlove groaned, recalling all the hours spent trailing Pedlar and his cronies.

Parlour shrugged. "It was always in the back of my mind that this could be some unrelated personal matter, but of course we had to investigate Pedlar and co in the circumstances."

"Salik beat you all to it, though," Michaela observed with loyalty to her late friend.

"It's just a tragedy he didn't think to report his findings to us instead of going it alone," Parlour replied to a murmur of sober agreement.

"And how's Alicia?" Beauville enquired, not wishing to forget the widow of Briscoe's first victim.

"Distraught," Parlour replied. As predicted, Alicia Munroe had been simultaneously devastated and deeply embittered by news of the double betrayal she had suffered at the hands of her late husband and business partner, Lindsay Briscoe. "We're leaving her alone for a couple of days. She's going to fly back for the funeral some time next week, once we've tied up all the loose ends."

"Well, send her our very best regards, won't you?" Beauville responded immediately.

Parlour nodded and left the room.

Goodlove rubbed his hands together and rose to his feet also. "Come on, Micks, got a train to catch."

The shutters were pulled down and padlocked when Parlour arrived at Gani's Mini Mart just after 1pm. It was unsurprising in the tragic circumstances, despite the conscientious and stoical nature of the tenants in question.

Parlour mooched around to the scruffy rear of the building and trod over some sodden cardboard boxes to knock gently on the back door. There was no response - hardly surprising, since *Sky Sports* could be heard blaring loudly through an open window. Parlour recognised the cosy tones of the golf commentary he had himself dipped into at intervals that week, during those rare instances, and instances they indeed were, when he found himself with a spare moment.

He knocked far more firmly this time, and then again until the volume was turned down on the surround sound television and the anxious, pinched face of Zoreena Gani appeared at the upstairs window. A look of relief came over her, as she realised it was the friendly local DI, and not more riff-raff with notepads.

She appeared at the back door a moment later and he followed her upstairs to the cramped flat above the shop, where Nazrul Gani was attempting to follow the golf whilst the Play Station bleeped and zapped on the other side of the room, the Gani offspring spread out on the floor before it, squealing and squawking as they wrestled the controls from one another.

Nazrul saluted Parlour without bothering to rise from the leather armchair. Normally Parlour would find that rather boorish, but he was inclined towards leniency on this occasion.

"Black coffee, wasn't it?" his wife smiled wanly.

"You know me so well," Parlour replied, not intending to sound flirty, though he couldn't deny he found Zoreena Gani rather attractive with her pouting lips and glossy dark eyes. He followed her into the tiny galley style kitchen, where barely an inch of work surface could be found among sky-high towers of dirty dishes and cooking ingredients, not to mention dozens of empty cola cans, crushed, perhaps in despair or vehemence.

"Scuse the mess," Zoreena sniffed. "It was Bangladesh Independence on Monday, we had a big family meal Sunday night… minus Salik. And then…"

"It's OK, Mrs Gani, I haven't come to carry out a hygiene inspection!" Parlour smiled, trying to put her at ease.

"No Grandpa Gani?" he enquired, leaning back against the doorframe, in the absence of an uncluttered worktop to rest his weary back against.

Zoreena nodded in the direction of the back bedroom, rolling her dark eyes. "Hasn't got up since he heard the news about Salik. Nazrul's not much better, think he's got Velcro pads on that armchair of his. Leaving me to sort out all the burial and stuff."

Parlour nodded in sympathy. He knew a little about the rituals surrounding the death of a Muslim family member; it was a lot of hard work for Zoreena to take on alongside caring for six others at home and dealing with her own grief at the loss of a loved one.

"When will Salik's body be released, you know, to take to the mosque?" Zoreena enquired, filling the kettle.

"Very soon," Parlour comforted her. "The cause of death has been established. There'll be a post-mortem, of course, but I can't see any reason why we can't proceed as soon as possible."

He nodded towards the back room. "Is old Mr Gani alright in there?"

Parlour baulked at the thought of the frail and wizened figure of the most senior member of the Gani family left to his own devices at this desperate time for them all.

"I looked in on him ten minutes ago," Zoreena reassured Parlour. She shrugged and looked rather balefully at the skinny ginger Inspector. "He's lost the will to live, I'm afraid. I take him in cups of tea but he barely touches them. He was always far closer to Salik than Naz. Second son syndrome and all that – far less responsibilities on Salik's shoulders, Dada put far less pressure on him. They had a much more relaxed relationship."

"Unfortunately, I think Salik felt he had the weight of the world on his shoulders the day he died," Parlour commented soberly. "Just a shame he didn't think to share his load with the police. We could have had that monster locked up without Salik having to sacrifice his life for the cause."

"You can't blame Salik for being wary of the police, now, can you?" Zoreena responded, an edge to her voice this time.

"Well he knew he could have come to me," Parlour frowned, rather peevishly.

"It wasn't you who hounded him out of Alicia Munroe's garden shed."

"DC Denton was rather heavy-handed in the circumstances, I grant you that," Parlour conceded. He held his hands aloft. "Hey, I didn't come to fight with you. I just came to offer my condolences and… well, to say that I hope you stick around in Deverton. You're a valuable part of this community, you know."

But Parlour wasn't convincing. Zoreena laughed hollowly. "What community?"

"I suppose you'd better come in," Lindsay Briscoe mumbled listlessly to the female half of the Parlour pastoral unit later that afternoon. Juliet followed her into the kitchen and assumed a position opposite the chair into which Lindsay had sunk, hands cradled once more around a giant mug of a milky substance that could equally have been chicken cupasoup or Horlicks.

"Is Baby Josh asleep?" Juliet enquired.

Lindsay just nodded in reply.

Juliet decided to take the initiative. She reached her hands across and placed them around Lindsay's, noting as she did so, that her friend had removed her gold wedding band from her ring finger.

"Look, Lins, I haven't come to judge or to poke my nose in, or to be intrusive in any way. I know we've not spent much time together lately, but I just came to say that I'm here for you. Anytime you want to talk… perhaps I should rephrase that… anytime you just want to be with someone."

There was a moment of silence before Lindsay briefly looked up and met Juliet's eyes.

"Thanks Juliet… Jules." She let out the tiniest of weak smiles, like a sudden streak of late afternoon sunlight across a grey winter sky, Juliet thought to herself.

Juliet paused before asking the obvious question.

"I'm not prying, it's just as a friend, I feel I need to know…"

"Where Charles is?" Lindsay interrupted. She gave a wry smile, not meeting her friend's eyes this time. "Gone to lick his wounds at Mummy's house, of course."

"He'll come around," Juliet comforted her, squeezing her hands once more. "He must see … why things happened the way they did."

"He's in a complete state of shock, and I can't blame him." Lindsay's shoulders started to heave. Juliet hastily got out of her chair and came around to her side. She pulled a sobbing Lindsay Briscoe to her breast as the eldest Briscoe child with his father's blonde good looks appeared alarmed at the bottom of the stairs.

"Mummy's just very tired, Thomas," Juliet informed him unconvincingly, shaking her head to herself as the eight year old hurtled back upstairs.

So much for the perfect façade, she thought to herself, feeling warm tears soak through her cheesecloth top.

***

"So how was Lindsay?" Parlour enquired of his wife, flopping down on the sofa beside her for a much needed veg, glass of Shiraz in hand.

"Shell-shocked as you might expect," Juliet replied, brow furrowed. "Those poor kids. Baby Josh is too young to understand, but how on earth do you tell an eight and six year old that Grandad's in prison for double murder and Mummy's had an affair with a man Grandad's age?"

"You don't until they're older, I guess," Parlour mused, sinking his bottom lower into the sofa and resting his heels on the coffee table.

"But when *is* it a good age to break that sort of news to your kids?" Juliet wondered.

Parlour shrugged. "When they're of an age to find out from someone else, I guess."

"But what age is that?" Juliet persevered, pressing a fluffy pink cushion with a snout and two piggy eyes to her stomach.

"I guess we'll find out when we get kids of our own," Parlour yawned.

"Well, it won't be next January," Juliet stated disconsolately, who, like most women trying for children, could, at any given time, come up with a date 40 weeks from now.

Parlour looked up at her and saw the faraway expression in her eyes. He squeezed her hand in sympathy, noting the porcine hot water bottle clutched to her abdomen.

"Got the cramps?"

Juliet nodded then broke into a watery smile. She looked down fondly at her husband. "We really do have a lot to be thankful for, Mark."

"I know."

They sat in silence for a moment before Parlour hauled himself up and with two quick strides, grabbed the remote control from the top of the bass speaker to the left of *his* baby, the 32" plasma television screen that dominated the open plan living area downstairs.

"Owt on telly?" Parlour enquired of his wife in a poor attempt at a Northern Accent, flinging himself back on the sofa.

Juliet shook her head distractedly. "I've already looked."

Parlour flicked the television onto News 24, his default channel when all else failed.

He sat upright. "Hey look, Jules, that's the RAT Race, isn't it?"

"The *what*?" Juliet frowned.

"You know, the Respect and Tolerance fun-run through Hyde Park that Micky's been organising for months. She told us all about it at our dinner party."

"The dinner party, how could I forget?" Juliet groaned, the hangover the following morning still uppermost in her mind, not the conversation around the table.

"Cape Cod!" Parlour suddenly exclaimed, moving closer to the television. "There's Micky right there!"

"Oh yes!"

Juliet perched on the edge of the coffee table beside him. Michaela Brevitt was jogging along amid a throng of brightly attired fellow RAT fun-runners, being pursued by a BBC cameraman and a jolly ex-children's presenter who still had the requisite energy to cover a couple of laps of Hyde Park and shout at the same time.

"They've had a good turnout," Parlour observed, eyes taking in the colourful moving mass of runners. It was a sort of cross between the London Marathon, Notting Hill and *Pride*, he thought to himself. Michaela Brevitt, though, was dressed more conservatively in a black RAT UK t-shirt and Nike running shorts, as perhaps befitted the leader of a burgeoning pressure group.

"Thought Micky was running with Cam?" Juliet frowned, as the camera panned out to reveal Brevitt running with a group of women dressed as cartoon characters.

Parlour paused then chortled. "I'd say she was a little bit more interested in the Latin Lovely beside her!"

Juliet leaned forward and peered at the screen. She swallowed, noting that Brevitt's fingers were firmly entwined in those of her running mate, a young Mediterranean woman dressed as *Dora the Explorer* in orange shorts and a tight-fitting pink t-shirt. As if to confirm Parlour's suspicions, Brevitt squeezed her friend's shapely bottom once the camera had zoomed away from her face and planted a fond kiss on her cheek.

Juliet looked perplexed, as much by her failed matchmaking efforts as her complete shock at discovering there was a whole side to Michaela Brevitt that had completely bypassed her, though to be fair to Brevitt, she had in no way lied to Juliet concerning her orientation.

"So where did Sacha come from?" she wondered aloud.

"In a test-tube by courier, at a guess!" Parlour chuckled, enjoying the crestfallen expression on his wife's face. It served her right for laughing at him at the dinner party. Now it was her turn to lose face.

"Oh, look, it's the Village People!" Parlour continued as Juliet sat brooding beside him.

Suddenly he leaned forward so that his pimply nose was almost touching the plasma screen.

"Cape Cod!"

Parlour had turned a curious shade of pink. Juliet almost felt the heat radiating from his cheeks.

"What is it now?"

"That's Cam… Jules, that's Cam isn't it? *Isn't it?"*

"Which one?" Juliet peered at the screen.

"The bloody New York cop, of course!" Parlour exploded, putting his hands behind his head.

Juliet put her hand over her mouth, speechless, before collapsing in a fit of mirth on the living room floor. Cameron Goodlove was live on national television, swinging a huge leather truncheon and marching arm in arm with a male gym instructor dressed head to toe in pink lycra.

"How does the adage go?" Juliet queried, regaining a small degree of composure as Parlour paced the room, considering the implications at Billock HQ. "Assume makes an *ass* of u and me… with ass being the operative word?"

She burst into peels of laughter again, but her husband was lost for words. Who would have thought that a strapping young chick magnet like Cameron Goodlove would be a couple of hormones short of the full Alpha male, thought Parlour, hitching his trousers up his skinny waist a few more inches. Perhaps the signs had been there, but Parlour surely hadn't read them.

He was disturbed from his reverie by the sound of *Take That* blasting from his rear end.

"Parlour," Parlour snapped, once he'd extricated his mobile phone from his back pocket. *"What?"*

Juliet watched with fear as Parlour sank down on the coffee table. No more murders, please, she said to herself. She was looking forward to the first relaxing evening in with Mark in weeks.

Parlour put the phone down two minutes later. He turned slowly to meet his wife's concerned gaze.

"It's the Sewer," he informed her, clearly in a state of shock. "He's been killed in a car crash!"

Juliet gasped. Detective Chief Inspector Brian Sewell dead? What implications would that have on Parlour's career – and their life here in Deverton?

About the author

Carol A Shepherd is an author, college lecturer and LGBT faith activist from Eastleigh, near Southampton, UK. You can find her books at www.carolshepherdbooks.info

If you enjoyed this book, the author would greatly appreciate a review on Amazon to spread the word and support independent publishers.

You can also subscribe to Carol's newsletter, The Bi Christian Writer and claim a free novella: https://www.subscribepage.com/bichristianwriter

More titles from Easy Yoke Publishing can be found at www.easyyoke.org

Also in the series:

Death by Peanuts (Parlour 1)
You Shop You Drop (Parlour 3)